IP

Pisgah Press

Pisgah Press was established in 2011 to publish and promote works of quality offering original ideas and insight into the human condition, the realm of knowledge, and the world around us.

Copyright © 2013 R. F. Wilson

Printed in the United States of America

Published by Pisgah Press, LLC
PO Box 1427, Candler, NC 28715
www.pisgahpress.com

Book & cover design: A. D. Reed, MyOwnEditor.com

All rights reserved. No part of this publication may be reproduced, stored in a retrieval system, or transmitted, in any form or by any means, electronic, mechanical, photocopying, recording, or otherwise, without the prior written permission of Pisgah Press, except in the case of quotations in critical articles or reviews.

Library of Congress Cataloging-in-Publication Data
Wilson, Robert F.
Killer Weed/Wilson

Library of Congress Control Number: 2014904401

ISBN-13: 9780985387594
ISBN-10: 0985387599
Mystery/Fiction

First Edition
March 2014

This is a work of fiction. Any resemblance to actual events or persons living or dead is coincidental.

THANKS TO:
- The Asheville Mysterians, for their on-going support, criticism, harassment, and affection
- Jossie Wilson, Charley Morris, Alice Sabo, and Jeanette Phillips for their willingness to slog through the manuscript and provide cogent feedback
- Cammie "The Grammar Nazi" Wilson
- Beth for her cheerleading and love
- All the others who, with their encouragement and repeated questioning, "When are we going get to read it?" have kept me going.

Killer Weed

by RF Wilson

For Pat

Killer Weed

1

I rode shotgun as my young colleague, Jay McIntyre, drove the ancient Jeep up a gravel and dirt road, climbing through old growth pine and hardwood forest. Spring was giving way to summer, bright white rhododendron taking over from the soft pink mountain laurel, flame azaleas blazing on the hillsides. I asked him to stop at a narrow bridge over a bold creek, where I stood, watching the water, breathing deeply of the cool mountain air, smiling.

"What's the grin about?" he asked.

"Smug satisfaction," I said. "Doesn't get much better than this, does it?"

"Oh, I don't know. Sure you wouldn't like to be back in the office pushing papers?"

I filled my lungs a couple of times before returning to the Jeep.

Another half-mile up the road, the woods opened onto an area devoid of trees except for those standing sentry around a two-story frame house perched at the crest of a rise.

A woman of some years walked off the porch toward us, ruggedly handsome in blue overalls over a white T-shirt, long white hair pulled back in a ponytail. Her well-worn boots suggested she was not of the idle gentry. I could imagine her with a shotgun in her hands if she hadn't been expecting us.

"Saw you comin' up the road," she said, her hand held toward me as I climbed out of the Jeep. Her grip was firm, businesslike. She was an inch or so shorter than my five-foot-ten with a trim figure.

"I suppose you know I'm Queenie Weaver. Taken a lot of abuse for that name over the years, but I'm glad I hung on to it. You must be Rick Ryder."

I had told her on the phone I'd be the guy with one arm. I like to warn people ahead of time—it avoids that awkward moment when people notice something missing on my left side.

"And this is Jay McIntyre," I said.

She beamed, as many women do on meeting the handsome twenty-one year-old. Six-foot-two, solid two hundred pounds, wavy brown hair, blue eyes and the complexion of a man who spends as much time as he can outdoors.

"This is Sonny," Queenie said, nodding toward an Australian Shepherd who had come up to stand alongside his mistress. His tail was wagging but the look on his face was all business.

"Care for a cup of coffee?" she asked. "Just made a fresh pot."

I said I would. Jay said he'd just have some water if he could.

After Sonny herded us onto the porch, Queenie motioned toward a couple of rocking chairs. "Be back in a minute."

We were ten miles or so northwest of Asheville in western North Carolina, looking southwest, into north Georgia and the southern end of the Great Smoky Mountains. A topographical map I had with me put this peak close to four thousand feet. The sky was an unblemished expanse of Carolina blue, the humidity below fifty percent, the kind of day the Chamber of Commerce would like to bottle and use for marketing.

Queenie pushed the screen door open with her shoulder. "Thanks for comin' up," she said as she placed a tray with mugs, condiments and pastries on a small table between us.

"It's our pleasure," I said. "One of the perks of working where we do is that we get to come out to places like this. This is spectacular."

"It is that. And I don't want developers rapin' this property like they're fixin' to do all around me. I understand you might be able to help keep it this way even after I'm gone."

"That's the idea," I said.

We sat in silence, looking into the distance.

Her gaze didn't waver as she began to narrate. "My great-great-granddaddy came here in the late seventeen-hundreds. According to his journals, this was a bald up here then like it is now. Seems like a strange place for trees not to grow, but it might have been like this for centuries before he arrived. Suited Maxwell. Saved him a lot of work getting a spot ready to build a house on. This place isn't the original, of course, although I'm told some of the stone in the fireplace goes back to the first cabin. I'd sure hate for this to turn into some kind of gated condo development. I've even heard there are people talkin' about building a ski place around here, like that one over in Maggie Valley."

She paused as she sipped her coffee.

"Good brew," I said.

"Yeah, I get it at that Country Café place down where the four-lane ends."

"I know the place," I said, remembering that time in my life, two years ago, when I'd first come across it. It was a bittersweet memory.

"Don't get me wrong about development," she said. "I'm not against it. Hell, we Weavers have made most of our money over the years sellin' land. This was an original grant from King George III, tens of thousands of acres. Old Maxwell, he was a preacher, came here as a Presbyterian missionary. Built a church and a school and all that. He was also a shrewd businessman, a trait that seems to have been passed along. But some of this has gotta be saved." She was quiet for a minute or so before she said, "Let's go take a drive. I'll show you what it is about this place that gets me so worked up."

Sonny led the way down the steps toward an old Ford pickup. Although he had been friendly when we were introduced, he became sullen as we all piled into the truck, me seated between our hostess and my co-worker, leaving no place for him except on the floor between Jay's legs.

"You're sittin' in his place," Queenie said. "He'll get over it."

The vintage vehicle backfired, belching black smoke before heading down the way Jay and I had come up. Queenie pulled the truck to the side of the road just past the creek Jay and I had admired on the way up. Sonny led us into the woods where there wasn't a path that I could discern. Skirting rhododendron and mountain laurel thickets, what the locals call "hells," we clambered over deadfall and fought back brambles until we heard the sound of water rushing. Two minutes later the undergrowth opened up and I was looking across the precipice of a waterfall. I guessed the drop to be thirty feet.

We were admiring the panorama before us when Sonny began barking ferociously. He took off down the slope toward the base of the falls.

"Maybe a bear," Queenie said.

I looked to see if she was putting us on.

"Out here, that's more likely than meeting another human."

The barking got louder and more insistent.

"Guess we better go down and see what all the commotion's about," she said.

A trail ran parallel to the falls about ten yards into the woods away from the water. Having a second arm would have helped me balance down the steep decline. Jay scampered down, and Queenie—

in spite of her years—was close on his tail. I was a few yards behind when I heard Jay yell over the roar of the cascading water.

"Hurry up!"

It was a demand rather than a request. Sonny kept up his racket as well. It took me another minute to get creek-side. The waterfall was to my right, cascading into a deep pool bounded by a row of boulders that formed a natural bridge to the other side of the creek. Jay was lying prone on the far side, hands in the water, holding up what appeared to be a backpack. Queenie had made it about half way across the rocks when Jay hoisted the pack and turned it sideways.

"Oh, my God," Queenie cried, seeing the pack was attached to a body.

Sonny ran up and down the far bank barking. I maneuvered across the rocks as quickly as I could to join the others and get a closer look. The body was snared in the branches of a tree that had fallen into the creek. The face was partially visible and covered with long, stringy hair.

I heard Queenie call out over the sound of cascading water, "It's Brian," as if we all knew who that was. Then she yelled at Jay. "You can move faster than we can. The keys are in the truck. You may have to get back up to the house before you can get a cell phone signal. Call nine-one-one and tell 'em to come on out to Queenie Weaver's place. Wait for them at the bridge and bring 'em down here."

"Shouldn't we get him out of the water first?" Jay asked.

"Don't mess with him," Queenie ordered. "This is a crime scene."

2

After Jay had scampered back across the rocks and was on his way up the trail, I asked Queenie what she meant about it being a crime scene.

"This was no accident," she said, biting her words through clenched teeth.

"Happens all the time," I said. "Just yesterday there was an article in the paper ..."

"Not to Brian."

"Why not?"

"Because he was smarter than that. That kind of thing happens to idiots who have no respect for nature, who've never been in this kind of country."

"Who was he?"

We found a log to sit on, away from the pool and the body and the mist blowing off the falls.

"He was just a kid, Rick. His name was Brian McFadden. He had to profile a local person who might have a unique view of the history of the area for a journalism class at the university. He wanted to do the attorney, Nate Chatham, the former civil-rights champion.... You're smiling. You know Nate?"

I nodded. "He's probably my best friend other than my wife.

I also do a little work for him from time to time."

"Small world, huh? Turns out one of Brian's classmates had gotten to him first, so Nate suggested the boy talk to me. I know Nate from the civil rights struggles—he got me out of jail more than once—but I was surprised I was the one who came to his mind as an interesting local person. I am aware I do have a reputation as a curmudgeonly old broad, this wild woman of the mountains."

The wan smile that had begun to slip onto her face disappeared as she continued. "He came up to talk to me. I told him about my family back to old Maxwell, what it's like to be a bachelor woman in these parts, the kinds of changes a person in their seventies has witnessed in the mountains. He was a nice kid. Really nice."

Her voice caught and she got quiet.

"Sorry," she said. "He was a damn nice kid. Had that kind of hippie thing going on. You know, long hair, wasn't going to be co-opted by the system, whatever that is. That's what people used to call me, you know, a hippie. Maybe still do, I don't know. Anyway, he really liked it up here, got into an Emerson-Thoreau thing, talking about how to get back to nature. I let him have the run of the property, something I don't let many people do, except my hand, Stan, and his wife, Martha Jo, although she's not what you'd call the outdoors type. And he liked to fly fish. Said that was the one thing besides money he got from his father. We'd eat whatever he caught, or he'd take it back to his apartment and share it with his roommates."

She stopped talking again. When I turned to look at her, her eyes were closed.

"You don't have to do this now, Queenie."

She inhaled deeply again. "No, it's okay. The first thing I thought of when I saw it was his body in the water was he'd been fishing and somehow had gone over the falls, kinda' like you thought, I guess. But he wasn't stupid. He'd never get that close to the edge. Something else had to have happened to him."

Sonny had curled himself below her feet. The three of us sat still for a few minutes hearing only the rushing water and the occasional outcry of a bird. Finally, Queenie said, "I suppose this is as good a time as any to tell you about the death threats."

3

She said it casually, the way she might have said, "Want me to tell you about the new dress I bought?" Although for Queenie, buying a dress might be as strange as receiving death threats.

"Yeah, this would probably be a good time," I said.

"Started about three months ago. It was one of the reasons I decided to come to you folks at the Mountain Center. People have been trying to get their hands on this land for a long time, maybe as long as it's been in the family." She'd been gazing into some indefinite place in the creek. She turned her head toward me. "You can understand why, after seeing some of it today. There's nothing like it around. There are places where the views are just as good, but no place with the kind of waterfalls and virgin timber stands this place has."

Her face wrinkled, like she was worrying over something.

"I hadn't thought about this 'til now, but one of my neighbors sold their land a couple of months ago, right around the time the calls started. When I talked to them about it, they seemed almost embarrassed, like they'd done something they weren't supposed to. The whole idea of property rights is you can do with your land what you want. I've got no gripe with that. They want to sell, make a lot of money, that's their business. And then last month, another neighbor sold his land. The thing is, they'd been people like me. Never gonna sell out. And then, all of sudden, they did." She shook her head and turned her gaze back to the creek. "I don't know what's goin' on up here, but it's nothin' good."

"You think the people buying the land are the ones making threats?"

She shrugged. "Can't say for sure."

"But you suspect."

"Like I said, people have had their eyes on this place for a long time. Could be something else, but I haven't had anybody threaten me since I was supporting the rights of black people back when it wasn't a popular thing to do. You know, Nate and I were pretty tight in those days. Some people thought we were an item. Drove folks mad. There were a whole lot of people then who couldn't abide the idea of a white woman with a black man. Still are, for that matter. Maybe some holdover racist has decided to harass me, someone who's just heard about me, this old white lady who was responsible for those people gettin' so uppity. Just coincidental it happens when somebody's buying up all the land around here."

She took a deep breath, rocked forward a little, stood up, and stepped to the edge of the creek. Bending over, she picked up a small rock, cocked her arm and threw it across the water, barely missing a tree on the other side.

"Good arm," I said.

"Used to play ball with the boys around here until we went to high school. I was about as good as any of them, better than a lot. Then all of a sudden they decided girls didn't know how to play. What a bunch of ..." Her voice trailed off.

I waited a few seconds before asking, "What do they say?"

"The threat-makers? Just stupid things like, 'Get out, Queenie, or you're a dead woman.' Stuff like that."

"Have you told the Sheriff?"

She gave me a look that suggested she didn't think I was too bright.

"How long you lived around here?" she asked.

"About twelve years."

"I don't want to impugn the man. The one we got now's a pretty good boy as far as I can tell. Seems like he's honest and all. Wish I could say the same for everybody who works for him. The guy we had before this one's in prison now and I don't think they were able to clean out everybody who was messed up with what he was into. And going back into the sixties, I was one of the enemy to a lot of them. Now, I try to stay clear of them. That way I don't have to wonder whose side who's on."

As much as I wanted to believe there was a bright line separating the good guys from the bad guys, I understood what she was saying. But, I still thought this was the kind of thing those sworn to uphold the law should know about. I was about to say something when Sonny started up again and we heard voices on the trail.

A minute later, Jay appeared, followed by an older guy in civvies wearing a hat with "CHIEF" emblazoned across the brow. I recognized him as Bobby Headley, Chief of the Leicester Volunteer Fire and Rescue Department. A few steps behind came another man and a woman, both with EMS insignia stitched on their blue shirts.

"What took you so long, Bobby?" Queenie called to the Chief. He was a solid six-four with a full head of salt and pepper hair—heavy on the salt—and the upper body of a man who has split wood all his life.

"Well, just for future reference," he said, "it would be helpful if people who died out here would do it someplace a little more accessible."

"Hey, Bobby," I said.

He squinted in my direction. A blank expression quickly gave way to a broad smile. "Rick Ryder. What the...? Never mind, we'll talk later."

When they reached our side of the creek, we shook hands. "You look good," he said. "See you haven't grown a new left arm, yet."

"Pretty much given up on it. Besides, it's a good conversation piece, once people get past that, 'I wonder if it's okay to point out to him he only has one arm' awkwardness."

"And how about you, Queenie?" he asked, leaning over to give her a hug. "Haven't seen you in a month o' Sundays."

"Yeah, I stay pretty well hunkered down up here," she said. "You know I'm just an old country gal, Bobby. I've even got that DVD-by-mail thing so I don't have to go to town to rent movies anymore."

By now the two volunteers who had accompanied the chief were in the water, examining the body.

"How long do you think he's been there?" I called down to them from the bank.

The woman looked up.

"I'm no expert, but based on other bodies I've seen in cold water like this, I'd say probably not more than a day or so," she said, confirming what I'd surmised.

"Queenie thinks he was killed, Bobby," I said to the chief.

He turned to her. "Why do you think that?"

She was forming an answer when Sonny once more set up a racket and raced back across the creek.

"That would be the sheriff's people," Headley said.

The county's crew was led by Detective Adam Parmeter. He was a small man, probably no more than five-five, and overweight. But his reputation around the county was that of a dedicated professional. At his direction, Queenie, Jay, and I clambered across the rocks to the side of the creek we had come down, getting out of the way of the crime scene people and the medical examiner. After a brief consult with the newcomers, Bobby said he guessed his folks had done all they could and would be on their way, ready for the Leicester community's next drama to unfold.

"Always good to see you, Queenie," Bobby said, then looked at me. "Don't be a stranger, Rick. Seems like you and corpses keep showing up together. Come by the station house. We'll drink bad coffee and you can tell me what's up."

"It's a date," I said.

After Bobby and the other volunteers headed up the trail, I turned my attention back to the creek. The backpack had been removed from the corpse before the body was moved into a small clearing on the bank. One of the investigators emptied the pack, putting the contents—mostly clothes and books—into evidence bags. Then he held up something that looked like a plant cutting. He called a colleague over and after a discussion he dropped it into one of the clear, small bags.

A noise gathered force overhead until it became a roar, drowning out the nearby torrent of water, the unmistakable "thwup, thwup" of a helicopter. The propeller wake lashed trees and undergrowth like the full fury of a hurricane. As the chopper hovered above, a line was lowered and the corpse, now enclosed in a body bag, was lifted skyward, disappearing through the foliage and, presumably, into the hold of the aircraft.

Queenie, Jay, and I were huddled in our own little group, watching as the sheriff's people continued to scour the area for evidence after the body was gone.

"When they all leave, I want to have a little ceremony," Queenie said to Jay and me. "I want it to be acknowledged that this is where he died."

Jay and I nodded in unison.

"Then I want to find out what really happened. Parmeter," she hollered across the water. "I need to talk to you."

The detective stepped cautiously across the rocks.

"What is it, Ms. Weaver?"

"'Queenie'll do fine. This wasn't an accident."

"I understand that's a possibility. That's why those folks over there are looking around. The M.E. says the deceased's head injuries are consistent with falling on the rocks but could also have been made by some blunt instrument. He'll examine the body to find out if he was alive or conscious when he went in the water. We do this stuff for a living, Ms. ... Queenie. We know the obvious is not always the right answer. It's not always the wrong answer, either. We'll get it sorted out."

Queenie offered her hand to the man. While they were shaking, she said, "I've heard good things about you. I expect you'll do your best."

She looked over at Jay and me and said, "Nothin' more we can do here. Might as well get on up to the house and talk about what it was you actually came here for today."

As the three of us turned to go, Parmeter said, "You all going to be in the area for a while? We need to get your statements."

"Yeah, we'll be at the house," Queenie said. When we were out of earshot of the others, she said, "I do think he'll do his best to find out what happened. I'm just concerned that some other folks he works with ... or for ... may not be as interested in the truth."

I remembered the look she'd given me when I asked if she'd talked to the sheriff about the threats she'd been getting.

4

"Well, boys," Queenie said when we were back in the truck, me in the middle and Sonny curled up under Jay's feet again, "that's not really what I had in mind for today's outing." Said with a chuckle, but wiping her eyes with the back of a hand at the same time. "I just can't believe it. Brian."

"You think this is related to the threats, too?" I asked.

"You've gotta think so, don't you?" she said.

Jay turned to us with a puzzled look. "What threats?"

Queenie filled him in.

"Could just be a weird coincidence," he said.

She gave him what I had already come to think of as "the look."

"A kid gets killed for no apparent reason at the same time people are trying to get me to skedaddle from my property and other people who have sworn they'd never leave have sold out might just all be coincidental?"

My young colleague shrugged.

The road seemed rougher going up than it had been coming down, and I hoped the beating my kidneys were taking wasn't doing irreparable damage. When we pulled up alongside the house, there was another truck parked in front, shiny, maybe a few years old, well kept.

"Stan's here," Queenie said. "Probably heard the helicopter, wonders what the hell's goin' on. You boys wanna come on up, have some tea, maybe something stronger under the circumstances."

A man came out the front screen door onto the porch as we approached. Probably mid-fifties and, like Queenie, he looked like he'd spent a lot of time outdoors. He was about her height, just the suggestion of a gut under blue jeans and matching chambray shirt. The cowboy boots he wore were not just for Saturday night's show. It was apparently unremarkable to Queenie that Stan had been in her house while she was gone.

"Hey, Stan," Queenie said as she took the steps. "Thought that commotion might have got your attention."

"What's goin' on?"

"Brian's dead," she said.

"What the hell?"

"Yeah. We found him at the bottom of Weaver's Falls."

"What? He fall over?"

"Come on, Stan. Brian wouldn't fall over the falls, for crying out loud."

Stan looked past Queenie to Jay and me standing at the bottom of the porch steps.

Queenie turned and said, "Oh, come on up, boys. This is Stan, my caretaker."

We moved up as she introduced us. "They're from that Mountain Center place I was telling you about, come up to have a look at the property. Go ahead, sit down," she said, signaling to the rocking chairs, then turned back to Stan. "He was killed. The cops are down there now."

"How're you so sure it wasn't an accident?"

"He knew how to behave around the water, Stan." She said it in a voice that implied she didn't think it was something she needed to say.

"Maybe he was high."

"High? Like pot-smokin' high?"

"Yeah. He did that, you know."

"Well, I didn't know. I suspected. But even so. And how do you know he got high?"

I thought it might be time for Jay and me to take our leave.

"'Cause he'd asked me if I wanted to join him."

I looked up at the two figures facing each other. It was as if each was waiting for the other to blink. After several seconds, Queenie turned away from Stan and said, "What about those drinks? Stan, you want to join us for a little something. You know, mark the occasion?"

"I was just fixin' to drag the lower road. Got pretty washed out that last storm we had."

Queenie shrugged. "Well then, say 'hey' to Martha Jo. You gotta come up for dinner one of these days."

Stan nodded without comment and headed down the porch steps.

"Did you call the office while you were getting EMS," I asked Jay, "let them know what was goin on?"

"I did."

Queenie said, "Got some twelve-year-old Dickel. Nice sippin' whiskey."

"I'll stick with the tea, unsweetened if you have it," I said.

"A teetotaler," she said. "I'll bet you're a Yankee, too." I nodded. "Well, what about you, young man? You gonna make me drink alone? They say that's not healthy."

"Have any beer?"

"My God, short hitters and abstainers. Yes, I've got some beer. Somebody brought me some from one of those local breweries in town. Pretty good stuff, too. For beer."

She went into the house and Jay looked at me.

"It's okay, isn't it? The beer, I mean?"

"Yeah, just don't get snockered."

Queenie loaded up the tray she'd brought out earlier and Jay got up and held the screen door for her. She was back with the libations in less than five minutes, along with some cheese and crackers and apple slices. "Might hold us 'til someone decides it's time for a meal."

We sat with drinks in hand, rocking gently, enjoying the vista, avoiding the event of the day, when a County vehicle came up the drive. Detective Parmeter and two deputies got out and started up the steps before being accosted by Sonny, loudly defending his territory. When Queenie had him settled, the trio came up. The bottle of George Dickel from which Queenie had poured herself a couple of fingers seemed to catch the detective's eye.

"Sorry to interrupt your party, Queenie."

"Don't get all righteous, Parmeter. We're drinking to the memory of a good friend who died much too young. It's a solemn occasion."

The detective held up a hand, palm open, an apology of sorts.

"We need to get your statements. And do you know who would be a next of kin?"

"I would suppose that would be his parents. I think his father is Richard McFadden. They live around the country club. If that doesn't help, call the university. He was a student."

"Yeah, we've got his student ID but no emergency information."

"Yeah, kids," Queenie said. "They think they're invincible."

The deputies were introduced as Aaron Presley and Norris Peebles. Presley said they appreciated us taking our time, as if we had much choice in the matter. Although Parmeter was in charge, Presley gave off an air of condescension, like he was the baddest guy in the room. He wore a khaki suit, the kind that seemed to be the summer uniform for TV detectives. I didn't like him.

Peebles was assigned to me. We went into the house and sat on opposite sides of the kitchen table for our talk. The guy didn't seem old enough to be out of high school, although I assumed he must have had some kind of higher education. He asked what I was doing up here today.

I explained that Queenie had called our office a couple of days ago. "She wanted to talk about how she could protect her land from developers even after she'd passed away. She'd heard about the idea of a land trust from a lawyer friend who also told her about us at the Mountain Center for the Defense of the Environment. I don't work with the Center full-time anymore, but help out as a consultant, specializing in land transactions. She was showing us her property, telling us about the people buying up the land around hers and the telephone threats she'd been getting."

"Telephone threats?"

I repeated what Queenie had told us.

"But she never reported them?"

"That's what she said. You'll have to talk to her about them."

"Did you know the boy?"

I thought he was kind of young himself to be referring to Brian as a boy. "Never saw him before."

"But Ms. Weaver knew him?"

"Apparently was quite close to him, the way she tells it."

"Why were you down at the falls?"

"Like I said, she was showing off the property, wanted us to know why she didn't want it to be 'raped.' That was her word. Didn't want developers raping her land. According to her, this place has been in the family since the time of the first European settlers. She has some pretty strong feelings about it."

"You know any reason someone would want to hurt him?"

"Brian? I told you, I didn't know him, never met him. Only just met Ms. Weaver this morning."

I was getting irritated with the young officer, thought he wasn't listening very well. I wondered how deputies got assigned to homicide cases.

"Anything else you can think of that might be important?"

"Just the threatening phone calls," I reminded him.

When they had gotten all our statements, they piled back into the sheriff department SUV and headed down the hill the way Stan had gone. Sonny followed for a few yards, giving them a noisy goodbye and good riddance.

"They're gonna go interview Stan and Martha Jo," Queenie said. "That oughta be rich. Martha Jo'll give 'em hell about something. She's one of those people doesn't seem to think anybody should interfere the least little bit in her life. Narcissistic personality disorder, I believe the shrinks call it."

I looked at her wide-eyed.

"Oh, just showin' off. Done it all my life. A lot of people don't like it. Think it's, well, narcissistic."

After we resumed our positions on the porch, a silence lingered as we each held our own thoughts, until a now-familiar sound intruded. Within seconds we could see the helicopter coming our way. At first I thought it must be the one from the hospital, off on some other mission of mercy. Then it came low over the area we had just been walking.

"What the hell?" Queenie said. "You don't suppose they've found another body, do you?"

The aircraft hovered around the falls before expanding the diameter of the circle it was tracing. It was gone no more than five minutes after it showed up.

"Aerial reconnaissance, maybe," Jay said. "You know, get a

view of the area you can't get on the ground."

"Maybe so," she said. "Anyway, I want to go back down there. Want to come along, see how the land lays, give our respects to the place?"

We piled back into Queenie's truck and headed down the mountain, parking a few car lengths away from where we had earlier in the day.

"I try not to go in and out the same way every time so I don't make an obvious path," Queenie said. "I've had to shoo more than a few lost sightseers out of here over the years, people who may have heard there's some waterfalls, think that the 'NO TRESPASSING' sign down below doesn't apply to them."

"People know about the falls?" I said.

Sonny again led us into the woods at a place that didn't look passable. Queenie kept talking as she trail-blazed ahead of Jay and me. I had to keep close on her behind to hear what she was saying.

"Hard to keep something like that secret. But I don't want to make it easy for them to find the place. If I do decide to turn it over to a land trust, you all won't turn it into a tourist spot, will you?"

"No, Queenie, that's exactly what won't happen. The whole idea is to keep property from being developed."

"And Stan'll still be able to live here?"

"If that's what you want, you just spell it out."

"I've got to think on it some more. I'll tell you, though, Stan doesn't think much of the idea."

"Why not?"

"He's pretty conservative about property rights. Thinks they ought to be inviolable. Shouldn't need things like land trusts to protect yourself."

"But you know the pressures on you to develop the land. And after you go …"

"Yeah, yeah, let's just not go there today, all right? Had enough of that for one day."

The brush opened up near the bottom of the falls where yellow crime scene tape was strung among the trees. We could have just walked under it but agreed that we shouldn't disturb the site any more than it already was.

"So, gentlemen," she said, "will you join me for a moment of silence, just to mark this space."

Standing on the bank, we watched and listened to the water pound down the rock face and crash into the pool below. Queenie picked up a rock at the edge of the creek and threw it toward the place Brian's body had been found. I couldn't see her face but I could tell her chest was heaving before she turned and headed back into the brush.

When we'd gotten back to the truck, she said, "I'm sure glad you boys were out here today. If you hadn't come along, who knows how long it would have been before somebody found him. Maybe after he'd been missing long enough someone would have.... Anyway, I'm glad you were here."

"I don't imagine you want to talk any more today about the future of the property," I said, "but is there any chance you have a copy of the deed and a plat? Of course, we can look at the originals at the courthouse."

"Yeah, I thought you'd probably want to see it so I retrieved it from my safety deposit box. Got it all laid out on the dining room table."

When we'd gathered up the paperwork from Queenie and gotten back to the Jeep, I said, "Not your typical day at the office."

"I don't know, Rick. Is there a typical day at the office with you?"

I knew he was referring to the time two years ago, just a few months after he'd begun an internship with the Mountain Center, when I'd been arrested for the murder of a young stripper. I'd spent the next several weeks investigating the case to clear myself and, when it was resolved, I quit full-time work with the agency and hung out my shingle as a private detective.

The director of the Mountain Center, Zella Jefferson, was standing at the reception desk when Jay and I returned to the office a few minutes before five. Zella had been my boss at the state environmental protection agency, and when she had been offered the job of running MCDE, she recruited me to come with her. She was an exotic woman of Asian, African and Arabian ancestry with wits to match her beauty. Although she'd heard about the murder hours before when Jay had called her after calling 911, I could tell she was shaken by our report from the way her mahogany complexion had turned dark.

"Do they have any idea who might have done it?" she asked.

"Queenie's been getting telephone calls telling her to get off the land and making vague threats. A couple of neighbors, people who said they'd never sell their land, have recently sold out and she thinks whoever's making the calls has something to do with that and probably to the murder, as well."

"If you don't hear from her tomorrow," Zella said, "it would be a good idea to get back to her. She might have some understandable reservations after something like that, but it's all the more reason for her to go ahead and try to protect the property."

"First thing tomorrow, I'll check out the recent land transactions around her. Besides getting an idea of what property around there is going for, I want to find out if the same person or persons are involved in the sales."

"That's fine. But if this turns into more of a murder investigation than research into a possible land trust deal, you'll have to go on someone else's clock."

5

Queenie called the next day to say she was okay and we could come on up and talk about a land trust. I had thought she might want to let things rest a bit, deal with her feelings about Brian's death. But she was, as she said, a mountain woman, and my experience with mountain people was that they tended to take things as they came. Although I was tied up for most of that day, I did have time to do some preliminary paperwork. Jay was in court for the Center in a case involving an egregious local polluter, so at nine o'clock the next morning, I was on the road up to her house by myself.

I heard the sirens coming up the mountain behind me before I saw the flashing lights. My first thought was that something had happened to Queenie, that she had been right about Brian's fall not being an accident, and that she was the next victim. I pulled as far to the side of the road as I was able while four black SUV's, each emblazoned with" SHERIFF" on its side, slowed to squeeze between my Honda and the foliage flanking the road, before resuming a speed I assumed was commensurate with the urgency of their mission.

I pushed my little car to the maximum of its climbing ability. The front-wheel drive kept good traction, but its four cylinders were no match for the behemoths that were leaving me in their dust. When I got to the clearing just below her house, I saw Queenie coming out, flanked by two uniformed deputies. It wasn't until I got closer that I saw her hands cuffed behind her back. Her escorts were helping her step up into one of their vehicles just as I pulled alongside.

"Call Nate," she hollered. "They're sayin' I murdered Brian."

The door to the SUV slammed shut.

I left my car where it was, got out and went up one of her escorts.

"What the hell's going on?"

"You heard what she said."

"That's outrageous. Queenie a murderer? Who's in charge here?"

"That would be Sergeant Ponder."

"Where is he?"

"In the house."

I was on the porch in five seconds, just as the vehicle holding Queenie started up. I watched as it turned around and headed down the mountain.

It took several seconds to register what was happening when I stepped inside. Two men dressed in black were moving methodically about the room, pulling things out of cabinets, emptying drawers. It was only then that I noticed SWAT emblazoned across the backs of their shirts. From their upper body bulk, I assumed they were wearing flak jackets. They were immersed in their task and didn't notice me step inside.

"What the hell's going on," I said. "Where's Sergeant Ponder?"

The two men turned to me. One spoke.

"Who the hell are you?"

"A friend of Ms. Weaver."

"You can't come in here. This is a crime scene."

"What crime?"

"Sir," the officer said. He was probably a little over six feet tall, a solid two-twenty-five or so, standard military/law enforcement type haircut. "You will have to leave. This is a crime scene."

"Yeah, you said that. Where's Ponder?"

The officer stepped around to the bottom of a set of stairs.

"Sergeant. Guy down here wants to talk to you."

"Who is it?" came the voice down the staircase.

"Ryder," I yelled up. "Rick Ryder."

"Don't come into the room, sir," the officer said. We heard heavy footsteps descending.

When Sergeant Ponder hit the bottom, he turned and quickly scanned the room, his view landing on me.

"And who are you? Hey, you're that one-armed guy we've heard about. Ryder."

"Yup. That's me."

"What're you doing here?"

"Wondering what you're doing here."

"What business is it of yours?"

I had to think quickly.

"I'm a lawyer."

Those weren't the magic words.

"So what?"

"I came up here to do business with Ms. Weaver this morning and saw her loaded into a paddy-wagon, handcuffed, and she's yelling at me that she's being arrested for murder."

He stared at me.

"And?" he said.

"I'm just wondering what's going on."

"First of all this is a crime scene and you have no business here. Second, I have no reason to speak to you."

From the sounds I heard above me, I could tell they were

searching upstairs just as they were doing down below.

"And," the sergeant went on, "if you don't back yourself out of this house right now ..."

I held my hand up in surrender. I knew the next words from his mouth would include things like "impeding" and "interfering." Might even involve "accessory after the fact." I backed out through the front door and hurried down the porch steps before someone decided I might know something about whatever it was they were looking for.

6

I steered the Honda down the mountain, the way I'd seen both Stan and the cops go the day before. When I'd gone far enough that I couldn't be seen from Queenie's, I called Nate Chatham from the car. Katrina, his paralegal and office manager, answered. Her deep Slavic tones sent quivers down my back and to places beyond. I'd known Katrina for more than a decade, as long as I'd known her boss. I was sure she could articulate clearly in English and used the accent for effect.

"The old boy in?"

"Yes, and good morning to you, Mr. Ryder."

"Good morning, Katrina. Please excuse my bad manners. Is he in?"

"Yes, although I'm supposed to be holding his calls."

"Tell him it's urgent. They've arrested Queenie Weaver."

The hold music was some old jazz, Thelonius Monk maybe. It was not more than fifteen seconds before he was on.

"Yo, my pale friend."

"Salutations. I was just up at Queenie Weaver's place, in time to see her handcuffed, loaded into a van and driven off. She said she was being arrested for the murder of Brian McFadden."

"That was quick," he said.

"What was quick?"

"I just heard they'd gotten the warrant signed. They're also gonna bust her for growing marijuana out there."

"Queenie? Growing pot? That's crazy, Nate."

"Well, as this business constantly reminds one, you never know what people will do."

"But murder? That is ridiculous."

"Well said. Unfortunately, the D.A. will not take 'ridiculous' as a defense."

"How do you know all this already?" I asked, knowing even as I asked the question.

"I've still got ears over there. They also tell me the D.A. was particularly interested to hear that you'd been out at her place when they found the body. You know, I don't think he's gotten over how your last involvement with him turned out."

He was referring to the murder I had been charged with. In exonerating myself, I had implicated some Very Important People and there were still questions about how assiduously the D.A. had pursued the investigation. If I hadn't become my own investigator, I could still be languishing at state expense.

"So you've managed to get yourself involved in another one."

"I didn't manage anything, Nate."

"I know, this kind of thing just happens to you. At any rate, I know you have a professional interest in Ms. Weaver—she told you, I believe, that I was the one who suggested she talk to you about the land trust business—so this all has some relevance for you. I image the land trust thing is kind of on hold since the property in question is probably going to be seized by the narcs. I don't know how busy you are with your private eye biz, but I do know you have experience investigating murders. Ordinarily," he said, "this is the kind of thing I'd just turn over to Dominic to look into," Dominic being an investigator Nate used in his practice.

"But he just got married ..."

"Dom?"

"Yeah, who'd have guessed, huh? Anyway, I've got him on another case and his home life is making certain demands on him. See where this is headed?"

"Do you really think a murder charge against Queenie has legs, Nate?"

"You know how it is over there, they've got a scenario they've come up with and unless someone else presents a more compelling one, that's the one they're going with. We'll see if they can make a case for it at the preliminary hearing but they had enough to get a judge to sign the warrant. So, you want the gig?"

"To find out what really happened to Brian McFadden?"

"You're clever, my man. See, you ought to be a private eye."

With that encouragement, I headed down the mountain to get out of the law's sight before they decided they had more business with me. When I was sure they couldn't see me, I stopped to call Zella and told her what Nate had asked me to do.

"According to Nate, the land is probably going to seized because of the pot, so there's not much that can be done on the trust deal until we get her exonerated."

"You sound very confident."

"I know she didn't murder the kid. What possible reason could she have?"

"And growing marijuana?" my boss asked. "From what I've heard about Ms. Weaver, that wouldn't be much of a stretch. You're the one who's always saying, 'You never know.'"

"If she was growing the stuff, then the whole land trust deal is moot anyway," I said. "So I think we should terminate my contract with MCDE for the time being. Don't drag the agency into another tawdry affair."

"That's probably a good idea. I am not one of those who think that all publicity is necessarily good publicity."

7

A half-mile down the road, unfinished wood-plank siding gave a rustic appearance to a new or recently refurbished house. I pulled into the small graveled parking area in front. A woman stood up from tending a kitchen garden, strawberry blond hair tucked up under a wide-brimmed straw hat. She was five-five or so, wearing snug jeans and a man's white oxford-cloth shirt tied up under her breasts. She had a pretty face with freckles and was very tan wherever skin was exposed. I placed her in the mid-thirties.

After twenty years without a left arm, I am often not aware of its absence. This is not true, however, when I am in the company of an attractive female. My wife, Kathy, suggests it goes back to my childhood and my inability to hold the attention of a narcissistic, emotionally cold mother. In spite of having the attentions of a very foxy woman in my adult life, I continued to feel an unmet need. Or so Kathy says. Whatever the reason, I was acutely aware of my abnormality when I stepped out of the Honda.

"Can I help you?" she asked in a honey-tinged southern drawl mixed with Appalachian twang, Blue Ridge Mountains by way of Alabama. Her smile had me believing we were already friends.

"I'm Rick Ryder. You must be Martha Jo."

She stepped toward me. We shook hands.

"How'd you lose the arm?"

No nonsense. I liked that.

"Car accident, twenty years ago."

"Must be a bother," she said.

"Sometimes. Although it does get me the good parking spaces."

"How do you know me?" she asked, ignoring the joke.

"Queenie mentioned your name. The short of it is," I said, overcoming my self-consciousness and the urge to flirt, "Queenie's been arrested for the murder of Brian McFadden, and for growing pot. I wanted to find out what, if anything, you or Stan could tell me about what's going on."

"Queenie? Murder? Oh, that's ridiculous."

"My thoughts exactly, although her lawyer points out that ridiculous is not a defense. I'd like to find out what you knew about Brian, his comings and goings as well as any credence to this pot thing. Is Stan around?"

"I believe he went to town."

"Know when he'll be back?"

"Could be an hour. Could be supper time. Not likely to be later than that. Stan doesn't miss many meals."

I'd caught a passing look at Stan the day before and they seemed an unlikely couple. I guessed her for at least twenty years his junior. You never knew.

"Care to come in for some coffee?" she asked, making a small drama of pulling off her gardening gloves, smiling at me. I rarely refused coffee, often went out of my way to find some. This would be the opportunity to ask questions I might not get the same answers for if Stan was around. I ignored the intimations of what might be on offer besides a hot beverage.

We went up onto a deck off the side of the house and into a very modern kitchen. A skylight filled the room with sun. She dumped some coffee beans into one of those machines that grinds them, then brews them, all with one push of a button. I sat at a table in the breakfast nook while she did the preparations.

"How long have you lived out here?" I asked as she stretched to get cups out of a cupboard. When she reached up, the undersides of her breasts showed below the shirt. I tried not to stare.

"Two years," she said.

"That how long you've been with Stan?"

"Actually, we've been married almost three years. When I first met him, this place was just an old cabin, nice if you like pioneering. I don't. When he asked me to marry him I asked where we'd live and almost laughed in the poor man's face when he said 'out at Queenie's,' 'cause I knew this was the place he was talking about. I said I'd marry him if we lived in a modern house. Took him the better part of the year to get the old lady to pop for it and then do the work."

"Stan did this?"

"He had some help. But that's what Stan did before he came to work for Queenie. Built houses, environmentally friendly homes, now what they're calling green. That was twenty years ago, and he was a little ahead of his time. He's not the greatest businessman, anyway, so he jumped at the opportunity to come out here and be her 'superintendent.' That's his formal title. He's the caretaker of this whole place."

"It looks great," I said. The coffee had made itself and she was pouring.

"Cream, sugar?"

"Black, thanks."

"Yeah, he is handy. The old ... Queenie doesn't really appreciate him, I don't think."

"But he's been working for her for twenty years?"

"Yeah, it's safe, you know? No worries, he thinks. I keep telling him with the green craze now setting in, he could be making a shit— a boat-load of money building houses again."

"But he doesn't want to do it?"

She shrugged, then stood again, moving back to the cupboards.

I struggled to keep my gaze at eye level, hard to do while I was sitting and she was standing. Although not skinny by any means, she didn't seem to have any excess on her bones. I wondered what else she did besides gardening to stay trim. I was sure she was aware of how the eyes of men—and likely some women—would graze over her figure.

She returned with a bottle of Jack Daniels, setting it on the table between us. "Want something to make it interesting?"

"No, thanks."

"You must have one of those employers has an attitude about drinking on the job," she said, pouring a finger of the smoky brown liquid into her mug. "Anyway, it's like he's stuck here. Quicksand. Whenever he's mentioned the idea of leaving, Queenie ups his salary, or gives him another perk, just enough to keep him here. Every time he tries to make a move, he just gets in deeper."

"How about we go out on the deck?" I asked. "Seems like too nice a day to be inside."

We gathered our drinks and went outside where we sat at the shaded end of a picnic table.

I took the move as an opportunity to change the subject back to my real interest.

"You think the idea that Queenie would kill Brian is ridiculous."

"I've forgotten. Why it is you're here asking questions about it?"

"I don't think I said. Up until about a half-hour ago, I was working for the Mountain Center for the Defense of the Environment, helping to put together a land trust deal for Ms. Weaver. Then the Brian thing happened and she's been arrested and her lawyer assumes the land will be seized so that puts the land trust on hold ... and I've now been hired to investigate."

She gave me a queer look. I pulled out one of my "Richard 'Rick' Ryder, Investigations" cards and handed it to her.

"I'm also a private eye."

Her eyes widened, one of the fun things about telling people you're a P.I. She said, "I really can't see Queenie doing something like that. Although I had been getting the feeling that the kid was wearing thin with her, if you know what I mean."

"No, I don't."

"He was always around, like a shadow stuck to her."

"I got the impression from her that he was out around the property a lot, fishing for trout, whatever. I didn't get the impression she accompanied him."

She stood up with her cup.

"More?" she asked.

"About half," I said. I caught myself staring at her as she walked away.

When she returned with the refills, she said, "He was a nice kid and all, but he seemed to have this weird kind of infatuation for her."

I remembered Queenie saying something about her taking a shine to the boy.

"I mean," she went on, "I don't think there was anything ..." She paused.

"Sexual?"

"God, no. Nothing like that. It just was kind of, I don't know, just weird."

I wondered if Martha Jo had been jealous. Brian was apparently a very good-looking young man, and he and Martha Jo would have been near their respective peak sexuality, chronologically speaking. I wondered what Stan thought of the boy. So I asked.

"Stan? He thought Brian was some spoiled rich dabbler. Playing at being an adventurer out here in the Blue Ridge Mountains."

"Rich?"

"That's what Stan thought. Thought the kid might be trying to figure out a way to get his hands on some of Queenie's money."

"If he was rich, why would he have to do that?"

"You know rich people—there's never enough."

I thought that was true about some people with money. Or power. Especially true of people with both.

"What about the pot growing? Wouldn't Stan know if something like that was going on out here?"

"It's a big piece of property. He didn't go trudging around all of it. Just what needed to be maintained. The roads, the houses, fences, that kind of thing."

"And that's a full-time job?"

"Is when Queenie's your boss."

"Queenie talked about how a lot of land adjacent to hers had recently been bought up. Know anything about that?"

She shook her head. "Don't pay attention to that kind of thing," she said. "Doesn't really affect us one way or another."

I doubted that was true, didn't imagine there was anything remotely connected to this place that she didn't know about.

"Is Stan in Queenie's will?"

"What the hell's that got to do with anything?"

She gave me a hard look, like I had just changed shapes in front of her eyes. "You think if Stan's in the old broad's will, maybe he was afraid she'd put the kid in there, too? So he offs the kid to protect his inheritance? Kind of a stretch, isn't it?"

"I was just wondering how tight their relationship was. I didn't mean to suggest ..."

"Yeah, yeah, yeah," she said with the wave of a hand.

I figured the sheriff's people would be along any time and I had probably just worn out my welcome.

"Thanks for the coffee," I said. "I guess I better see what's happening to Queenie. I'd like to come back and talk some more."

"See if you can find out about our secrets," she said.

"And what secrets would those be?"

"Now, they wouldn't be secrets if I told you, would they?"

She got up as I walked off the back deck. When I turned to get back in the Honda, she was leaning over the deck railing, smiling. I wondered what it would be like to talk to her later in the day, assuming the finger of bourbon in her coffee would not be the last she'd enjoy before sundown.

8

I called Nate's office and asked Katrina to tell her boss I was headed into town. She put me on hold for a few seconds before coming back and telling me he'd meet me at the Downtown Bakery.

Martha Jo gave a little wave from her perch on the deck as I drove off. Apparently, I was back in her good graces.

Cop cars were still sitting in front of Queenie's when I passed by. I didn't slow down. Twenty minutes later I lucked into a parallel-parking space directly across the street from the cafe. My Honda slipped in easily, a modest challenge as a one-armed parking maneuver.

Nate was already in a booth. Were it not for the color of his skin, I might have walked right past him. I still hadn't gotten used to his new look. Since a heart attack three months ago, the former Brown University tackle had lost forty pounds. That left him at about two hundred twenty on a six-two frame, still an imposing – even intimidating – figure, a fact about himself he was known to use to his advantage around the courthouse.

I got some coffee and joined him. He chewed an ever-present stogie between his teeth as we shook hands and exchanged pleasantries.

"Looking good, big man," I said.

"Wait'll I hit two hundred. Then you'll really know what a lean, mean, fighting machine looks like."

I asked him what he'd learned at court.

"Apparently," he said, "when the helicopter went in to extricate Brian's body from the woods, the pilot spotted some suspicious-looking shrubs growing in the forest. He thought they might be marijuana plants and called it in. That's what the second helicopter was doing out there, confirming there was pot growing on Queenie's property."

"How does that translate to murder?"

"The backpack Brian was carrying? Or was on him in the river, anyway? It had a couple of very sizable buds in it, that sinsemilla stuff, like six inches long, couple of inches around when they dried it out. The theory they are espousing is that Queenie was growing the stuff with Brian's assistance and he started helping himself to the fruits of their labor."

"Isn't that kind of a stretch?" I asked, hearing myself repeat Martha Jo's words.

"Absolutely. Unfortunately, the judge was Thomas Earwood. You know Thomas?"

"Vaguely. Pretty conservative, I understand."

"That's a gentle way of putting it. During the heyday of the civil rights action around here, he was very much an obstructionist. The course of history has favored the likes of Ms. Weaver and myself. He's never gotten over it."

"Was he one of the folks who thought you and Queenie were a twosome?"

It's a good thing his cigar wasn't lit because it came flying out of his mouth and across the table at me like a guided missile. I put my hand up to stop it from exploding on my face. He shook in silent laughter.

"Yeah, I suppose he was. But you know, I'm not sure which

was most disappointing to them: thinking we were a couple, or finding out we weren't."

He sipped from his coffee mug, then leaned forward, elbows on the table, fingers meshed, making a lean-to of his arms. His voice was low as if he was taking me into a conspiracy.

"So, anyway, here Queenie and I come this morning waltzing into his court. Now, I happen to think our system of jurisprudence is, overall, a pretty good system, better than a lot around the world. One aspect of that system is that we give judges a whole lot of discretion in their courts. There are checks and balances, blah, blah, blah, but the reality is that someone like the Honorable Judge Earwood can let his animosities play out in his courtroom."

He lowered his arms and drank some more, then let his spine fall against the back of the booth.

"I don't think for a second that Queenie's had a thing to do with any of this. But there are some interesting questions."

I waited a few seconds for clarification and finally asked, "Questions like ...?"

"Like, why is it you just happened to be down at the falls?"

"Me?"

"The bunch of you. Why did Queenie want to go there?"

"How does that play into it? I mean, if she did the murder, why wouldn't she just leave the body there, wait until somebody came looking for him?"

"Because by going down there, it would seem to remove blame from her. People would think like you just did. Surely she wouldn't have killed him and then taken people to the body. Ergo, she must be innocent. That's what she is hoping people will think. Or so the thinking of the prosecutor goes. Ergo, she's really guilty."

"Meaning, if you act in a way that would tend to demonstrate you're innocent, you're guilty?"

"Don't play naïve with me, Richard. You're a lawyer. You

know how it works."

"I presume you've talked to her about why we were down there."

"I have. And I'm hoping what you have to say will be in accord with her story."

"Jay and I were out there talking to her about creating a land trust and she was showing off the property. That's it."

"Pretty big piece of property," Nate said, rolling the stogie around with his teeth. "Could take days to see it all."

"I guess Weaver Falls is the crown jewel of the place."

Nate nodded slowly as if coming to agreement with some unseen commentator.

"So, there's work to be done," he said, looking at me with no particular expression.

"Like looking into who was really growing the weed. Did she tell you about the threats?"

"Yes, and we told the judge about them. Made no difference, but at least we're on record."

"I've been assuming they have to do with all the property that's been bought up recently and somebody's desire to buy her land."

"Reasonable assumption. Unless it was somebody who wanted her away from the marijuana. Even if she wasn't the one growing it, somebody may have had reason to believe she knew about it. I'm just makin' that up, but it's another scenario." He began to slide out of the booth. "Time to go defend the downtrodden against the weight of the system."

When Nate smiled, he brought to mind Samuel L. Jackson in a conservative suit and tie, black hair combed straight back from his forehead. With the stogie, he looked like a man from another era.

9

Layers of white clouds moving in from the west heralded a change in the weather as I walked the two blocks to the courthouse. Madeline Bennett greeted me in the Register of Deeds office. She was a tall, good looking, middle-aged – that is to say, about my age – woman. Her hair was black and she wore it straight, a style I guessed hadn't changed much since high school. She had on black slacks and a silky white blouse buttoned to the neck. I find those silky blouses sexy. I wonder if the wearer feels the same way.

"Hello, Mr. Ryder," she said. A blind man would know she was smiling.

"Hi, Madeline. I'm doing some work for Queenie Weaver. Need to see what people have been paying for land around her place recently."

"I'd noticed activity out there. She's not going to sell the place, is she?"

"No. Just looking to see what she can do to take care of the property in case of, oh, eventualities."

Madeline gave me an "are you going to tell me more?" look. When I didn't, she said. "Well, I hope she can hang on to it. It's beautiful out there."

"You know the place?"

"Yeah. I'm kind of kin to her. Third cousins twice-removed, that kind of thing. When I was a kid, there used to be family reunions out there. Not sure why they stopped having them."

I enjoyed the banter, but I needed to get down to business and Madeline turned me loose among the stacks. Everything is kept digitally these days, and they have computer terminals in the Register of Deeds office for the public to use, but I'm old-fashioned. I like to have the books in my hand. I doubt that I'll ever get one of those gadgets you can download books from the Internet onto for the same reason. I plan to keep messing around in the hard copies of things in the court house as long as they let me. Within five minutes of beginning my search, I was lost in the arcane language of real estate transactions and the small dramas it documented.

Time passed as it does when you're oblivious to what's going on around you. It took a second to realize Madeline was talking to me again.

"It's almost one o'clock, Mr. Ryder. I'm going down to the deli to pick up a sandwich. Can I get you anything?"

My look must have reflected the void that came over my mind.

"I'm getting a club sandwich. It's very good."

After my brain had reengaged, I asked, "They have a Reuben?"

"I heard about Ms. Weaver," she said. "It's kind of the talk of the courthouse." We were eating our sandwiches in a break room tucked into a corner of the old building. "No one really believes it," she went on. "They know she and Judge Earwood have a history, figure he's just settling a grudge and they'll drop the charges."

"I don't know. Nate ... you know Mr. Chatham?"

"Who doesn't?"

"He seems to think they're serious. It's not only the judge, but the D.A."

"I wish they'd just go ahead and make him a judge, too. Get him out of that office. You didn't hear me say that."

"Say what?"

By mid-afternoon I had turned up some interesting information. An outfit calling itself HPB Holding, LLC, a name I presumed was intentionally obscure, had bought a couple of large parcels near, but not adjacent to, Queenie's property. The agent of record on both sales was Pete Haywood. I copied down the salient information and put the books back in the stacks.

"Don't be a stranger," Madeline called as I walked toward the door. I smiled in return.

Pete Haywood's machine answered my call. I left my name and home phone number and asked that he call me back. A man answered when I called my wife's office. A young man. Her assistant. A very young man. She hired him about six months ago when her business had begun to take off. Good looking young man. He was working to pay his way at the local branch of the state university where he was studying the universe of computing. His name was Warren. I liked Warren. I was jealous of Warren. Not that I thought anything would actually happen between him and Kathy. It was more that I coveted the amount of time he got to spend with her. We exchanged hellos and he put me through to my wife.

I told her about the morning's drama and my conversation with the caretaker's wife.

"She was drinking whiskey in her coffee this morning and my guess is it wouldn't be her last drink of the day. She may be a little looser of tongue by the time I get out there again. Depending on how it goes, I could be a little later getting home than usual."

"That's okay. I got another contract today. Call me when you're done and we can go out to celebrate. I'll buy."

Sometimes it bothered me that she didn't take more of an

interest in my work, letting the whole idea of a murder investigation go without comment. On the other hand, while she was clearly excited about what was happening in her professional life, I was too wrapped up in my own stuff to be very enthusiastic about some new work she had.

Sonny greeted me noisily as I crested the rise at Queenie's house. When I got out, he immediately stopped barking, maybe because there was no one at home for him to protect. I scratched under his chin and along his haunches and told him I'd be back. The place was eerily quiet. I got back in my car and headed down the hill toward Stan and Martha Jo's. Sonny followed me about twenty yards before turning back.

No truck was in sight at the caretaker's house. There was a recumbent figure on the deck as I pulled up.

I said "Hi" as I approached.

It wasn't until I got closer that I became aware that all she was wearing were bikini bottoms, a straw hat and sunglasses. That's unless you counted the drink in her hand as part of her attire.

"Come on up," she said.

I tried not to stare.

"Do my boobs bother you?" she said.

The truthful answer would have been "yes." But then she might cover up and then I wouldn't be bothered anymore, and where was the fun in that.

What I said was, "Yes, but I'll get used to it."

"It?"

"Them."

"Okay. Back so soon?"

She didn't sound as loaded as I thought she might be and the hat and glasses effectively obstructed her face so it was hard to get a reading.

"Yeah, I was hoping to talk to Stan," I lied.

"Me, too, the son-of-a-bitch. Been gone all fucking day. I thought we were goin' in to town. Wanna drink?"

I amended my previous assessment. "Tea," I said, "unsweetened, if you've got it."

"Oh, come on. The sun's way over the yardarm."

She was sitting up, drawing attention to the uncovered parts of her body. She was very well put together. If any of it was due to the miracles of modern medicine, it didn't show.

"That's okay. Tea's fine."

"What are you, a fucking teetotaler?"

"Yes."

"You aren't in fucking AA, are you?"

"Yes."

"Well, goddam. I tried that once. Didn't work."

There's a saying in AA that the program doesn't work you, you have to work the program. I kept my mouth shut. She was on her feet now, headed for the kitchen door, wobbling slightly before getting her sea legs.

"Have a seat, I'll be right back."

She returned with my tea and was standing alongside me, the interesting bits of her torso at eye level, when the pickup truck pulled into the yard. She stayed where she was, waiting for her husband to come over.

When he got within earshot, she said, "Fuck have you been?"

"Hell's it to you?"

"Shit, is it going to be one of those afternoons?"

"Depends on if you can keep your mouth under control." His eyes let go of Martha Jo and latched on to me. "And the fuck you doin' here, Ryder?"

What with the melodrama going on, it was hard for me to tell if he was pissed off just because I was there or pissed that I was sitting there with his wife's bare boobs in my face.

"I thought you might take me down to the falls from the other side. I'm working for ..."

"I don't care who the fuck you're working for. Get out of here. And stay out. This is none of your business."

"Actually, it is my business. I'm working for Nate Chatham, Queenie's lawyer."

"Damn ni ..."

He caught himself before the "n" word came out.

"Whatever you think of the man," I said, "he's a damn good attorney. If anybody can get her out of this mess, he can."

"That kid never should have been allowed the run of the land. I told her that."

"Why?"

"Get me some Jack," he said toward Martha Jo as he came up on the porch. "And cover yourself up. You're not on stage anymore." Then he turned back to me. "'Cause something like this could happen. That's why. But, like with everything else, she never listened to me."

"You've been working for her how long?"

"Twenty years."

"And she's never listened to you in twenty years. Think you'd get tired of it."

Martha Jo returned carrying his whiskey and wearing a top. Not much of a top but enough to satisfy the requirement.

"I think it's me," she said. "I think she paid attention to him before I showed up. Then she thought everything he was saying came out of my mouth."

This stuff was better than watching daytime TV.

"So you don't get along with her," I said, using the active listening technique I'd picked up in my years on a therapist's couch.

"Oh, I get along with her okay. She just doesn't think I'm

good enough for her Stan."

"I'm not her Stan," the man said.

"Yeah, and the Pope don't wear a pointy hat. Oh, and by the way, the cops came by."

"What'd they want?"

"Well, you know, somebody died and they think he was murdered and they found pot growing on the property. Wanted to know what I might know about any of it."

An expressionless look hovered between them, like that between a hypnotist and his subject. I wasn't sure which role to ascribe to whom.

"What'd you say?"

"What could I say since I don't know anything? And, of course, they also wanted to know where the fuck you were. I don't think they believed me when I said I didn't know."

As if on cue, they both turned to look at me.

"What are you still doing here, Ryder?" Stan asked.

I wanted to say, "enjoying the show," but was afraid it would not be well received. Instead, I said, "Just leaving, Stan." Nodding toward his wife, I said, "Martha Jo, good to see you again," hoping the "again" might give them grist to chat about for a while. Walking off the deck toward my Honda, I did not get the hospitable, "Y'all come back."

10

Much of the time the sleuthing game is like watching an impressionist painter at work. Dabs of color get added a little at a time so that, slowly, something recognizable begins to take shape. I had gotten an impression of Martha Jo and Stan, but the picture was still far from clear. Queenie hadn't suggested anything was amiss with her employee, but how much had Stan's relationship with Queenie changed after he married the younger woman? Were they people likely to conspire to get Queenie's land away from her? And, remembering Stan about to call Nate the "n- word," I wondered how he could carry around such barely suppressed racism for twenty years while working for a radical integrationist.

Sonny ran down from the porch as I approached the big house, tail waving at half-mast. He might have been semi-happy to see me, but he'd rather have seen his mistress. Although Stan would probably see that the dog didn't starve, he might also be reluctant to cross the yellow crime-scene tape designed to keep the place under wraps. I, however, was not burdened by such qualms. I assumed the front door would be locked and a jiggle on the handle proved me right.

Sonny followed me around the side of the house. More yellow tape confronted us at the back door. I poked under flower pots and over the door jamb, and then stepped off the back porch to look around for other likely places where Queenie might keep an extra key.

Sonny trotted over to an old garage behind and off to one side of the house. He sat straight up as if he was a sentry, like one of those lion dogs outside museums and palaces. More yellow tape warned that this, too, was off limits. There was no lock on the big doors, the kind that opened out from the center. When I shook their handles, carefully, so I wouldn't break the tape if they were to open, they didn't give. I looked back over at Sonny and noticed the cinder block he had sat down next to. I lifted it up. Voila! Around to my right, a side door to the garage was also adorned with bright yellow ribbon. Turning the key in its lock resulted in a satisfying clunk.

The smell of petroleum hit me as soon as I pushed open the door and ducked under the tape. It took me right back to the Ohio of my childhood, in my dad's workshop. Gasoline and engine oil, paint thinner and lubricating grease. For an instant, I forgot where I was. It took a few seconds for my eyes to adjust to the low afternoon sunlight falling in through two small windows. Reaching around on the wall, I found a switch. The added artificial light made little difference. My eyes wandered. It appeared to be an ordinary working garage. A lawn tractor parked in the middle of the concrete floor. A work bench. Shelves with jars of screws and nails. Tools arrayed on boards. Lawn tools on hooks. This was primarily Stan's province, I guessed. A few cobwebs adorned the upper reaches, but other than that and a very thin layer of dust, it was clear that whoever worked in here was of the "a place for everything and everything in its place" school of maintenance. I saw the latch that secured the big doors from the inside. A quick walk around the inside perimeter revealed nothing of interest until I noticed a bare spot on a shelf over the workbench. Perhaps six feet long, it was conspicuous for the absence of dust except at the ends of the board and an uneven edge along the front, as if a row of books had recently been removed. As I got up close, I noticed that the dust that formed the outline was whiter than what had accumulated elsewhere. The cops must have dusted for fingerprints before removing whatever had been there.

It was getting late and I had a date with my wife. My eyes swept the room one more time before I grabbed an old rag off the workbench. While I assumed the police had already gathered finger prints, I still wiped off the light switch and the door knob as I headed out, slipping back under the tape. To my surprise and good fortune, the garage key also opened the house. My companion showed me directly to the pantry where his food was stored. After he made short work of a bowlful, I filled his water bowl and put it on the back porch before calling Kathy. We agreed to meet at our favorite Mexican restaurant in forty-five minutes.

I used the garage rag as I went on into the house through the kitchen door. Given the noise I'd heard when the SWAT team was here, I was surprised things weren't in greater disarray. Just as in the garage, dust patterns showed where things had been moved around but I couldn't tell if anything was missing until I got to her office. Drawers from a four-drawer file cabinet lay empty on the floor. The surface of a desk had been cleared except for a phone and computer monitor. There was a printer, but the CPU was gone.

It was time for me to leave if I was going to be on time to meet Kathy. Sonny had stayed at my side throughout my explorations, like Watson to my Sherlock. When I got back in my car, his tail stopped wagging altogether. For an instant, I thought about taking him with me, then thought about our cats. And, if I took him, Stan would probably file charges for dog-napping.

I was already seated at a table, drinking a glass of tonic water with lime, when Kathy arrived. She lingered in our kiss an iota of a second longer than the customary end-of-the-work-day greeting.

"Feeling good?" I asked.

"Having people tell you they'll give you a lot of money for doing what you like to do can have that effect on a person."

A waitress brought her a glass of the house red without Kathy having to ask.

We had long ago gotten beyond the "does it bother you if I drink" stage and it was her habit to have one or two glasses of wine in the evenings. I asked her about the contract.

"You remember the town I'd been consulting with, the one that got sued after a kid fell last year and broke his neck?"

"Yeah?"

"They finally settled with the family out of court. Part of the settlement was to get the city's playgrounds up to standard. The family was willing to settle because the city had already hired me to tell them what they had to do. Now I get to do it."

Kathy had been a phys ed teacher before getting her MBA. After several years as a sales rep for manufacturers of playground equipment, she became a consultant and now worked with school systems, municipalities, day care centers, anybody who had recreational space for children.

"So, I'll be going to Georgia for a couple of days."

My stomach dropped as it did every time she mentioned traveling out of town. Last year, when I had been caught up in the drama of being accused of murder and trying to exonerate myself, she had had a "brief" affair with a man in Charlotte. "Twice," she'd said, "and it's over, and we're not going to talk about it." She did admit it was probably a pay-back for my dalliance – as chaste as it had been – with a young stripper. After her third or fourth trip out of town after all the turmoil had settled, I told her I was having trouble letting go of the Charlotte episode. "It's over," she said. "It's been over. Maybe you need to go back to therapy," she said, making it clear my insecurity was my problem to deal with, not hers.

When I was eighteen and had been drinking heavily, I caused a car wreck in which a young girl died and I lost my arm. My drinking progressed in the wake of the tragedy even as I was seeing a succession of counselors. Eventually, I got involved in AA and had been sober for ten years before my one-day relapse a year and a half ago. I hadn't had a drink since. I did talk to my sponsor about being jealous and insecure and even brought it up occasionally at AA meetings. I had come to accept it was just something I was going to have to live with, like the phantom pains that sometimes inhabited my non-existent arm.

"Try not to go there, okay," she said just before the waitress came for our order. "You're my guy, you know?"

"I know," I said, wishing my brain was able to make my gut understand as well. A shoeless foot began to caress my ankle under the table. The demons disappeared.

The cats, Wilbur and Gladys, had let themselves in through their little door and were pacing the kitchen by the time we got home. I fed them and they disappeared, back out the way they came in. They would return sometime during the night after they had augmented their diet with whatever wildlife they could outwit in the woods. I tried not to think of them as the nasty little predators they were.

Kathy and I retired early but, in spite of the bedtime athletics that ensued, I knew my fear would rear up in a couple of days when she packed her bags in the Infiniti and headed out.

As I was ascending from the basement gym the next morning, I heard a message being left on my business answering machine. A woman's voice, youngish, with a slight tremor.

"Mr. Ryder. A friend gave me your name and said you might be able to help me. Please call as soon as you can." She left the necessary information.

I suppose everybody who gets in the sleuthing game has romantic notions of being a latter day Sam Spade or Philip Marlowe – flirt with murder, drink whiskey in the middle of day, associate with dangerous women. My first case actually involved a woman and drugs and people with guns. Since then, the bulk of my work had consisted of background checks for people involved in Internet dating. Most of that was accomplished sitting at a computer. Every phone call offered a moment of exotic possibility. Even so, I took time to shower, dress, and get a cup of coffee before returning her call.

"Thank you for calling," she said after I'd identified myself. And said nothing else.

"How can I help you?" I offered, to break the silence.

"I'm being followed."

I let that sit a few seconds.

"By someone you know?"

"I don't want to talk about it on the phone."

She could have been paranoid or histrionic. Or, reasonably fearful. Her name was Audrey Hollingsworth, she had given me that much, and we agreed to meet in the back room of the Sunshine Café on the west side of town. I said she should come at 8:30. I would already be there. I would be the guy with one arm. That's one time when it's convenient – I don't have to wear a flower in my lapel or have a newspaper folded a certain way to identify myself.

It was early enough and warm enough outside to enjoy a cup of coffee and an English muffin on the deck with Kathy before heading out. The cats graced us with their presence, lolling in the sunlight that had made its way over the ridge and down the hillside behind the house. The creek murmured contentedly to us as it passed near the house.

The ringing of the landline stopped me in my tracks as I was headed out the door. Again, I debated the merits of not answering but couldn't stand the not knowing.

"Mr. Ryder. This is Pete Haywood. You called yesterday. Sorry it's taken so long to get back to you."

We agreed to meet at his office north of town at ten. It was shaping up to be an interesting day. I was excited and recalled the Chinese curse: "May you live in interesting times."

11

I got Katrina on the phone at Nate's office. I told her about my appointment to meet Haywood later in the morning. I didn't mention the Hollingsworth woman since she had no connection to my business with Nate. Driving from the house along Cove Road, native and hybrid azaleas in purples and reds adorned the properties of people who had more interest in yard work than I did. Honeysuckle filled the air with its sweet perfume. The ubiquitous rhododendron ran amok through the woods. By the time I'd reached my destination, I had almost forgotten that my life was once more mired in murder and other mayhem.

The Sunshine Café was one of the few businesses that had flowered in the heyday of the west-side community thirty years ago, survived its demise, and blossomed again with the neighborhood's rebirth in the past half-decade. Espresso machines had replaced the multi-gallon coffee pots, scones and bagels joined donuts on the breakfast menu, polyurethaned blond wood tables had displaced Formica and aluminum. I got a coffee at the counter and found a spot in the back.

At five minutes past nine, an attractive woman, late twenties, maybe early thirties, wearing a white skirt cut on the bias so that it fell below one knee and stopped about mid-thigh on the other leg, stood atop the two steps that dropped down into the back room. A gauzy black blouse left an inch of midriff exposed, a black bra was visible beneath the blouse. The two buttons not fastened gave rise to intriguing possibilities. Black leather boots with four inch heels reached up over her calves. She had long, black hair styled in the carefree manner that requires much attention.

She looked in my direction. I stood up as she walked toward me. For a woman worried about being followed, I thought, this is not the way to be unobtrusive.

"Mr. Ryder."

I took her hand. "Rick," I said.

"Rick," she repeated. "Audrey Hollingsworth."

"Want coffee?" I asked.

"Don't drink it. You could see if they have any bottled water." A woman used to being waited on.

"Anything to eat?"

"No thanks."

She was not anorexic but she didn't have any extra fat on her, either. Avoiding scones and pastries was no doubt part of the plan.

I got her water and refilled my cup. She was sitting at an angle to the table with one leg draped over the other when I returned.

"So," I ventured, "you're being followed."

"Yes," she said, apparently taking more delight in exposing her body than in sharing her thoughts.

"Want to tell me about it?"

"What's to tell. Somebody's following me."

This was going to be like picking nits off a chimpanzee, but less nutritious. I figured I might as well be earning some money while I was at it.

"Do you want to hire me?" I asked.

"Yes. That's why I called you."

"OK. Here's what it's going to cost." I mentioned a number for a retainer and told her when we would revisit it. "Plus expenses."

"What kind of expenses?"

"Mostly gas, probably. I'll let you know if other things come up."

"So, we're on the clock now?"

I nodded. "And the quicker you give me something to go on that I don't have to pry out of you, the less it's going to cost."

Her face, which until now had the appearance of something chiseled from granite, softened a degree, a hint she might have a human spirit under there. I realized she wasn't just cold. She was scared.

"It's a little white convertible. It's hard not to notice."

"How often have you seen it?"

"Five, six times."

"Have you seen it today?"

"No."

"When did you first see it?"

"Two, no, three days ago. I think. It's a car that catches your eye, you know. I just noticed it behind me. I didn't think anything of it. But then later in the day, it was there again. I thought it was probably just a coincidence. And it was there the next day."

"Where is there? Near your home? Work? Tell me the story of this. You know, one day I was driving from …"

The first time she saw it she was on her way downtown to work at the advertising agency Hensley, Presley and Associates. On her way home she saw it again. The next day she didn't see it until she had gotten home after work and was on her way to a party in the evening. That was when she first thought something was up, but tried to talk herself into believing it wasn't. The car was behind her again yesterday morning.

"I called the police before I called you. They said there was nothing they could do. He hadn't really done anything. If someone contacted me, you know, let me know they were following me, or started making harassing calls, that kind of thing, then they might look into it."

"You know it's a 'he'?"

"Well, I just assumed, you know. All I can see in the mirror is sunglasses and a ball cap."

I looked at my watch. I had about five minutes before I was going to have to leave to meet Pete Haywood.

"We need to talk more, but I have another appointment this morning. I should be back in town about noon. Maybe we could have lunch." I said I'd call her when I was done with Haywood. "Why don't you wait here while I leave. I'll see if there's a white convertible out there. If there is, I'll maneuver behind it, so I can get a license plate number. I'll call you one way or the other."

There was no white convertible. I called . She thanked me and said she'd be waiting to hear from me later in the morning.

I had to make good time which meant driving on major highways, something I avoid whenever possible. (Friends who live in Charlotte and Atlanta think this is quaint.) There was compensation, however, in being able, when cresting certain rises, to see all the way to the ridge line that formed the boundary with Tennessee. I had the windows down, the air-conditioning off.

On the way, I thought about what I hadn't had time to ask my new client. Was there anybody she could think of – an ex-boyfriend, maybe, or someone she'd turned down for a date – who might do this kind of thing? Because of her earlier reluctance to talk on the phone, I thought it entirely reasonable for me to meet her again in person to have this discussion.

Approaching my highway exit, I shifted mental gears, ready to meet with someone I didn't know but who I had already decided was nefariously mixed up in Queenie Weaver's life.

12

Pete Haywood was a throwback. In a time when most real estate agents I knew reflected the upward-striving consciousness of their clientèle, Pete was a good ole boy who looked like the part-time fundamentalist Baptist preacher he was. Silver hair combed into a pompadour in front, black slacks, white shirt and tie. In cooler weather, I was sure he would have worn the jacket that matched the pants. He had a glad hand and I knew he would never express distaste or negativity to a stranger, saving that for his family and congregation when speaking of the Devil and liberals like myself. He greeted me on the steps of the log house that served as the offices of Realty North as if I was a long lost relative he'd been looking for all his life.

The make-believe dwelling was situated at the edge of a small, recently-built strip mall just off the divided four-lane a few miles north of the city, a made-to-look old-timey house in a trying-to-be up-to-date shopping center.

"Mr. Peters," he said as I approached him.

When I called to set up this meeting, I identified myself as "Rick Peters," Peters being Kathy's maiden name and the name she uses in her business. I was gambling that he wouldn't get suspicious and start asking around about me. It wouldn't take long to find someone in town who knew a one-armed snoop.

"Rick," I said, as we shook.

"Call me Pete," he said, a broad smile stuck onto his face.

"By any chance are you a preacher when you aren't selling real estate?" I asked. I knew for a fact that he was, having inadvertently seen him on TV a couple of Sunday mornings while surfing channels looking for the news.

"Yes, I am. What made you think so, may I ask?"

"I don't know. You have, something, a light about you that makes me think you'd be good at it."

If he detected the smoke I was blowing up his hind end, he didn't let on. What he did do was momentarily let go of the smile, replacing "happy" with "sincere."

"I'm honored you would think that. I'm blessed to have been called. James Creek Free Will Baptist Church. We'd love to have you visit us sometime." The smile crept back. "Come on in."

Other than the country motif which was replicated inside the house, the building looked like any real estate office I'd been in. To the left was a round wooden table surrounded by four matching chairs, a laptop computer and an array of brochures lain out on the surface. On my right was some living room furniture of the same style, a cut above what was standard issue in manufactured homes. The smell of burnt coffee drifted out from a kitchenette.

"So, you want to move up north," he said, responding to the explanation I'd given him for my interest in property out this way.

"Kathy and I really like it out on Cove Creek," I said, "but new subdivisions are going up all over the place out there. Of course, I don't have to tell you about that." The look on his face was a blend of satisfaction and condescension, as if I'd said, "I don't have to tell you about God."

He nodded sagely. "Yeah, that whole area is getting mighty popular."

"I was looking into what property's going for in various parts of the county and saw that you'd handled some recent transactions for an outfit named HPB. That's why I called you in particular. What they paid seemed very reasonable. Got any idea what they're planning for the property?"

The smile slipped for a fraction of a second before he caught it.

"What line of work did you say you were in, Rick?"

"I don't think I did. My wife and I have a playground equipment business." Technically, this was true. When she changed from being a sole proprietor to a limited partnership, I became the partner.

"Playground equipment," he said, as if trying to imagine how one made a living at that.

I nodded. "The county has our equipment," I said. If he felt like it, he could check that out and see the name Peters Playgrounds, PC on the paperwork.

"Well, Rick," he said, apparently satisfied, "I really can't say what HPB has in mind. I think it's reasonable to assume there'll be some kind of development there, but I don't really know. They just told me the kind of area they were looking for, and I knew a couple of the families out there. I was able to put them together."

I nodded again. Thoughtfully.

"So, if I was able to acquire some land in that area, I guess I'd have to be concerned that the same thing would happen that I envision happening to Cove Creek."

"Well, Rick, unless you're looking to buy a whole lot of acreage, that's a risk anywhere in the county. Now, farther north, out of the county, you could find yourself a big enough tract that could protect you from encroachment. But there's really no way to get entirely away from development. People keep coming here, Yankees getting out of the rat race, half-backs – you know, people who go from the north to Florida, then come half-way back –

along with people who grew up here in the city and want to, well, if you live out Cove Creek, you know what I mean. We can look up some stuff on the computer, if you'd like, then go take a look at some places."

What I really wanted to know more about was the HPB property.

"What you're talking about is probably farther out than we were thinking," I said. "That area around the property HPB just bought seems like the perfect location."

"I can talk to them," he said, "see if they're interested in reselling any. You'd have to pay more than they did, of course. And if they've bought it for speculation, I'd think they'd want to hold onto it for a while, especially now that prices are down. I could talk to some other folks out there. See if anybody else is interested in selling."

I heard a car pull off the road into the gravel lot. "Sounds like you have more business and I've got to get back to town. I appreciate your time. Let me know if it seems HPB is interested in dealing or if you come across anything else you think I might be interested in."

He reached out his hand.

"Don't forget that invite to come to church," he said, a tag line I was pretty sure he used with anybody except people with dark skin and those he suspected might be Jewish.

I called Audrey and we agreed to meet at a small bistro on the south side of town in half an hour. Although there were a myriad of good restaurants downtown, the drive would give her another chance to see if she was being followed.

When I called Nate, I was flabbergasted that I got the man himself on the phone.

"Yo, Bro," he began. "Sometimes you gotta love the way the

universe works. The DA wants a million for bail. You know, the usual B.S. Outrage on behalf of the American Public, blah, blah. I, of course, suggest something more modest, in the $100,000 range. Judge says, two-fifty. I go across the street to put up her land as collateral. Turns out that the drug guys were supposed to have seized the property for having been used in the manufacture of an illegal substance. But they didn't get the paperwork done, so now we've got the land tied up with the bail bondsman. You know somebody's going get their rear end chewed for that snafu."

"Queenie's out of jail?"

"Sure is. And spittin' nickels. I'm not sure which has her more upset. Being accused of murder or of growing pot on her land. I told her you were working for me so she's going to want to talk. You might give her a little while, though. Let her cool down some. It can be entertaining listening to her rant, but it's not a very productive use of time."

13

The voice-activated phone in my Honda rang. I called a greeting to it.

"I understand you're going to be working on my case," the voice said.

"Queenie! Good to hear from you," I said, wishing I'd let the call go to voice mail.

"I'm not in the mood for pleasantries. I wanna find out who's behind this."

"Of course," I said, "the sheriff will also be investigating."

"Yeah, and we both know that if this involves anybody other than certifiable low lives, they are going to be tippy-toeing around. Don't want to make waves. Don't want anybody with money and influence unhappy."

"Why, you sound downright cynical."

"Come off it, Rick. You know how it is."

I did. I had my own experience going up against the powers-that-be. The outcome of my run-in with that network was that I didn't get hanged for something I didn't do. But neither did the man most responsible for the murder of which I'd been accused.

"We don't have to turn the world upside down, Queenie. We just need to get you off."

"And protect my property. That's why you came to see me in the first place."

"Queenie, I've got to go now, I'm driving through town to a lunch meeting. I'll come out to your place when I'm done."

"They've got me on a leash, you know. Condition of my release. So, I'll be around."

The Southend Café was tucked into the corner of a moderately upscale huddle of businesses near the southern edge of the county's suburban creep. I parked and stood outside, waiting for Audrey's car and to see if the white convertible was following her. A minute after her blue sports car pulled into the parking lot, a white, topless Miata went by. The driver was wearing a red ball cap turned backwards and sunglasses. Traffic blocked my view of the license plate.

On the drive down, I'd been thinking about how challenging this woman had been when we'd met earlier and what a pain in the neck she could turn out to be. Nonetheless, I smiled when she stepped out of her car, long left leg leading the way. Maybe it wouldn't be a terrible gig.

"Did you see him?" she asked.

"I did," I said, assuming, as she did, that it was a man behind the wheel.

We were not an inconspicuous couple. Audrey dressed in a way to insure she would be noticed and my missing arm were both attention getters. Although it was a perfectly legitimate business lunch, I wouldn't be able to explain my relationship with this woman without violating her confidentiality and was relieved when were seated immediately upon entering the restaurant. After ordering – a small chef's salad and a glass of white wine for her, crab cakes and unsweetened tea for me – I got right to business.

"The logical place to start is, who might have an interest in either stalking you or just annoying you? It doesn't seem like this is a person trying to avoid notice." I thought, but didn't add, much like yourself. "Is there anybody you've broken up with recently, anyone who you've turned down for a date or otherwise, you know, pissed off."

"I'll have to think about that," she said and I wondered if that meant there was a long list.

"The sooner the better. So far he's just following you. But we want to put an end to it before it escalates."

"Escalates?"

I wondered if she was being disingenuous or naïve.

"I've been followed," I said. "It's annoying, disconcerting. Then I got shot at."

Her eyes widened.

"Shot at?"

I nodded.

"Is that how you lost your arm?"

This struck me as a non sequitur. Rather than registering fear for herself, she was more interested in me. I shook my head.

"No. That happened years ago. I'm suggesting that being followed can lead to other things. And I think you know that and that's why you called me."

She picked up her wine glass and leaned back in the booth. "Yes. Of course. That's exactly why I called you," she said in a voice without inflection.

"This shouldn't be too hard, really. I'll follow you at random times, far enough back that he won't know I'm there. Eventually, he'll get behind you, I'll get the plate number and we'll find out who it is. Or at least, who owns the car. In the meantime, if you think of any men, or women for that matter, who fall into the whole 'unrequited love' category, I'll check 'em out, see what kind of cars they drive."

"Then what?"

"You need to keep a diary of every time you see your pursuer. Then you can go to court – I work with a lawyer I'm sure would be happy to represent you – and get a restraining order."

"Even if he's not really done anything to me? If it hasn't, like you said, escalated?"

"If it happens often enough, its harassment."

After our food arrived, she asked what it was like being a private detective. "It must be very exciting," she said, leaning toward me, one elbow on the table, eyes wide, like they were when I said I'd been shot. My sight-line dropped for a fraction of a second to the cleavage made visible by that second unbuttoned button before I recovered eye contact.

There is a place near the middle of a tennis racket known as the "sweet spot." If the ball hits there, the force transmitted to the hand is so small that the player is almost unaware that the impact has occurred. People have sweet spots as well, that place in our psyche where something happens, often with great force, and about which we are unaware when it happens. It's the place where the interest pretty women show in me connects.

"What are you working on now ... besides me?"

"I'd love to tell you all about it," I said, truthfully. "But, just like I won't tell anybody about my work for you, I can't tell you about any other work I might be doing."

"Not even your wife?" she asked. At the time, it didn't occur to me to wonder how she knew I was married. Not having a left hand means I don't wear a ring in the customary place.

I smiled.

"See, you do tell her, don't you? Can't you just tell me what it's about? I mean not with names and all." Her voice became hushed. "Do you catch wandering husbands, that kind of thing?"

"I have and it's not very exciting."

"Less exciting than following around a woman who is herself being followed around?"

"Depends on the woman, I suppose," I said and knew as it came out of my mouth that it came very near to crossing a boundary that should exist between us.

"I hope it doesn't get too exciting," she said, the smile on her face at odds with her words.

To get back on a professional footing, I asked her for her daily itinerary. I said I'd be at her house some mornings when she left for work or at the office when she was done for the day and told her to call me if there were changes in her routine, evening activities, that kind of thing.

"With any luck it should only take one or two outings to get this thing wrapped up," I said, not sure I really wanted it to end that quickly.

The check came and I said we could handle it one of two ways. Either I could pay it and charge it to my expenses which she was paying. Or, she could just pay the check. She chose the latter. When we were outside, she asked when I would start following her.

"No time like the present," I said. "If he follows you back to town, Bingo. If he doesn't, I'll have to earn that retainer."

Then she gave me the names of two men and a woman she thought might be worth checking out. She had worked with one of the men. The other was a friend of a friend whom she'd met at a party. The woman had hit on her at a bar.

"It's not even a gay bar," she said. "I don't know why she thought I'd be interested."

"Hope springs eternal," I said. "You never know."

"It was too creepy."

"Could that have been her under the ball cap?"

"I don't think so. She was more, I don't know. She wasn't

butch at all. Very good looking, I will give her that. She gave me her card. I think I still have it." She fished around in her purse for a minute before saying she guessed she'd thrown it away.

It wasn't until I got back in my car and had a moment to sit with myself that I realized how much I was looking forward to the chase and to finding out more about this woman, how much I was indulging my voyeuristic inclinations. I justified it by reflecting that, if they were honest about it, it was why most P.I.s got into the business.

14

I was going to have to tell Kathy about Audrey and get to an AA meeting soon. The last time I had consorted with an attractive young woman – although nothing more racy than conversation had taken place – I relapsed and wound up charged with murder.

I called Dominic, Nate's other PI, the one who recently got hitched. I knew he was busy but I also knew he had an in at the DMV who often tracked down names for him. That person could get fired or worse for doing it, but seemed to be willing to oblige Dom whenever he called. I presumed it was a woman and wondered if the investigator's recent marriage would put a chill on the relationship. I didn't ask him, just gave him the names.

"Addresses would help," he said.

"I'm sure. But I think they're all in this county. That should narrow it down."

He said he'd do what he could.

I waited for five more minutes with no sign of a white Miata convertible before I headed back up north to see the alleged murderess and illicit drug grower.

"I can't goddam believe it," Queenie said. "I would have expected this kind of thing, wouldn't have been surprised by it, anyway, forty years ago. Hell, I had my life threatened back then and I didn't think they were bluffing. But this ..."

I told her what I'd found out about HPB Holding, LLC, a name I presumed was intentionally obscure, buying five hundred acres from Jesse and Sally May Jenkins and three hundred and fifty acres from Curtis and Pearl Pruitt. The land wasn't immediately adjacent to Queenie's but they bordered on each other and were separated from the Weaver property by some acreage owned by one Ira Ivey. Queenie knew all the parties, all old families, each of them here for at least two generations.

"People get land poor, you know," she said. "Can't afford to pay the taxes and maintain the place. All those Yankees coming in here and jacking prices up. That's OK if you want to sell, but it just screws with your taxes otherwise. And a lot of the developers are local. They're the ones who really frost me. And the real estate guys who make a killing. And the banks who give 'em the money to build a bunch of McMansions, put a fence around 'em, lock 'em in. Oh, geez. I'm sorry to go on like this, Rick. I get to ramblin'. Too much time alone, nobody around to vent on 'cept'n Sonny here. He listens good and all, but he's not much of a conversationalist and I think he misses the finer points of the debate."

The three of us – Queenie, myself, and Sonny – were on her front porch, the non-canines among us drinking iced tea. Although the sky above was unblemished azure, a layer of haze obscured our view of the distant mountains and valleys.

"You know, "she said, "it wasn't that long ago that you could see all those ridges out there, see into Georgia and Tennessee and South Carolina. Not like now, when maybe once in a while on a good day you can see forever, if the wind's right and there's no humidity. Over the last twenty years the southeast has lost more visibility than any other section of the country. Oh, listen to me. I don't have to tell you this stuff. You're the environmentalist."

"But you're right," I said. "And, if we keep cutting down

forests, it's going to get worse."

We were shaded from direct sunlight by the porch roof, but the warmth and after-lunch carbohydrate plunge made me lethargic. I closed my eyes and rocked. I realized I had dozed off when I heard a soft "woof," Sonny barking to something in a dream. I looked around the immediate environs and remembered what my friend in the Register of Deeds office had said about family get-togethers.

"Madeline Bennett said you used to have reunions up here."

Queenie nodded. "Sure did. We'd have fifty, seventy-five people. I think we had five generations represented here one time. The oldest was ninety-eight, I think, and the youngest was a month old."

"What happened?"

"People moved away. My side of the Weavers kind of, you know, petered out – you'll excuse the expression – me bein' a spinster lady and all. They still have 'em, one of the other lines of the family gets folks together. I still get invited and may go some year before it's all over. I think they go to some state park down around Winston. Get a good crowd, I hear."

"So, who gets this property when you die if you don't set up a land trust?"

"Well, let's just cut to the chase here, huh Rick? It's a good question, though. Not having immediate heirs, I've never been too worried about it. But Earle Boyce, know him, over at Boyce Carlyle Boyce …?"

I nodded. Earl was Old Asheville gentry. His family had been lawyering to the aristocracy of the area since the late 1800's. I'd had some conversations with him about families he represented who were interested in land trusts. He met the description of "gentleman" in the sense of a well-born person as well as a courteous and honorable man.

"He's my personal lawyer. Been buggin' me to do a will and

I got to thinkin' about what I wanted to do and then there were those death threats. That's when I called you. You think there's some long lost relative who's heard I might put some of my land in a trust and set me up for murder and a pot growing rap?"

"Might be good to know who stands to lose if you park some of your land where nobody can get at it, someone who might have had visions of one of those McMansion developments for themselves."

Her gaze turned toward north Georgia. She closed her eyes, as if it was all too much to think about.

The drone of cicadas and the wind shshing through the pines were the only sounds until Sonny barked. I thought he might still be dreaming until he jumped up and ran to the bottom of the porch steps. He kept barking as a dust plume swelled in the road coming up from Stan and Martha Jo's place.

The now-familiar pickup appeared over the rise. Sonny assumed his lion-dog stance as Stan got out of the truck and came up the steps. Sonny's tail was still. The man made no indication he was aware the dog was there.

He nodded in my direction as he said, "Ryder."

"Stan."

That was the extent of the social amenities. He turned toward Queenie. "You not answerin' your phone?"

"Been out here with Rick, left my cell inside. Can't hear the land line. What's up?"

"We gonna have a conversation about all this?"

"All this? By that you mean murder, pot growing, my arrest. That kind of 'all this'?"

"Yeah."

"Well, I thought we would. I figured Mr. Ryder'd like a little of your time, as well. I'd thought maybe the two of us'd come down and see you and your lovely bride."

There was no hint of irony in her voice.

Stan looked back at me with barely masked disdain.

"You know he's working for Nate," she said, "investigating the murder and the other stuff. So, I expect you'll cooperate with him."

He looked over at me again then back to Queenie.

"Yeah, he told me. Sure. I'll help any way I can."

I kept my skepticism to myself.

"So," she said, "you know anything about pot being grown on my property?" Very matter-of-factly, like an attorney asking a question in a court room.

Lawyers are used to dealing with liars among clients and adversaries, not to mention our own colleagues. The hesitation. The shifting of the eyes. Hardcore sociopaths can get away with it, can even beat polygraphs.

Stan was not a sociopath. He may have had anti-social inclinations but I could tell he was getting ready to prevaricate.

"Why're you even asking me that? Of course I don't. What would I know about it?"

"Don't know. That's why I asked."

"Well, I'm kind of offended you even thought about it."

"Yeah, well I don't like being arrested, either. I'm like my man here," she said, giving a slight nod in my direction, "just checking all the possibilities."

The less kindly look reappeared on his face as he looked my way.

"Now, Queenie, you know I only ever have your best interests in mind around here."

"I always assumed that, Stan. So, how could someone be growing enough pot that it could be seen from the air and us not know about it?"

"It's over in that southeast corner neither of us ever go to any more. There's really nothing there, just a bunch of scrub growth and rhododendron hells and that little stream that's kind of dried up these days."

"Don't we have fence along there? Don't you check on it?"

Here comes another one, I thought.

"Well, not as much as I should, I guess."

"You guess? Goddam, Stan. That's why the fuck we have fences. Excuse my French."

It surprised me and seemed to take Stan equally unprepared. I thought this was a good time to go on the offensive.

"Like Queenie said, Stan, I would like some of your time. I was hoping you'd drive me around the property."

"Why you wanna do that?"

"To snoop around. That's what I do."

"I dunno. I'm kinda busy today."

"With stuff for me?" Queenie asked.

"Well, uh ..."

"Stan. I've been charged with murder. The feds want to take away my land because there's been pot growing on it. Gettin' that stuff cleared up is my priority and while you're on my time that's your priority, too. Got it?"

"Yes, ma'am," he said with a face that looked like it had been chiseled out of ice.

"Don't do that, Stan. He's here to help me. Be nice."

He loosened the glare he was holding on her and looked back over to me, his face thawing a degree or two.

"OK. Sorry. I guess we're all kinda stressed out."

"That we are," I said. "So, Queenie, we done for now?"

She agreed we were. I told Stan I'd follow him to his house, and then he could drive us from there, keep him from having to come back up here. I saw him pull out his cell phone before he got in his truck and imagined he was calling Martha Jo to tell her to get dressed.

15

Martha Jo was nowhere to be seen as I pulled alongside Stan's pickup. He came promptly out of the house and climbed in the behind the steering wheel, wearing the expression of a kid who's been made to do chores instead of being out playing ball. I grabbed onto the door frame to hoist myself into the passenger seat.

Scanning the interior as I buckled myself in, I noted the leather seats and the dashboard that made me think of the cockpit of an airplane. "Nice," I said. "What year?"

"'2009."

"Looks brand new."

He waited a few seconds before saying anything else. "It's a repo. I bought it from the bank. So, where you wanna go? This is a big piece of property. We could spend all day and not see all of it." The edge was gone from his voice, maybe because I'd admired the truck. Maybe he liked the idea of roaming around, getting away from the women in his life.

"Can you take me to where the pot patch is, or was?"

A second passed before he answered. "Don't know exactly where that is."

"But you have an idea. You said it was off in some corner you never went to, or hadn't been to recently." Until just then, as the words came out of my mouth, I hadn't wondered how he knew even that much.

As if he'd read my mind, he said, "The cops were like Queenie, giving me a hard time about, you know, if I was the caretaker of the property, how come I wasn't aware there was this big plot of pot growing on it? I said I still didn't know where it was and they described the place."

Possible, I thought, although in my experience, the police ask for information; they don't give it out.

The road from Queenie's house at the crest of the ridge down to Stan and Martha Jo's place was a continuation of Weaver's Mountain Road. It continued to descend slowly, carving a horseshoe with two long legs through the woods and fields. When we came to a gate, Stan got out, opened it and returned to the car.

"The property line?" I asked.

He nodded. "Gotta go down, pick up an old logging road, that would be how they got up in there without us knowing about it," he said. "That's what this is, too. Old logging road. Area's full of 'em. Haven't been used in years. Queenie got religion about timber operations up here a long time ago." His head turned toward me. "Don't get me wrong. I don't blame her or anything but she could have made a lot of money harvesting some of these trees. There's some virgin hardwood out there. You know, back, way back, the time her people first showed up out here, folks just cut whatever they needed. Then the timber companies started showing up. There were sawmills all over these mountains. They'd cut down everything. Didn't have the technology for clear-cutting, that came later with the big guys. Georgia Pacific, outfits like that. Eventually, things grew back, and then they came for the second growth. And now that's gone in a lot of places." He nodded. "Yeah, I think the old girl's doin' the right thing, there."

"So," I began, slowly segueing into the big question, "who do you think was growing it?"

"The pot? Oh, it was that kid, Brian." Answering this time without the syncopation.

"You know that?"

"That's what makes sense. Kid used to roam all over. Knew we never came down here. He would have found this old road."

We were at a fork where a road connected at about a thirty-degree angle from behind us and he had to do a serious K-turn maneuver to get us heading in the right direction. After going half the length of a football field, he stopped. Tire tracks went off to the right, up to a barbed wire fence into which a makeshift gate had been fashioned. It was decorated with more of the ubiquitous yellow tape.

"See, this is what Queenie thinks I should have been checking. I guess if I had been, I'd of found it and all this mess wouldn't have happened."

Beyond the gate, the tracks ran up to a line of scrub pines beyond which I couldn't see. We got out of the truck and I walked up to the fence. The barbed wire was springy. If it had been strung tight, I might have been able to climb over it. As it was, with only the one arm, I'd need some assistance from the other side.

"You want to climb over and give me a hand?" I asked.

His face was the now-familiar deadpan for two seconds before he broke out into a grin.

"'Give me a hand.' That's a good one."

Nice to know he had a sense of humor. "Funny. I meant, would you climb over then help me over."

He shook his head. "Naw. I know they arrested Queenie but I think they've got their eyes on me, too. I'm not crossing that tape line."

"Well, shit, Stan. I'll get all tangled up in it if I try."

"Sorry, Ryder. I'm just not goin' there."

He didn't sound angry, just matter-of-fact. A reasonable person would probably have agreed with him.

"Well, how do you know the pot's back there, or was?"

"That road we just come up? That's County Road 1782. The cops asked me how much time I spent down around the county road. Wantin' to know if I wouldn't have seen people comin' and goin' with the amount of traffic there must have been cultivatin' that stuff. Like I said, kind of like Queenie. What was I, slack or something? I explained to them like I did to Ms. Weaver that I hardly ever came down here. I mean, I hate to say it, but look at the condition the fence is in. Obviously, I haven't been tending to it very well."

I wanted to get in there and poke around, but at least now I knew where it was. Maybe there was another way in.

We got back in the truck. Stan turned us around and headed back down the county road before having to do the K-turn maneuver again. We were halfway back to his house when I noticed another set of tracks off to our right.

"Where do they go?"

"Down to the falls."

"The side across from where we came down the other day and found Brian?"

"Um hm," he emphasized with a nod.

"Let's go," I said.

He said, "Man, I got work to do," but at the same time, he was slowing down.

"Should I get Queenie on the phone?" I asked.

He glanced over at me with what I decided was "the look." I smiled in return.

"We're goin, we're goin," he said.

The road was nothing more than two tire tracks across mostly open field and it petered out at the edge of the woods. I could hear the roar of the falls somewhere off to my left when I stepped out of the truck. A few dozen paces got us through the woods and onto a granite outcropping. The creek was visible through the trees. Our way was blocked by more yellow tape stretched between two small pine trees.

"Might want to buy stock in that stuff the way they fling it around," Stan said.

I ducked under the barrier. Stan held back.

"You not coming?"

"I told you, man."

"Well, If you hear anyone else coming, give a call," I said and headed toward the sound of cascading water. Within thirty seconds, the rock curved around to the right and I was standing almost directly atop the falls. I felt the need to get away from the edge but was mesmerized by the view. When I was finally able to take a step backward, there was something behind me. I froze, then turned.

"Stan! What the hell?"

"Sorry. Didn't mean to freak ya out." He was grinning. "See how easy it might be for someone to take one step too many? 'Specially if he was stoned?"

My heart thrumped inside my chest. "God, I felt stuck out there. And you scared the hell out of me. I thought you weren't going to cross the tape."

He shrugged. "Got curious."

"That's how it could have happened," I said. "Bryan out there and someone comes up behind him. Wouldn't even have to touch him. Just scare him a little."

"Yeah? And who do you think that someone might be?"

He sounded like a playground bully, daring some kid to say the wrong thing. I was acutely aware of the precarious position I was in.

"Whoever was growing the pot."

"You think it was me, don't you?"

"Were you growing the pot?"

His eyes narrowed. "I told you I didn't know nuthin' about it."

One part of my brain told me it was unlikely he'd actually push me over. If he had been the cause of Brian's death, he wouldn't want yet another body found at the bottom of the falls, especially since Queenie knew we were together. At the same time, I knew that all he had to do was take one step toward me and shove. I hedged my bets. "Then I guess it wasn't you."

"Just so you know," he said, "I don't think Queenie did it, either. I think it was an accident, pure and simple. Kid was stoned, got too near the edge, took a wrong step, slipped. Whacked his head on the rocks below. That's it." He looked past me, toward the top of the falls. "We done here?"

"Guess so," I said and took a deep breath.

At the place where the path went off of the rock back toward the car, a less obvious trail went straight ahead.

"Where's that go?" I asked.

He looked back at me. "Dunno. Never noticed it before."

And the pope don't wear a pointy hat, I thought.

16

We walked back to the truck without a word. In the silence that carried into the truck's cab, I wondered why he would lie to me about a little used path in the woods. I could have misread him and he really didn't know where it went, but he knew the geography of the area well enough to have hazarded a guess.

Back at the house, Martha Jo was out on the deck with all the interesting parts covered, a drink in her hand, stretched out on the chaise lounge to absorb what was left of the late afternoon sunlight. I made a point to shake Stan's hand and thank him for his help. I said I'd probably be back in the near future. His face registered a lack of enthusiasm. Martha Jo gave a little wave as I got in my Honda. I gave a smaller one in return before I started up.

I spoke the words "Kathy cell" to the car phone. After the recording telling me to leave a message, I said, "I'm heading over to the university and probably won't be home 'til six-thirty or so. I'll pick up something on the way."

Although I did not believe Brian McFadden was the pot grower, I thought it might be prudent to check into his using habits. Late afternoon, when kids would be back from classes and had not yet gone to dinner seemed like a good time to stop by. A couple of false statements about who I was and why I was calling got the necessary information out of a pleasant sounding receptionist in the Registrar's Office.

Brian McFadden had lived in an off-campus student apartment where a plain-faced young woman wearing gray sweat pants and an Arctic Monkeys T-shirt greeted me. Her short straight hair was black and pink and she had a small ring in her right nostril.

"This where Brian McFadden lived?" I asked.

"Who wants to know?"

Spunky kid, I thought.

"I'm a private investigator looking into the circumstances of his death and I wondered if I could ask you a few questions." I showed her my I.D.

"The police've already been here."

"I'm not the police. Do you have a few minutes?"

She didn't say anything and I was about to repeat myself when she said, "Yeah, come in."

The room looked like a set for a movie about college kids. Random items of clothing hanging on the backs of chairs, CD cases and magazines vying for space on a coffee table with a covey of remote control devices, more CD cases cascading into a heap in front of a stereo. An empty pizza box was perched precariously on the kitchen counter along with a handful of dishes. On balance, about midway along the continuum from compulsively clean to squalor.

The girl pointed me toward a clear space on an old couch, in between piles of books and papers. She sat on an over-stuffed chair that had begun leaking its guts.

"You're a private dick, huh?"

I smiled. "Yeah."

"Never met one before," she said. "Always wanted to say that, though. Private dick."

"Has a certain ring to it," I said.

"So, why are you investigating the murder?"

"Because my client has been accused of it. I'm trying to find out who the killer really is."

"'Cause your client's innocent."

"That's right."

"Aren't they all?"

I liked her attitude. "Except when they're not," I said. "I happen to believe her."

"You think one of us did it?"

"Who's us?"

"Us. Who live here."

There were three of them, she told me. Had been four with Brian. She said Brian had been the perfect roommate – the kind who's never around. "He was always out at that lady's place, what's her name?"

"Queenie."

"Yeah, that's it. Queenie. Old lady, isn't she?"

"In her seventies," I said. I asked if Brian went to classes.

"Oh, yeah, he was good about that. He was a good student, planned to graduate early, that's why he was going to summer school."

"How much pot did he smoke?"

Her eyes narrowed slightly, like she was gauging what I knew. I had learned not to ask questions like, "Did he smoke pot?" to which people automatically answer, "No." When you asked "How much?" people assumed you knew something whether you did or not.

When she continued not to answer, I said, "I'm not the cops. And I don't give cops information." That wasn't entirely true. There are instances when private investigators are obliged to share what they know with the police. This wasn't one of those times.

"Not much," she said. "Like a lot of us. If somebody's some and sharing. Or, sometimes we'd go in together and buy some. We're poor. Shit's too expensive these days."

I nodded. I knew there was something else she wasn't saying. I looked at her.

"What?" she said.

"That look on your face. You've got something else to say."

She squinted and turned her head slightly, trying to figure me out.

"A couple of weeks ago, he had some stuff. Some really good shit. I mean, really good. You ever smoke?"

"I'm familiar with the substance," I said.

"Well, this was the kind that makes you feel like there's a hole in the top of your head and you're flying out of it? Ever had anything like that? You can't move? I mean, physically, can't move. He had this bud, must have been six inches long, two inches across, some kind of sinsemilla."

This was not good information for our side, considering what had been taken out of Brian's back pack when they pulled him out of the creek.

"This was a month ago?"

"Yeah, about."

"Was he selling it?"

"No, he never sold shit. If he ever had any, he always shared it."

"Did you ever see anything other than the one bud?"

"Yeah. Two weeks ago he had another. He said it was just a little more mature, had a more reddish color to it."

"As good as the first?"

"Better, if you can imagine. But you could only smoke a little of it, man, or like, you'd be out of commission for hours. It was as good as eating it in stuff. You ever do that, in brownies or cookies?"

"Alice B. Toklas," I said.

"Who?"

"Never mind. Old friend."

"Anyway. It was primo shit."

"So, that was it? Two buds?"

"Yeah. All that I know of, anyway. And I don't think he'd have any reason to keep it from me if there was more."

"Or if he was selling it?"

"I told you, man, he didn't sell stuff."

"OK. Got it."

We talked some more about how he got along with the other roommates and people in general (good); if his habits had changed any recently (not that she knew of); if he'd been secretive or there was any kind of personality change (no). I thanked her for her time and gave her my card.

She looked down at the small piece of paper and said, "Rick the dick. I like that, too."

"Thanks. Call me if you think of anything that might be of interest. You know, new friends, anything you or any of your roommates think was strange or out of the ordinary for him, anything at all."

She said she would. I believed her.

My cell phone had buzzed in my pocket while I was talking to the roommate. Kathy left a message saying she had just picked some lettuce and tomatoes in the garden. She suggested I get some fresh feta cheese and Kalamata olives on my way home so we could have a big Greek salad for dinner.

Driving into town, I kept thinking about the possibility Brian could have been high standing at the top of the waterfall. If what he was smoking was as potent as the roommate described, he could easily have misjudged where he was. And maybe he was the one growing it and that's all there was to it. I didn't like the scenario but at least it would get Queenie off.

17

When I came into the kitchen from the garage, I was immediately joined by Wilbur and Gladys, the cats who had adopted us shortly after we'd moved in. They would quickly consume what I fed them and return to the woods to augment their diet with whatever wildlife they could outwit. That chore accomplished, I joined Kathy on the deck. She was wearing khaki shorts and a flower-embossed T-shirt. Her feet were bare. She had a glass of wine in one hand and a cigarette in the other.

Although her drinking didn't bother me, I resented her smoking. She was the kind of person who could smoke one or two or no cigarettes a day. She often had one after meals, although never the clichéd one after sex. There were times I would have loved a smoke. But I was addicted to mood-altering drugs and couldn't have just one. After giving up a two-and-a-half packs a day habit when I'd quit drinking twenty years ago, I'd tried a few times to use them the way she did and always wound up at over a pack a day within a week. She stubbed hers out as I leaned over to give her a coming-home kiss.

"You look comfortable," I said.

"I am. Join me and we'll dissect the workings of the universe before we make a salad."

I fixed myself a glass of tonic and lime and rejoined her on the deck. She was still on a buzz from her recent contract signing and being immersed in all the work that ensued. I told her of my travels with Stan and how he'd come up on me at the top of the falls.

"You think he was trying to make you fall over?"

"It occurred to me but I can't imagine he'd want to have to explain another corpse in the creek. He already thinks he's a suspect along with Queenie."

"Wouldn't they have arrested him if they suspected him?"

"Not necessarily. If they do think he had something to do with Brian's death or the pot growing or both, they may just be keeping an eye on him, see what he does. Like if he goes into town, who does he see? Maybe they have his phone tapped."

"Do you think Brian could have accidentally fallen over the falls?"

"If he was high, absolutely. When I was out on that ledge, I was so entranced by the view, I couldn't move." I shivered as I recalled the scene. "It's not much of a stretch to think he could have stepped the wrong way. And, the way the roommate describes the pot he had, it sounds like the same stuff that was found in his backpack. On the other hand, if he was as savvy in the woods as Queenie claims, you'd think he'd know not to get stoned up there."

"Do you think he could have been the one growing it?"

"If he didn't sell it like his roommate contends, what would have been the point? Maybe a few plants, but I think we're talking about a pretty big operation."

"Got a plan?"

"I'm going to go look the place over again without Stan."

"He's your chief suspect?"

"He and accident are the two at the top of my list."

The sun had begun its evening slide toward the western

horizon, leaving the deck in shade. We adjourned to the kitchen to prepare the dinner. I chopped garlic while heating olive oil. When the oil was hot I dumped in the garlic, letting it release its fragrance, added stale bread I'd ripped into crouton-size pieces and sprinkled it with basil and oregano. Kathy washed lettuce while I sliced tomatoes and red onion. We piled all that onto plates, adding crumbled up feta, the olives, and home-made Greek dressing before returning to the deck. Dessert would wait until I got home from an AA meeting.

I got to the First Presbyterian church in time to help set up chairs. My sponsor came in and sat next to me just before we said the Serenity Prayer. Afterward, we slipped around to the side of the building, avoiding the cigarette smoke and car exhaust that would accumulate in the parking lot. I told him about Audrey and how much I looked forward to seeing her again.

"So, what are you going to do about that?"

"What I've just done. Tell you."

"Anything else you can do?"

"Try to be honest about getting together with her and make sure it's absolutely necessary for the work."

"Have you told Kathy about her?"

"No. Well, she knows I have a client. But not what kind of a client."

"What does that tell you?"

While my sponsor had turned his shirt collar up against the cool evening breeze, I was beginning to feel some heat.

"It tells me I'm feeling guilty," I said. "And, I know that if I don't tell her, she'll find out and then there'll be a real mess."

"So?"

"I'll tell her."

"When?"

"Tonight. Jeez, you're annoying."

"My work isn't to make you feel good, you know."

We were in bed eating vanilla ice cream with fresh strawberries when I told her.

"So? You have a client who's being followed around."

"She's very attractive. And young."

She looked at me over the top of her reading glasses.

"Have you had sex with her?"

"Come on."

"You plan to have sex with her?"

"Of course not."

"Well, just don't be a jerk. You are inclined to get stupid around pretty young women." She leaned over and kissed me on the cheek. "Thanks for telling me about her. If you hadn't, you'd have started getting all weird and I would have figured there was something going on and I'd have started to get weird and pretty soon I would have found out and I'd be pissed and—"

"Yeah, I get it. I'm glad I told you, too."

We put our empty dessert bowls on our respective night stands and wrapped our arms around each other. Five minutes later, I had to get up to pee. When I got back, she had turned the other way and I spooned up against her, lying there until I fell asleep.

18

After my morning workout, and coffee and a bagel on the deck with Kathy before she left for her office, I called Audrey. She said she'd was planning to leave for work in half an hour. I told her not to go before I called.

"How will I know you're behind me?"

"If I'm doing my job right, you won't."

Twenty minutes later I pulled to the side of the road outside her condo complex. Two cars were behind her as she came by. I fell in at the back of the line. When she drove into the parking garage under the bank building where the offices of Harper Presley Beatty were housed, I kept on going. Her cell phone went to voice mail. "No sign of him," I replied to the disembodied voice. "Give me a buzz when you're getting ready to leave this afternoon."

I called Queenie and told her I was on my way out and it wouldn't hurt my feelings if she had some coffee ready when I got there.

"I ran out of that good stuff I had from the County Café so you'll have to settle for plain old Maxwell House."

"That'll be excellent."

On the front steps, warmed by the morning sun, Sonny lay

on his stomach, keeping guard for us. I told Queenie I wanted to retrace my steps from the previous day. I did not tell her that I thought Stan knew a lot for someone who denied he knew anything.

"I've found in this sleuthing business, you've got to get a feel for a place, wander around, not really looking for anything, but aware enough so you notice stuff that pops up."

"Yeah, yeah," she said, "seen it on TV. You just do whatever it is you have to do and find out who's behind all this."

"That's the plan," I said.

She got out a forest service map so I could get my bearings. I found County Road 1782 and Weaver's Falls. The way I figured it, the little-used path that led away from the falls, the one Stan denied knowing where it went, headed straight toward the county road. The marijuana had been grown somewhere between the falls and that road and the path should take me right to it. I thought it unlikely that Stan didn't know it.

There were no signs of life when I passed the Dillingham place. Stan's truck was gone, which seemed to be routine, and Martha Jo had yet to find her place in the sun. I parked the Honda where Stan had left his truck the day before and got a pair of soft-soled moccasins out of the trunk.

I retraced the route Stan and I had taken, slipping under the crime scene tape and heading toward the sound of water. Standing again at the precipice of the falls, I imagined what it would be like to be there stoned.

When I was nineteen, on a trip to the coast with some friends, we ate hash brownies one morning and went down to the ocean. I stood in the surf feeling the tide pulling me inexorably out to sea. It took a huge exertion of will to get myself turned around and crawl back up the sand, knowing I had to get out of there before

I drowned myself. Yes, I thought, it was absolutely possible that someone high on pot could make a misstep up here. That didn't, however, rule out other explanations for what happened to Brian.

I took a few deep breaths and turned back the way I'd come. At the place where the main path right-angled back to the road, I kept going on the lesser used trail, as much as possible walking in the woods, parallel to the path. Although no yellow tape actually cut off access to this area, I didn't want it known I'd been here. After a quarter mile or so, the woods thinned out ahead of me and more yellow tape was visible. Stan might have been onto something when he suggested buying equity in whoever made the stuff. I ducked under it.

The field ahead of me looked like a harvested Christmas tree lot. In ten minutes, I counted the trunks of twenty-four plants, all about three inches in diameter. Each plant was separated from its neighbors by several feet, not at all like the marijuana plantations I'd seen pictures of where the stuff grew in rows as tight as fields of corn. At the far edge of the lot there was a stand of scrub pines, like those I'd seen from the barbed wire fence the previous day. The entire area couldn't have been more than about a quarter acre, what I'd heard referred to as "boutique" growing. I assumed the cops photographed the plants before and after they cut them down and wondered if Nate would be able to get his hands on the pictures.

A car door slammed. Dropping into a crouch, I began to duck-walk out of the open field. It was either Stan or the cops, I figured, and neither would be happy to see me there. My heart pumped adrenalin. I'd be in deep shit if caught by the police. Stan wouldn't be quite so bad unless he was involved in criminal activity out here and needed to be sure nobody knew about it. The cops could jail me for violating a crime scene, but Stan might take stronger measures. In my mind's eye, I saw a body in the pool below the falls. Another door slammed. Voices were audible but indistinct. I moved into the woods and began circling back the way I'd come in, trying to get to a place where I could see them without being seen.

I stepped farther back into the woods without losing sight of them. They seemed to wander aimlessly, moving close to the edge of the open space nearest me. Two of them. One wore a suit. The other was in khaki slacks and a sport shirt. I couldn't get a good look at their faces but began to make out snippets of their conversation.

"... heartbreaking ... a shitload more money ... I told her to wait ... days, we'd have it all harvested. I think ... nervous ..."

"Maybe it ... her. Maybe it was him. She ... nervous type ..."

"She's ... brains of that ..."

"Whatever ... how much ...? Five-hundred an ounce ... believe that? I remember ... thirty-five ..."

I slipped behind a large oak tree. When they were within twenty feet, I could hear them clearly.

"You smoke any of it?"

"Nah. Done with that stuff. You?"

"Tried it."

"Good?"

"Whew. I understand why cops tell high school kids, 'this isn't your parents' pot.'"

"You think people can get hooked on this stuff now?"

"I don't know ... pretty heavy ..."

Then they were heading away from me and it was all muffled again. One of the voices was familiar but I couldn't place it. Could have been from anywhere, in line at the grocery store, renting a movie. The conversation had me confused. Her? Him? Queenie and Stan? It was no stretch to think Stan was involved. But could Queenie really be mixed up in it? And if so, how far? Murder? She was an independent, self-sufficient, country woman who, nonetheless, was very cosmopolitan. Maybe she had some philosophical thing about pot, thought it should be legal, something like that. And, since she had the land, why not use it? I knew I was making things up, but where there is a vacuum of information, our imaginations fill it. I wondered what would happen if I told her what I'd heard.

When a car door slammed again, I started into a run. Another door slammed, two engines started up. The uneven ground made it hard to get much speed and by the time I made it through the scrub growth to the barbed wire fence, there was no sign of them. I knew I was going to lose sleep that night if I didn't remember where I'd heard that voice.

19

There was still no sign of life when I passed Stan and Martha Jo's place. Back at Queenie's, Sonny roused himself from his lookout station on the porch, gave out a "woof" and came down to escort me up the steps. I called in through the screen door. The mistress of the house called back and told me to have a seat and she'd be right out. Three minutes later she appeared with iced teas for us, festooned with fresh mint sprigs.

"And you think they were talking about me?" Queenie said, when I told her what I had overheard.

"I don't know you all that well, Queenie, but I can't imagine you involved in some industrial pot growing operation."

Dark clouds thickened on the horizon. Every few minutes we heard a rumble as thunder bounced around the western ridges.

"Back in the mid-sixties," she said, "I did grow pot in my back yard. Hell, we all did. It wasn't very good weed, though, and there was better stuff for not very much money on the street. The authorities were getting worked up about pot around that time, lumping it in with heroin and cocaine, calling it a narcotic. What a bunch of crap. I never did think marijuana was much of a threat to the safety and well-being of the population. Certainly, not as bad for someone as alcohol. And you notice I don't have any compunction about using the latter. Anyway, I got out of the home-grown business over thirty years ago."

"Business?"

"Oh, I never sold any. But I did teach other people how to do it. Gave classes up here. It was a counter-culture thing. Us against the establishment. I didn't charge anything although people would leave love offerings, you know, loose change, maybe a little folding money. More often it was 'in kind' donations, homemade foods, pottery – it was back when everybody was into ceramics, macrame plant hangers, things like that. With all that stuff and the collection of rolling papers, pipes, bongs I got, I coulda' started my own head shop. Except for the food, I mostly gave it all away."

She looked out toward the horizon. "I believe we're in for some weather," she said and let out a laugh.

The clouds had turned ink black. Lightning flashed, advertising the thunder claps that would follow.

"You ever watch the weather on TV, Rick?"

"Occasionally," I said.

"Sometimes, it's the best amusement around. I keep wantin' to say, 'look out the window!' Thirty percent this, sixty percent that. Jeez."

"What happened to the, um, business? Which wasn't a business."

"Oh, I started getting too well-known. People I'd never met before would come up here on Saturday mornings. I figured it was just a matter of time till a narc showed up. And I didn't need the powers-that-be having more reason to harass me than they already did for my civil rights work."

She turned and looked at me. "I don't know if you can appreciate what it was like then. Communists and narcotics. They were going to destroy the American way of life. I guess today it's terrorists. Gotta be somebody to be against, somebody to justify our fear and the existence of the security state. Oh, Jeez. I'm sorry, Rick. I am goin' on again. That's not what you're up here to talk about. What the hell was it ... Oh, yeah, growin' pot."

"Yeah. Back to those guys down where there was some pot being grown unbeknownst to you. You think the 'him' they mentioned would be Stan?"

"I don't know. I hate to think my judgment about people is that far off, but he has been getting weird lately. More surly than he used to be. Although, he was never what you'd call Mr. Sunshine."

I told her about my expedition with him the day before.

"You're suggesting Stan knew more than he should have," she said.

"Let's say I thought his explanations were unconvincing."

"Do you think Brian might really have been mixed up in it?"

"Maybe Brian stumbled on the operation and started helping himself."

"Well, we can't talk to him, but we can talk to Stan," she said.

"I'd be careful, Queenie. If he is mixed up in this, well, one person's dead already."

We were interrupted by a loud crack at the same time a streak of bright yellow flashed nearby. I shivered. Hail the size of grapes began to thump the ground. Above our heads, it sounded like a thousand tiny hammers pounding on the tin roof. Within seconds, the front yard was covered in a filigree of ice. Less than a minute after it had started, it was over. Blue sky pushed the dark clouds off to the east. The air was as crisp as a starched shirt fresh from the laundry.

We sat in silence for a moment, stunned by the quixotic temperament of Mother Nature. By the time I'd regained my voice, all evidence of the storm had melted.

"Now that was weather," I said. "Don't suppose there was a message in all of that, do you?"

"You mean, God getting my attention, telling me to watch out?"

We both laughed.

"You've got to admit, it was pretty impressive."

"Yeah, well, I've had a pretty stormy six decades. My life's been threatened dozens of times. People got killed back in the sixties for standing up for what was right. I don't scare easy."

On more than one occasion when I was a full-time investigator for the Mountain Center for the Defense of the Environment, I'd had weapons aimed at me while I was looking into violations of environmental law. It was frightening, but I never really thought those people would shoot. They were just making a point. For Queenie, it hadn't been just for show.

"As my wife keeps telling me," I said, "don't go off and do something stupid."

She waved a hand in dismissal and walked into the house. I thought that might have been a sign for me to leave until she returned with a rifle in her hand.

"I got a shotgun and a handgun in there, too. I can take care of myself, young man."

"OK, Queenie. I get it."

"So, you want to go down to his house now?" she asked.

"No signs of life when I came past there."

"Hmm. Surprised Martha Jo isn't down there getting her boobies tanned. That seems like her major summertime occupation."

We heard a vehicle coming up the road from the direction of town. Sonny lifted his head, then strolled down to the bottom of the steps. He began to bark either a greeting or a warning.

It was a black van, much like the one that was here the day she was arrested, with 'SHERIFF' emblazoned on the side. It stopped in front of the house. Queenie called off Sonny. A man in a khaki suit got out and came toward us. I thought I recognized him.

"Ms. Weaver," he said as he approached.

My heart skipped a beat. It wasn't love. The man's voice was one of those I'd heard in the pot patch earlier in the morning. He'd been wearing the same suit the day we were interviewed by sheriff's deputies about Brian's death.

"That would be me," Queenie said.

"I'm Detective Presley. You may remember me from the other day. I just wanted you to know we're going to be on your property for a while."

I did a quick estimate of the time it would have taken him to return to town and get back out here with his crew. It was doable.

"I hope you find something that'll lead you to the real murderer while you're here."

An indulgent smile came on his face, like he was having to deal with a child.

"We'll be doing our job, ma'am," he said.

"Yeah, and the other day you boys were doing your job when you put handcuffs on me and hauled me away. I don't think I'll forget that, Detective."

"Yes, ma'am, I understand how you feel."

"No, I don't think you do. Just go on."

The detective turned and was headed toward the van when she called after him.

"And, if you see Stan, tell him I want to talk to him."

The cop nodded as he walked away. Sonny barked after him. Queenie did not intervene.

When the van was gone, I turned to Queenie.

"I believe that dog of yours is a good judge of character. I think Presley's one of the guys who was down in the pot field earlier."

"What do you suppose he was doing there if he was just going to be coming back out?"

I shrugged. "Dunno. Making sure the place was clean?"

20

I sat at the kitchen table while Queenie put together chicken sandwiches on home-made sourdough bread. She informed me that the starter for the bread was over a hundred years old.

"My great-granddaddy's wife brought it to the family. Supposedly, her family brought it from Holland. Hope you appreciate the lineage. Can't get this stuff down at the Bi-Lo, you know." While she was slathering on mayonnaise, she said, "You think that sheriff's guy had something to do with the pot growing?"

I didn't want to think that. I know there are good guys and bad guys in the world, but it makes finding the bad guys harder when they are masquerading as good ones. I pulled out my cell phone and found the number for Bobby Headley, my fire chief friend out in Leicester.

"Know a county detective named Presley?" I said when he answered.

"Well, hey, Rick. Let's just cut to the chase here, huh?" One of the nice things about caller ID is that you get to skip the introductions step in the transaction. "Seems to me I've heard about a new guy – 'new' as in since I was there – by that name. 'Course there's columns of Presleys in the phone book. You got your one-S kind and your two-S kind and ..."

"Yeah, I know. It's a common name around here. Know anything about this new guy?"

"Nope. Like I said, he wasn't there when I was. Want me to find out about him?"

I said I did and he said he would.

"Shouldn't take long," I said to Queenie. "Bobby's another one of those guys like Nate who seem to know everybody downtown. Glad there're some good guys we don't have to wonder about. And, in answer to your question, unless I interpreted his conversation in the field all wrong, yes, he was involved in the pot growing."

"So," she asked between bites of her sandwich, "what's next?"

I chewed for a minute while I considered. "When I was looking at property transactions the other day, I saw that Ira Ivey owns property adjacent to yours and between the two properties that were bought by HPB with the help of Pete Haywood."

"The Pruitts and the Jenkins," Queenie said.

"Yeah. So, I thought I'd go down and see Ira. Find out if anybody's been making overtures to him about selling, or if he had any conversations with his neighbors when they sold their properties."

"Not likely to find Ira. He passed a couple of years ago. But his wife's hanging in there. Maisie's a tough old broad, kinda like me, although folks would consider her a little more traditional, I suspect." Her brow wrinkled. "You think those sales have something to do with Brian being murdered?"

"Don't know, Queenie. But I do know you've been getting threats, and a young man has been killed and someone's been growing pot on your land and there's a sheriff's dick who may be dirty."

"A dirty dick?" she said.

I almost spit out my sandwich as I laughed. "Yeah, a dirty dick."

To get to the Ivey place I had to go back to the main road

and find the mailbox, turn left up a hill, then wind around what seemed like another old logging road for three miles or so. It was more isolated than Queenie's but at a lower elevation and had none of the vistas of the Weaver place. The house was a two story frame structure with a veranda around three sides. It was in good shape with a new tin roof. It could have been as old as Queenie's sourdough starter.

Two minutes after I "hallooed" from the bottom of the front porch steps, a woman of indeterminate age came out and looked me over. She was closer to the stereotype of a mountain woman than Queenie was, wearing a long, nondescript house dress, her gray hair pulled back in a bun.

"Mizz Ivey?" I said.

"That's me. Who's askin'?"

"My name is Rick Ryder and I'm doing some work for Queenie Weaver."

"What kinda work?"

"Talking with her about what might happen to her land, mmm, later."

"'Later?' Like when she dies?"

"Yes, ma'am."

"Why'nt you just say it. Don't have to pussyfoot around, mister. I know all about dyin'" She tilted her head a little, then said, "You fixin' to buy it?"

"No, ma'am, but I hear there are people buying up land around these parts and that's what I wanted to talk to you about."

"You want to buy my land?"

I held my hand up like a traffic cop. "No, ma'am, I just want to find out if other people have been talking to you about buying it."

She gave me that quizzical look again. "How'd you know about that?"

"Didn't," I said. "Just a guess. I do know two of your neighbors recently sold."

She invited me in for tea, meaning, of course, the iced and sweetened kind. Inside, the house was dark, heavy drapes over the windows closed against the light, as country people without air conditioning do in the summer. We went on into the kitchen and sat on oak chairs at a rectangular oak table. I guessed the furniture to be as old as the house. The rest of the kitchen was new, with up-to-date appliances, a spotless vinyl floor and modern cabinets.

After the tea at Queenie's, I really didn't want any more, but couldn't refuse the hospitality. When the drinks and a plate of store-bought cookies were on the table, I told her I'd heard about her husband.

"That's what I was meanin' when I said I knew all about dyin'," she said. "Passed away two years ago."

I said I was sorry to hear that.

"Why are you sorry?"

"I'm sorry for anybody's loss like that."

"You don't know nothin' about it. The old miser had put money away I didn't know nothin' about. That's how I got to fix this place up a little. He wouldn't a done it. I'd have had to fall through the kitchen floor before he'd put a new one in. As it was, the ceiling leaked and I couldn't get him to fix that."

I waited before saying anything.

"I do miss the old coot though. Gets lonely out here some times. My two boys are gone, too. Just me now."

She paused again, then looked straight at me. "Yeah, that preacher guy, can't call his name right off ..."

"Pete Haywood?"

"Yeah, him. He's been around a couple of times. Talkin' about some big money if I sell. Sally May Jenkins told me what they got for their place. Wasn't supposed to talk about it, she said. Her husband doesn't want people to know. She says he's kindly embarrassed. Thinks people will think he's a sell-out. Well, he is. But that's their business. It's a free country, they want to sell their land, ain't nobody can stop them. But I'm not sellin'. I told that preacher that and I'll tell you that. Now, there's times I think I ought to do it, give all the money to charity. I got this nephew, my late brother's boy, his wife's got her eyes on the place. Every time I see 'em, she looks at me like she's just a-waitin' for me to keel over. Gives me the shivers.

"Oh, just listen to me go on." She looked at my almost empty glass. "More tea?"

"No thank you, ma'am. Had some up at Queenie's. Have any more, I'll float down the mountain."

Under other circumstances, this would have been a good opportunity to talk about a land trust, but that wasn't my purpose today and I didn't want her to think I'd come selling anything. I asked her if she'd had any threats.

"Yeah, I did. But they can't scare me. I'm too old 'n' orn'ry."

"Before or after you turned down the offers to sell?"

She thought it over.

"After, I guess."

"How many would you say?"

"Oh. Three, maybe four. This guy would say in this deep voice like he was trying to hide who he was, something like, 'you'll get out of there if you know what's good for you.'"

"And you know he meant sell the place."

"Oh, yeah. That was pretty clear."

What else was pretty clear was that this HPB, LLC, outfit was trying to buy up the mountain and was not being very neighborly about it. Nor very Christian, either. What was not clear was what connection there was to a marijuana crop and the death of a college student.

It had gotten on to mid-afternoon and I wanted to go by Pete

Haywood's office before the day was over. I had no idea what I expected to accomplish there, except I believe if you give people enough opportunity to talk they will often tell you things they hadn't planned to. I thanked Maisie for the conversation and left one of my cards in case she got anymore threats or calls about selling.

The small strip mall that houses North Realty sits just beyond a traffic light on the four lane that marks the northern boundary of the county. I slowed when the light turned yellow and was at a full stop when a white Miata pulled out of the mall and turned right, away from me. Miatas did not seem as popular as they were when they first came out in the late 1980s, but there were still a lot of them around and white seemed to be the most popular color. Still, you had to wonder. By the time my light had turned green, the sports car had gone through the next light and on into town. I knew I'd catch a red at the next light and let go of the thought to catch up with him.

I pulled in alongside Haywood's Caddy and went on into the office. He looked up from the table that served as his desk.

"Rick Ryder," he said.

I wasn't surprised he remembered since he practiced two professions in which being able to recall peoples' name is an invaluable aptitude. It was also true that the one-arm thing tended to stick in peoples' minds.

"I was in the area and wondered if you may have come across my ideal piece of land," I said as he stood, extending his hand in greeting.

"Afraid not. But I'd be glad to take a ride with you to Madison County. There're still some good values out there. I really think that's likely where you want to go, if you want to be in the mountains. Or maybe even over to McDowell."

"Yeah, that's a longer ride than I wanted to take. I'm just on my way home now. Might take you up on it some other time."

"Give me a call," he said, with a broad smile. If he thought my spontaneous visit was in any way unusual, he gave no indication. But then, he was the kind of man I doubted ever let people know anything was other than just the way it was supposed to be.

I had cleared the door when I turned back.

"That Miata that just left here," I said.

"Left here?" he said.

"Yeah, just now, white one, was going out just before I pulled in."

"Must have been at one of the other businesses. I've been alone for the last little while."

I was sure I detected a shift of his eyes as he said it.

Kathy was on the phone in the living room when I walked into the house. Her body posture told me she was talking to her father. He was an addict like me, although his drugs of choice had been the pain killers prescribed to him after an accident years ago, while I'd pretty much just stayed with alcohol. Family patterns are hard to break out of, so it's not surprising that Kathy would wind up with someone like me. A familiar male type. The thing about me that drove her crazy.

"Dad, if you're sick, go to the doctor. I can't do anything for you down here ... Yes, I know that's why you'd like it if I lived closer to you ... I'm not having this conversation with you anymore tonight. Call David. I know he has a wife and children but that's no reason he can't come and see you."

I knew she was refraining from saying, and I know he doesn't come see you for the same reason I'd never move back to Ohio. I gave her a kiss on the forehead and went on into the kitchen. Somehow, Gladys and Wilbur know I'm the cook in the family. They don't come through their little door until I arrive. I have told them that Kathy is as capable of opening a can of cat food as I am, but they don't seem to listen. After answering their demands, I poured myself a glass of tonic water, squeezed the juice from a lime wedge into it and went out on the deck.

The morning paper was still on the table where I'd left it when I went off to tail Audrey. When I opened to the Mountain Section, three photos grabbed my attention. One was identified as a field of marijuana plants. One was a picture of a single plant. The last was of one "bud" from a plant. According to the article, headlined, "Million dollar pot bust," there were two dozen sinsemilla marijuana plants found in a raid on a half acre of land belonging to Queenie Weaver. It explained that unlike "regular" marijuana which is made up of ground-up leaves, sinsemilla uses just the non-flowering buds of the plants, which tend to have high levels of THC, "the active ingredient in marijuana." The plants looked like bushes, perhaps five feet tall and three feet in diameter, neatly manicured. The paper said there were up to fifty buds on each plant and that each bud was worth one thousand dollars. I imagined both the number of buds per plant and the value of each bud were inflated, the latter greatly so. Big numbers warrant big budgets. I wouldn't have to call Nate about any pictures the police may have taken during the raid.

Kathy was carrying a glass of wine when she joined me.

"I know it's just the way he is and will always be," she said, "and I am powerless over him. I try not to get sucked into his drama, but he sure can jerk my strings."

I no longer said things like, "he only can pull your strings if you let him," and other platitudes I'd picked up in recovery. She'd given Al-Anon a shot back when I was drinking. She said she thought they had some good ideas but they also seemed to do an awful lot of whining.

She put her drink down and walked outside, returning a few minutes later with a couple of tomatoes, a green bell pepper and a bunch of red leaf lettuce from the garden. I chopped some cold chicken breast and onion, cubed some sharp cheddar cheese and sliced a couple of hard boiled eggs to throw into the mix along with some of the leftover home-made croutons.

The gentle murmur of the creek was our musical accompaniment for dinner al fresco. A pot of decaf coffee had just finished brewing when the landline rang. We looked at each other, deciding who wanted to be the one to put an end the evening's tranquility.

21

I hadn't finished saying "hello" when the young female voice cut me off.

"I'm leaving in half an hour to go downtown to a birthday party for the CEO of a client. It's at The Circuit. You know where that is?"

"Well, hello, Audrey. And, yes, I think I do. That new place on Market?"

"That's it. Will you see if that guy follows me?"

We made a plan and I returned to the deck.

"That was Audrey, my client. She's going to a party downtown. I'm going to go see if that guy in the Miata follows her."

"Just be careful, Love."

"What kind of trouble can I get in? I'm just going to follow her. If the guy follows her, I can get a plate number and, voilá, case closed."

She shrugged. We kissed. It was one of her "I'm yours" kind of kisses. Or maybe it was, "You're mine."

My pulse sped up along with my Honda as I headed to Audrey's condo. I told myself it was the adventure and not the woman. This was why I'd gotten my P.I. license back when I'd been working in the state's environmental protection bureaucracy. I needed some excitement in my life after I'd given up drinking and all the drama that entailed.

I was about fifty yards away from the entrance to her complex when I saw the white convertible alongside the road behind a row of shrubs.

I called Audrey's name to the hands-free phone. "I'm at the entrance to your place," I said when she answered. "He's hiding behind some bushes just outside the gate. I'll wait until he gets behind you."

Five minutes later her BMW went by. I waited thirty seconds after he pulled out behind her before I joined the parade. I was close enough to see the license plate but the figures were obscured by dirt, or something painted on to look like dirt. It was just after nine when Audrey pulled into a parking lot across the street from the party place. The convertible went on past. I pulled into a No Parking-Loading Zone space and waited to see if he'd come back into view.

I watched Audrey in my mirrors as she crossed the street. She wore a shiny, slim, pale blue dress that didn't reach her knees. A white stole covered her shoulders. Her perfectly tousled hair shone under the street light. I don't suppose my sigh could have been heard more than twenty yards away.

There was a modest but steady stream of traffic, vehicular and pedestrian, typical for a summer night downtown. Cars moved slowly as drivers looked for parking spaces. It was a clear night, although the street lighting would interfere with any stargazing. Music spilled out from the second floor space that was The Circuit.

Five minutes later the convertible returned and pulled into a parking space on the street half a block up. Stepping off the sidewalk and into the street, I walked toward the Miata. When I was directly behind the car, I leaned over and brushed the dirt from the license plate. The driver got out and came back to me.

"What the fuck are you doing?" he asked. His tone was not conversational.

He wasn't wearing the shades now. In the light provided by street lamps, he looked middle-aged, a little older than me, maybe fifty-ish. He was clean-shaven, wearing jeans, a short-sleeved sport shirt and the ball cap.

"Trying to see your license plate," I said as I stood. I was going to show him my PI identification when he pulled a gun out of the waist band of his pants.

"Get the fuck out of here," he said.

I pulled my cell phone out and punched in 911.

"I said get the fuck outta here, asshole."

The 911 operator came on.

"I'm in on Market Street, just outside The Circuit and a guy is pointing a gun at me, telling me to tech.. Rick Ryder ... yeah, you maybe ought to hurry. I'm not sure how serious he is. Yeah ... he drives a white Miata convertible, license plate number, let me ..."

I saw him raise the gun and was able to move my head out of the way when he swung. I closed on him, dropped the phone and grabbed his arm, slamming it down on my leg. He dropped the gun. I stood over it and faced the man, not wanting to pick up the weapon since there could be traceable fingerprints on it. I kept facing him as I reached down for my phone and said into it, "Well, he's no longer holding the gun on me, but someone ought to get here anyway."

He stepped into me as if he was going to take another swing when somebody on the sidewalk yelled, "Hey!" My assailant looked around, paused for a second as if considering his options, then ran to his car. There was no reason to chase him. I'd gotten the plate number.

The bystander who had yelled came over. "You alright?"

"Yeah. My leg's a little sore. The police should be on their way."

City police headquarters was only four blocks away and a squad car was there in less than three minutes. I told them what happened and gave them the license plate number.

The cop looked at the place at the end of my left shoulder where most people would have an arm.

"You were able to get a gun away from a guy with just ... ?"

"The one arm? Yeah. He wasn't going to use the weapon. I was pretty sure of that. Too many witnesses. My leg hurts like hell, though, where I slammed his arm into it."

We hung around while they ran a trace on the license plate and five minutes later found out it had been reported stolen a week ago, just about the time Audrey had noticed she was being followed. I asked one of the cops if this didn't raise her situation to another level for them, one they could take action on, being followed by an armed man.

"Not armed anymore," the cop said.

"How long do you think it will take for him to get another weapon? And another plate?"

I gave him Audrey's number and said I hoped a detective would get in touch with her the next day. He gave me a "don't tell me how to do my work" look and suggested I stop by the police station and look at mug shots to see if I could I.D. my assailant.

Audrey didn't answer her phone. Busy partying, I presumed. I left a message recapping what transpired, ending with, "Call me."

It was hard to get the key in the ignition the way my hand was shaking and it took a couple of seconds before I realized my whole body was vibrating like cat gut under a violin bow. It was not a pleasant kind of buzz. For the first time since my relapse a year and a half before, I craved a drink.

Kathy was in bed with a book. I joined her with my nightcap decaf, and proceeded to regale her with the evening's adventure.

"Did you think even for a minute he'd shoot?"

"I told the cops I didn't, not out there with all those people around. But it's always a possibility when pissed-off people have guns."

She sighed and shook her head, as if she was suffering the burdens of motherhood.

I took a couple of pills for the ache in my leg. When I returned to bed and turned off the light on my side, she turned hers off and wrapped herself around me.

When the phone woke me at six-thirty, I was heavily involved in a dream. It took a while to realize the sound was occurring in the waking world. I assumed it was Audrey, calling for details of the night before. I was surprised to hear the older woman's voice.

"Hi. What's ..."

"Stan's dead."

22

She cut me off when I started to ask what happened, said for me to come on up, she'd be down at their house. The pain in my left leg reminded me of the events of the previous night and I simultaneously wished for and was glad we didn't have anything in the house stronger than over-the-counter medication.

Foregoing my morning routine, I yanked on some jeans and pulled a sweatshirt over a tee shirt. Kathy lay undisturbed in the bed. I gave her a peck on the cheek and wrote a note explaining where I was going. After feeding the cats, I was out of the house before 7:00.

The undulating whine of sirens met me half way up Queenie's drive. Fifty yards later, I had to pull over to keep from getting forced off the road by a sheriff's car. An EMT truck, the crime scene van and another sheriff's car in addition to the one that had passed me had already arrived at the Dillingham place. When I got out of the Honda, I could hear voices coming from behind the house. Queenie was seated at the umbrella table on the deck, hunched over a coffee mug. For the first time since I'd met her, she looked all of her seventy years.

She glance up as I approached. "There's coffee in the kitchen."

She held her mug out toward me. "Warm this up while you're goin,' would ya."

I sat across from her when I returned. "What happened?"

"Just before I called you, Martha Jo called me. Couldn't make out what she was saying at first. She was just abawlin'. Finally settled down enough that I could understand her. She said they'd had a row the night before and she went into town to stay with a friend. Didn't say what friend and I didn't ask. Anyway, when she got home early this morning, his truck was out front but he wasn't in the house. She called out to the shed and, when she didn't get an answer, went to check it out, see if he was still mad and not talking to her. She said she felt bad about leaving like she did. I wondered if she didn't feel bad because of who she'd been with, but I let that go, too. So, she goes out to the shed and sees him on the floor. Her first thought is he's had a heart attack."

Another sheriff's car came down the road in a hurry, dragging a rooster tail of dust in its wake and pulling up abruptly alongside the other vehicles. A woman was driving. Presley got out of the passenger side. A cold chill ran down my spine.

"They're all out back," Queenie called to them. The woman nodded. Presley ignored us. When the deputies were out of sight, Queenie turned back to me. "Anyway, so she goes over to him and realizes he's been shot and, from the looks of it, had done it himself."

That was a conversation stopper. I wondered if he'd been involved in the pot-murder affair and was afraid he was going to be found out. Or maybe marital problems, his younger wife tired of being stuck out here in the boondocks and he can't stand the thought of her leaving him.

I asked Queenie if he'd seemed depressed lately.

"Hell, like I've said before, he's never been Mr. Sunshine. Always reminded me of a Basset hound on medication."

Martha Jo appeared on the deck wearing tight short shorts, a man's white long-sleeve shirt, sleeves rolled up, tails tied up under her breasts. Her feet were ensconced in sandals, her toenails painted a bright red. I doubted she was wearing anything we couldn't see. Her hair was in order. A drink was in hand. It was not yet eight a.m.

"Anybody want anything?" she asked.

We declined. She joined us at the umbrella table. None of us spoke. Martha Jo looked off into the distance. The silence became oppressive, as if it was sucking the oxygen out of the air. The 'sorry for your loss' kind of thing seemed inadequate. Queenie opened her mouth, began to say something when Martha Jo said, "Now what do I do?"

People react to grief in strange ways. I thought she sounded petulant, imagining she might get dispossessed of her living quarters. Ice cubes clanked as she tipped her glass to her mouth. She stood and, as she headed toward the kitchen, asked again if we wanted anything.

"More coffee'd be good," I said.

"Yeah, you're the drunk who doesn't drink, aren't you?"

That was one way to put it. Queenie said she'd have more, too.

Whether the liquor had loosened her up, or she had just moved into another space, the bereaved widow began talking when she returned.

"We had a fight last night," she said. "I never should have left like that. I went and stayed with a friend. I got over whatever I was pissed off about, I don't ever remember what it was. When I got back this morning, his truck was here but he wasn't around. That's not unusual. He's hardly ever … was hardly ever … around the house. I called out to the shed and when he didn't answer I went out to see if he was there, if he wasn't answering because he was still mad, or thought he ought to still be mad."

Her eyes moved back and forth between Queenie and me,

as if she was daring us to say something. Then she homed in on Queenie. "It's your fault, you know. Always making him do more, nothing ever good enough."

Queenie looked back into Martha Jo's eyes.

"That's a bunch of crap, Martha Jo, and you know it. Come on, Rick. They'll know where to find us if they need us." To Martha Jo she said, "Let me know if you need anything when you get over your attitude."

I pulled into the driveway behind her. We walked to the back door and on into the kitchen in silence. She fixed coffee, more for something do, I thought, than because either of us really needed it. There were tears in her eyes when she sat across from me at the kitchen table.

She fidgeted with her cup for a time that seemed endless but was probably no more than three or four minutes before she got up and left the room, returning seconds later with a box of tissues. After wiping her eyes and blowing her nose, she said, "That stuff about nothing ever being good enough, it's a bunch of crap, you know? He liked being busy, doing stuff. He hated sitting around. It's true there were times I had to get on him to finish things. I think he may have had some of that attention deficit thing, you know, working on three different projects at once. But that's the way he worked, not what I made him do."

"Queenie," I said. "It's not your fault."

"I never understood what he saw in her," she said.

I raised my eyebrows.

"Well, yes, of course, there was that," she said. "Maybe the bigger question is what she saw in him."

I raised my eyebrows again.

"Well, yes, I suppose that could also be so. He does have ... did have ... those rugged good looks. I liked seeing him, especially when I could get him to smile."

I restrained myself from saying, I'm sure Martha Jo could put a smile on his face.

"You know," she said, "that story she told us on the porch, of the fight and leaving and coming back and going out to the shed. That was almost a verbatim repeat of what she'd already told me."

"You mean like people do when they've memorized something," I said.

"Yeah. Just like that."

The kitchen was still cool and, unless it turned out to be an absolute scorcher, would remain that way throughout the day. I sipped my coffee.

"You thinking she did it?" I asked.

"Just sayin', is all. Maybe she had a lover in town, feels guilty, you know, husband kills himself while she's off getting her ashes hauled and doesn't want anyone to know it. So, she has a story. I guess I'm more concerned about that Presley character showin' up after what you said about him, thinkin' he might be the guy you saw where the pot had been growin'."

"When he showed up this morning, I thought I might come out of my skin. It was a physical reaction. Guy gives me the creeps."

Queenie was about to say something else, when my cell phone rang.

"Rick?"

"Yes, Audrey?"

"I got your message about what happened last night. Did he really pull a gun on you?"

"Yes, he did."

"Weren't you afraid?"

"Happened too fast to think about it," I said, which was almost true.

"You know," she said, "girls like guys fighting over them. It's very exciting."

"A little too exciting," I said which also was not entirely true. Some people who treat addicts think we are addicted to adrenaline as much as anything in the drugs themselves. Excitement junkies.

"Have you heard from the cops?" I asked.

"Not yet. Have you heard from your friend about any of the names I gave you?"

"Nope. And I think we'll just put that on hold until we see what the cops come up with."

"Does that mean you won't be following me to work this morning?"

I looked at my watch. It was 8:45.

"I guess so."

I thought I heard a sigh.

"When will I see you again?"

"I don't know. Let me know when the police contact you. We'll see what they come up with over the next few days."

"Well, OK. I enjoyed our little time together."

"So did I, Audrey. Maybe we can have coffee and settle up when this is over."

After I'd hung up, I realized I was disappointed that the chase was off and that I would be displaced by sworn enforcers of the law.

Queenie asked me what I was planning to do next. I didn't have anything planned except my usual meandering around to see what turned up. I hoped to hear from Bobby Headley about Detective Presley and I thought I might just go see Pete Haywood again and take him up on his offer to drive around the neighboring county. I wondered how likely it was that I'd see the white Miata again. The cops had said the license plate on it had been stolen, but not the car itself. Maybe it would reappear.

"Gonna talk to Martha Jo anymore?" my hostess asked.

"I've got to be careful, Queenie. The cops don't like us private-eye types messing in their active cases. Gotta come up with some good reason why I should go down there."

"Couldn't you just make a social call? You know, how's she doing, that kind of thing."

"You mean, I just happened to be in the area ..."

"Yeah. I believe you can put down a line of bull if you need to."

"Thanks."

"Oh, it's a skill," she said. "Not everybody can do it well. Like Martha Jo, for instance."

I called Jim, my AA sponsor. I had been active in the program when Kathy and I moved to the mountains and I had a sponsor in Raleigh. The first time I heard Jim talk at a meeting, I knew he was a guy I'd like to work with, mostly because he never mentioned God. He did say, "one day at a time," but that was the only one of the sayings you hear repeated ad nauseum at meetings that he did invoke. That was one I happened to believe myself. My Raleigh sponsor became a kind of Sponsor Emeritus, a back-up when Jim wasn't available, but Jim was now my go-to guy. I told him the story of the night before, Stan's death, and Audrey's phone call.

"Want a drink?" he asked.

"Not right now. But I did last night."

He reminded me of the five o'clock meeting downtown, one that had been started years ago as a place to go on Friday instead of into the bars for Happy Hour.

As soon as I hung up, the phone buzzed in the car.

"This is Rick."

"Hey, Rick. Bobby Headley. Got some stuff on Presley you might be interested in. Aaron Presley. Used be a city cop. Worked vice over there. According to my source, his departure from the department was abrupt. He was never accused of anything. There's nothing on his record, just a rather speedy withdrawal. Went down to work for the McDowell County Sheriff for a year or so before coming back up and joining the Sheriff's Department here. My guy thinks there was a woman involved."

"Isn't there always a woman involved?"

"Sure seems like it."

"McDowell County," I said. "That's kind of small time compared to the city police up here, isn't it?"

"Way small. That's what makes you wonder. But hell, I mean people have all kinds of stuff in their closets, you know? People make mistakes, goof up, try to cover their tracks as well as they can and go on. But you also know my experience with the sheriff's shop. The top guy is new, and it seems like a lot of stuff has been cleaned up since I was there. But, what is it you're always sayin'?"

"You never know."

"Yeah, that's it. You never know."

23

Warren answered when I called Kathy's office. He really was a nice young man. I just wished he wasn't so damned good-looking. When she got on the line, we agreed to meet for Mexican after my A.A. meeting.

I got to the church in time to help set up the chairs. The discussion topic was how our ego is often our undoing – ego in the sense of our good opinion of ourselves and how important it seems to us that other people share that high opinion. I knew I had gotten high not just on the adrenaline of the previous night's fight but also, and maybe more importantly, on Audrey's reaction to it. People at 12-step meetings often say, "I heard just what I needed to hear." That is kind of the point, after all, and it was true for me that afternoon, being reminded of my need for approval and acceptance from others, especially those of the feminine persuasion. However, my experience also taught me that, as important as self-knowledge is, it is not always sufficient to prevent me from repeating past mistakes.

She was sipping a Margarita when I arrived. I had a tonic and lime. She ordered fajitas. I got the fish tacos.

"Big day?" she said.

"Yeah, it seems like almost any day that begins with finding out someone died under unusual circumstances is going to be a big day."

"How'd he die? What was his name? Steve?"

"Stan. Gun shot to the head. There's some thought is was suicide."

"Only some thought? Not universal?"

"There are some things that make me wonder. Like, no note. Like Detective Presley showing up again. I told you about him, didn't I?"

"He's the dirty dick?"

Our food came and our attention to the day's details waned. We had gotten all the way through the entrée and were waiting for some of the restaurant's famous tres leches cake before she told me she was going to be leaving for Georgia Sunday afternoon. I knew it was coming but it still blindsided me. I hoped it didn't show.

"How long will you be gone?"

"It might only take a day, more likely two. Should be home Tuesday night."

She must have seen it.

"Why don't you see if Zella can have dinner Monday night?" she said. "That'll keep you out of trouble."

"Thanks," I said. I didn't say what I wanted to, which was, yeah, but it won't keep you out of trouble.

"It's only two days."

"I know. I'll be OK. Work is pretty interesting. I'll see Nate, make a couple of meetings. Time will fly by."

When we got home, she suggested I go out on the deck and she'd join me in a few minutes. I anticipated what was coming. She'd bring me a cup of coffee, full strength. I'd say, "it'll keep me up," and she'd say, "I'm counting on it." She would be wearing something skimpy, something that didn't quite keep the good parts from view. She would sit next to me and lean close. She would have some fragrance on, something that smelled very good, something I'd want to get close to. I'd make a suggestion that we retire and she'd say we should just relax and finish our drinks. I'd say, this is not very relaxing, just the opposite. I would feel her bare foot climb into my pant leg. She would get closer still and kiss me on the neck, a hand would rest on my thigh. She would unbutton my top shirt button and kiss the top of my breastbone. Her hand would slide up my thigh, all the way up. I would ache for it to move sideways and she would sit up and lift the wine glass to her lips and take a small, slow sip. She would run her tongue over her lips. I would drain my coffee in one gulp. She would start to rise and take my hand and I would follow her upstairs. It was like watching a favorite movie you'd seen many times before and you knew how it was going to end and you watched it over and over again because it was so good.

The buzzing woke me. The clock radio showed 6:25. I hit the snooze button twice before picking up the phone.

"I wake you?" Queenie said.

"Uh, yeah," I said, walking away from the bed, hoping the noise hadn't wakened Kathy. My leg almost gave out, throbbing like it had the previous morning.

"What's up?"

"Sorry. Just saw something I thought was intriguing enough you might want to know about it."

I was out of the bedroom, heading downstairs to the kitchen.
"Go on."

"Sheriff's car just came by."

"Yeah? ... That's it?"

"Yup. Kinda early for the law to be out here roamin' around, 'specially on a Saturday, don't you think?"

I'd made it to the kitchen. The coffee maker was ready to go, just waiting for me to push the button.

"I guess so. Someone on their way to console the grieving widow, you suppose?"

"Something like that. I've told Sonny to let me know if someone's coming back up the road from down there. But you know, sometimes Sonny acts like he hasn't really heard me. Doesn't always take direction well."

"I've got a couple of cats like that. Well, they actually never take direction. I don't suppose you have any good reason to go down there yourself," I said, "check on how she's doing?"

"I'm not sure I'd be welcome. I might go tend to my garden a little, that one on the side of the house. With a little luck, I might be able to get a good look at whoever it is when he comes back this way."

"I've got an idea who it might be," I said.

"Probably same as mine."

I sat on the porch with my coffee, listening to the murmur of the creek as it meandered alongside the house. I remembered that I hadn't gone by the police station to look at mug shots the day before and thought I could do that on my way home from tennis. Four of us who had almost nothing in common except a love of the game had been meeting for doubles at eight o'clock on Saturday mornings for the past four years. Christmas and being out of town were considered to be the only reasons not to be there, although they had excused me the night I'd been in jail a year or so ago.

Later, I could see if the Reverend Haywood was available, ride around with him, see if anything interesting transpired. Maybe see the Miata again, although I imagined they – whoever they were

— would have ditched that car. I could go out to see the Widow Dillingham myself, see how she was getting along.

When the coffee was gone, I headed upstairs to get dressed. I had just stepped into the bathroom when she called to me.

"Why don't you come back to bed, hon?"

I turned toward the bedroom. She looked like she was still sleeping. I slipped back under the covers. We kissed.

"I know what you're up to," I said.

"What?"

"Trying to assuage your bad feelings about leaving me for three days."

"Two. And so, if I am?"

"Well, I may have to lose my attitude about you going out of town."

I rolled over and looked at the clock. It was seven-fifteen.

"I've got to get going, or I'll be late," I said, almost collapsing as my leg gave way again. It seemed like I may have gotten more than just a bruise from my assailant.

My phone rang while I was on my way from the tennis club to the police station.

"Ryder. Dominic." The thesaurus could list Dominic Hayes as a synonym for taciturn. "Got some info on those names you gave me," he said.

"Spill it," I said, sounding to myself like someone in a Mickey Spillane mystery.

Of the two men and the woman who Audrey thought might have reason to stalk her, the woman was the only one Dom had found anything about.

"And she got married about six months ago. Doesn't seem likely she'd be stalking another woman, does it?"

"People do strange things, Dom, you know that. Maybe it's the lady's husband. Maybe she and Audrey had more of a relationship than Audrey was willing to let on about. Could be embarrassing, I suppose, even in this day and age. Maybe her new old man found out about it."

"Yeah, well, the other thing that's surprising is I can't find a thing on either of those guys. It's like they never existed in this town. Want me to keep looking?" he asked.

"Where?"

"The state, the region. It'll take some more time."

"No, that's OK. Who knows? The cops might even be helpful. I'm on my way over there now to look at mug shots."

I told the desk sergeant why I was there. They had books of photos of known stalker-types. I took a break after half an hour for a cup of coffee and then went through the rest of them. No one looked like my guy. I had just gotten up to leave when I heard my name called. The voice belonged to Ted Henderson, the detective who had honchoed the investigation into the stripper murder of which I'd been accused.

"What have you got yourself involved in this time, Rick?"

"Oh, the usual – murder, drugs, naked women."

"Ah, right down your alley."

He knew about Queenie's arrest even though it happened on county turf. There aren't a lot of homicides in the area, and people who work that beat keep up with what's happening nearby. I also told him about Audrey and the altercation of the other night.

"You do OK with one arm, don't you?"

"Had twenty years of practice," I said. "Oh, since you're here, can I talk to you a minute about an ex-cop, guy named Presley, Aaron Presley."

He scanned the room. There was no one in close proximity. "Something going on that involves a woman?" he asked.

"Could be."

"Yeah, guy's got OK cop skills but seems to be easily led around by the gonads. You didn't hear that from me."

"Hear what from you?"

24

The machine answered at Pete Haywood's office. I told it I'd like to take Pete up on his offer to ride around the neighboring counties and that I'd be in the area all weekend. Then I called Audrey. Her voice mail had just started into its recording when she picked up.

"Sorry," she said, "just got out of the shower."

I stifled my imagination.

"I think the police are watching now."

"What makes you think that?"

"There're two guys just sitting in a car in the parking lot outside the condo."

"Jeeze. They might as well be in a patrol car, have a sign on it, 'we're watching you.' On the other hand, the guy tailing you doesn't seem like a pro at this, either, so maybe he won't figure them out. That why you called, to tell me the fuzz are on the job?"

"I thought you'd want to know."

"You're right, thanks. And, while I've got you on the phone, maybe you can tell me more about the guys whose names you gave me. There doesn't seem to be any information about them, like they don't exist, at least not in this county."

There was a long pause, the kind of empty air people fill up with made-up stories. I was waiting for something creative.

"I'm sorry," she said, almost whispering.

"For what?"

"The guys aren't real people. Oh, God, I'm such an idiot." I didn't say anything and she went on. "I thought it might make me seem more interesting if there had been guys who might want to follow me."

"Make you seem more interesting?"

It occurred to me that she was one of those very attractive women who have been treated for so long on the basis of their looks, they're afraid they don't have anything else that would be of interest to the rest of the world. She had to maintain appearances at all cost or else she'd be nothing.

"That's crazy," I said. "I mean, diagnostically crazy. You know that, don't you?"

She excused herself and blew her nose.

"I'm sorry," I said. "But my experience of you is that you are naturally interesting, you don't have to make stuff up to add to it."

"No," she said, stifling a sob. "I'm sorry. Am I going to be in trouble with the police now?" She sounded like a little girl who'd been caught taking cookies before dinner.

"No. I never gave them the names. And some guy really has been following you. Driving in a car with a stolen license plate and carrying a gun." I knew the answer to the next question was moot, but couldn't keep myself from asking.

"What about the woman?" I asked.

"She's real. That's another reason I wanted to give you men's names."

"So I wouldn't think you were gay?"

"I guess."

"You know, she got married about six months ago."

"She did?"

This was one screwed-up cookie, I thought. The kind who seems to attract trouble. Or be attracted to it.

"Does this mean we won't be having lunch again?"

I wondered why she wanted to. With the cops on the job, my work was done. I said I thought Monday would work. Looking back on it, I blame the crying.

I picked up some chicken and some prawns on the way home. The chicken was politically correct, having lived a free-range lifestyle, probably mostly in the shade, never shot up with hormones, raised by people who drove a hybrid. I couldn't vouch for the shrimp. They marinated in Rick's Secret Sauces for a couple of hours before I cooked them on the grill. After Kathy and I ate, we took a walk in the forest. Cove Road becomes gravel just past our driveway at a sign announcing you are entering the national forest. Cove Creek follows the road, picking up the stream that comes down the mountain past our house. We circled around from the road back up to the woods behind the house, seeing who could name the most wildflowers. When we got back to the house, she had her nightcap glass of wine while I drank a cup of decaf. Our lovemaking later was more subdued but no less gratifying than the night before.

The next morning she suggested tennis. There are a couple of well-maintained and not heavily-used courts at the community center down by the volunteer firehouse. She doesn't play as much as I do, and I figured that, having just played the day before, I'd have an edge. She beat me two out of three sets. I attributed the loss to the absence of a two-handed backhand in my repertoire. After we cleaned up and had a lunch of leftovers from the previous night's barbecue, she packed the Infiniti. I waved her away from the bottom of the drive.

When I got Zella on the phone, I told her Kathy suggested I might inveigle a dinner invitation while she was out of town. Until the murder and consequent fiasco of a year and a half ago, the idea of me having dinner alone with Zella was unthinkable. Zella is an attractive and sensual woman with whom I have been infatuated since the day she hired me to work for her as an attorney at the state's Department of Environment and Natural Resources. In spite of my attraction, I have honored both my marriage and the sanctity of her widowhood in my relationship with her. But in the midst of the murder and related investigations, she had asked me to come over for a meal. It was chaste and all business and a side benefit was the discovery we could do this and behave like proper grownups.

"Sure, come on. But I warn you, you're going to get leftovers."

I was a good cook. Zella was a great cook. Her leftovers would beat my leftovers.

My heart went arrhythmic for a few beats when she opened the door. When we had worked together, I had developed a kind of immunity to her good looks, like a drinker becomes tolerant to the effects of alcohol. Seeing her following a period of absence was like taking that first drink after being sober for a while. She stood an inch or two taller than I and carried herself as if royalty ran in her blood. African and Asian genes combined to give her a highly-polished mahogany complexion and her once jet-black hair was now seasoned with gray. The burgundy-colored sari she was wearing exposed one shoulder and highlighted her full bosom.

Our lips touched demurely and she led me into the house where the sumptuous aroma of curry vied for my attention.

"I'm glad you called," she said. "I've missed you around the office."

We moved into a room presided over by a grand piano. A richly matted and framed portrait of her late husband kept an eye on us.

While the pungent stew heated, she fixed a glass of sparkling water with a twist of lemon for me and a Scotch for herself.

"How goes the murder investigation?" she asked as we seated ourselves.

"I don't know how the police are coming along or if they're looking for possibilities besides Queenie. I know how that can be if they've decided on the outcome before they've begun investigating. But, if they don't come up with something less circumstantial – and the circumstances are tenuous at best – they're going to have to let her off. Especially in light of some recent developments."

"I read about the groundskeeper or whatever he was. Paper said his death was suspicious."

"Appeared to be a suicide," I said, "although I wonder if he wasn't helped. And, there's this sheriff's guy keeps popping up. Ted Henderson knows him and does not speak especially highly of him."

I told her Presley's history as I knew it and the circumstances of our paths crossing.

Zella checked the curry and pronounced it ready. We served ourselves in the kitchen and took plates to the dining room table.

"Then there's the recent flurry of land acquisition near Queenie's," I continued after we'd toasted our health.

"You think that's related to the murders? Seems like a stretch."

"You know me, Zel, I tend toward conspiratorial explanations for things. Often I'm right."

The conversation turned to what was happening at the Mountain Center for the Defense of the Environment. They had just filed suit against a mill alleged to be dumping untreated industrial waste into a river north of the city. Jay was talking with a family about how they could keep their land out of the hands of developers. Everything seemed to be running well without me. I told her about my conversation with Maisie Ivey and suggested that Jay might want to talk to her about possibilities of a land trust. After poppy seed cake and coffee, we moved back to the piano room where she regaled me with some Thelonius Monk she had just learned to play. We talked about what we were reading and movies we had recently seen before it seemed to be time to go.

When we kissed again at the door, a tinge of melancholy fell over me, hardly noticeable. I fought the urge to pull her into a full-body hug.

I felt guilty about that impulse when I got to the car until I realized it was nothing more than a natural inclination. An attractive, fun, smart, talented woman who was a close friend. Why wouldn't I want to hug her? Then I felt like a responsible adult, not acting on that part of me that has little regard for boundaries.

On the way back to the house, I realized I had not talked to her about Audrey.

25

It was almost nine-thirty when I arrived home from Zella's. I pulled on a sweatshirt and went out on the deck. A lonesome owl cried out for a companion. The murmuring of the creek had transported me to the twilight zone between waking and sleeping when the phone rang. Kathy's routine on the road was to call at ten o'clock. Her voice saying she loved me was often the last thing I'd hear for the day. Our conversation was comforting in its predictability. She told me about the drive to Columbus (uneventful), the motel room (fine and nondescript), dinner (a very nice seafood place). I told her about the evening with Zella. After we'd said good-night, I realized I hadn't mentioned my intention to have lunch with Audrey, the second person I could have shared this with. It had all the earmarks of a secret.

The morning sky was pale yellow when I took my coffee out back. The sun wouldn't appear above the ridge behind the house for two hours. Even this early, I could tell it was going be a day to gladden hearts at the Chamber of Commerce. I pushed myself hard during my morning workout to avoid feeling how much I missed Kathy.

An hour later, the gods were with me when I pulled up in

front of the Downtown Bakery on Biltmore Avenue right as a parking space was being vacated. I fed quarters into the meter and walked inside. Nate was already in a booth, prepared for our regular Monday morning get-together.

I sat down with coffee and a scone.

"Hello, Counselor," he greeted.

"Hello, Counselor," I greeted in return, our stylized exchange acknowledging our common professional background.

I'd met the big man at an AA meeting twelve years ago, soon after Kathy and I moved here. He had just gotten sober and was skeptical of the program, not in small part because, as he said, "ain't many people of the black persuasion at those meetings." I had been among those who had suggested that he might be more at home at Narcotics Anonymous, to which he countered he'd never done an illegal drug in his life.

"Being a reformed drunk has become acceptable," he said, "even in the black community. But the proper folks of my neighborhood still have a pretty low opinion about junkies. And, besides, I'd probably run into a bunch of my clients."

While he rarely goes to a meeting, he has never relapsed. Unlike myself.

I brought him up to date on my various activities in the service of his defense of Queenie. While I had yet to uncover anything that would, in itself, exonerate her, the authorities had also been unable to make a credible murder case against her.

"Unless there's stuff we don't know about, it's unlikely the grand jury's going to indict the old bird," Nate said. "So, you gotta ask yourself, why Queenie? I can't believe it's just to settle old political scores. Otherwise, they'd have been making my life a lot more miserable, too."

"It's the land, Nate. Someone wants it and, short of murdering her, this gets her out of the way."

"Seems like a pretty byzantine way to go about it."

"Good word, Nate."

"I did go to college, you know."

I did know, but the old homeboy persona he adopted often allowed me to forget that he graduated Phi Beta Kappa from Brown University back when you'd be more likely to see a black man at a Klan rally than on the campus of an Ivy League school.

"So, what's your take on Stan Whatshisname's death?" he asked. "Think it was suicide?"

"Nope."

"Then who?"

"Good question. I'd been leaning toward Stan as the culprit for Brian's murder, but I think this gets him off the hook for that."

"I'm sure he'd be grateful for your saying so."

"I just meant ..."

"Yeah, I know, bro. Unless of course, he killed the kid, and then he had to be killed to make sure he didn't spill the beans in case the cops started nosing around again. Even though it's unlikely the murder case against Queenie is going to go forward, I'd still be more comfortable if we had a reasonable alternative scenario. The grand jury doesn't convene again for a couple of weeks, so you've got some time to earn your keep."

A good looking, well-endowed teenager wearing a tank top and short skirt walked past our table. I watched Nate's gaze track her as if pulled by a magnetic force. He took a deep breath.

"Hard on an old man's heart," he said. "Well, I probably ought to get going. See that the wheels of justice turn for the downtrodden as they do for people of means." He began to scoot out of the booth when he said, "What's happening with that lady you were following?"

I told him about the gun incident, the stolen license plate and how it seemed the police had taken over the case.

"What does that do to you?"

"I suppose I'll be available to help out, if needed."

"Help her or help the po-lice?"

"I don't think the po-lice gonna want my help, Counselor."

"Hmm. So you're just, like what, hanging in the wings, see what happens?"

"I guess that describes it. I have gotten a retainer from her, after all."

"Just so you got your priorities straight. And since I put you on the clock before she showed up, priority one is working on Queenie's case."

I followed him to the cashier. We parted with a soul handshake, a gentle mocking of our collective hipness. This time I was sure that neglecting to mention my upcoming luncheon was absolutely unintentional, in spite of his specific questioning about her.

I left another message for Pete Haywood before driving out to Queenie's.

We sat at the kitchen table with coffee and slices of toasted fresh sourdough bread and blackberry preserves. I took a bite and my eyes lit up.

"You make this jam?"

"Yup."

"Man, you ought to be selling it."

"Well, you know, I did a few years back. Just when the whole farmers' market thing was comin' into vogue. Did the whole entrepreneur thing. Hooked up with the small business people at the community college. Got an accountant. The whole nine yards. Did it for about three years. But, it's hard work, you know. Just pickin' the damn berries is work. And it started bein' just work. The fun went out of it. Found myself worrying about how much money I was gonna make. That's no damn way to live. You know, some lady wanted to buy my business, offered me a lot of money. She talked about going on the Internet, catalogue sales, all that stuff. I said, can you guarantee me in writing you'll never touch the recipe? She just looked at me like I was from another planet. Said, once she bought it, she could do what she wanted with it. That was the end of that."

"Our loss," I said.

"Oh, I'll give you a jar to take home. How do you think I keep the friends I do?"

"Well, now that we've taken care of the preserve issue, did you see that cop again, the one went by here Saturday morning?"

"I worked out there about an hour, didn't see the car come back. Of course, whoever it was, they could have gone on down the back way. Most people don't go that way 'cause it's to hell and gone before you come back to a main road. Nice drive, though, if you just want to wander around the mountain."

She got up and brought the coffee pot back to the table. I nodded, she filled my cup, then hers, and returned the pot to the stove. I watched without comment. She sat back down and continued.

"I broke down and called Martha Jo, let her know I was over being mad at her, asked if there was anything she needed. She was passably gracious, said there wasn't and thanked me for the offer. Then I asked her if anybody'd been by the house, told her someone'd come up earlier and I didn't recognize the car and I was pretty edgy about who was on the property these days. I'm startin' to think like you, Ryder, because when there was silence for a few seconds, I thought maybe she was preparin' a story, like she didn't know how much I really knew. She said no one had been by, maybe she'd been in the shower and they knocked and she missed them. Well, I thought anybody comes out this far would notice her car and probably snoop around a little before they took off. And ...

well, a little suspicious, don't you think?"

"Maybe I'll go on down and have a talk with her," I said.

"On what pretext?"

"Still working on the murder. That's not a pretext. I'm wondering if anything else may have occurred to her that might be helpful."

"Don't suppose you're interested in seeing some more of those boobs."

My cheeks got warm.

"Why, Queenie. Whatever ..."

She stopped me with a wave of her hand.

"She used to dance, you know. I will say this about the woman. Whatever else she may or may not have going for her, she still has a fine figure."

"Stan make her quit?"

"I'm not sure. I think there was some kind of scandal out at the Dolls House where she worked. Something about her and a cop."

Our eyes widened in unison.

"You think?" I said.

"Could be."

26

Queenie's kitchen remained cool even as it approached midday. Old Maxwell knew what he was doing when he built the original cabin, leaving it surrounded by shade trees and situating it on the crest of a ridge where it would catch the prevailing west-east breeze.

"Probably ought to get on before the whole day slips away," I said.

"Before you go," she said, "there's something else I need to tell you. Probably need to tell Nate, too. Some books of mine are missing."

"Books?" I asked, a little ingenuously since I had an inkling of what she was referring to.

"Yup. A bunch I had out the garage. Been meaning to do something with them, they've been out there for years."

I nodded.

"You know something about this?" she said.

"After they carted you off to the hoosegow I came up and poked around. I saw the empty bookshelf out there."

"How'd you get in?"

"Sonny showed me where the key was."

Queenie scowled at her companion who looked up at her as if

to say, "Yeah, so what?"

"Well, he knows you're one of the good guys."

"Why would the sheriff by interested in them?"

"They're books about growing pot."

My eyes widened.

"They were all from the sixties and seventies," she said. "I told you about the classes I gave on growing the stuff. Those were my reference books. I'm pretty much an autodidact, you know. Taught myself anything I know that's of any use in this world. My folks did send me off to Meredith College in Greensboro, tried to make a lady out of me. You see how well that succeeded. But, they did try, I'll give 'em that. Anyway, I've kept those books as kind of historical artifacts. Thought about donating them to some library. Probably not something the county public library would want. The University, maybe."

"Wouldn't they get moldy and eaten by critters out there?"

"Guy at a used bookstore downtown showed me how to wrap them in special paper. And I don't know why, exactly, I kept them out there. I guess there was a part of me, the more appropriately socialized part, that thought maybe not everybody would think it was a good thing to have a pot-growing library in one's house."

"Maybe that college stuff did have an effect," I said. "At any rate, the cops now have evidence that you grew pot."

"Yeah. But it was nothin' like that stuff I'm supposed to have been growing now, what they busted me for. That sinsemilla stuff. We never knew anything about that. Knocked me over when I saw the pictures in the paper."

"I think the prosecutor will find that kind of splitting hairs. How many books are you talking about?"

She made an embarrassed shrug.

"Maybe, oh, a couple dozen."

"A couple of dozen!"

She nodded.

"Books on marijuana. But you never grew very much?"

"Really, Ryder. I know it sounds kinda outlandish. The most I ever had growing myself was maybe three, four plants at a time. And I haven't done that for forty years now. Since before Nixon started his War on Drugs."

"OK. I can see the transcript of the trial: The prosecutor asks for the evidence to be wheeled in. There are twenty or so books lined up on a library cart. Names like: Growing Your Own for Fun and Profit; The Homegrown Hobbyist; High in the Mountains..."

"Yeah, I get your point, Ryder. Tends to raise questions about the defendant's character."

"Not so much her character, Queenie, although that, too. Just about how unlikely is it that a woman who admittedly not only grew pot back in the day but who also taught others how to do it, is NOT the one responsible for pot being grown on her land now?"

"When you put it like that, it doesn't sound good, does it?"

"No, it doesn't." I was getting worked up and realized it wasn't my problem. It was hers. And it could wind up landing her in prison. For a long time. Dope growers are right up there with child molesters as the bogeymen of the day. As bad as commies back in the middle of the last century.

"Does Nate know about this? I mean, that you were the local doyenne of pot growing?"

"Don't know. That wasn't part of my world he shared."

There wasn't much to be done about it except to alert Nate. Maybe there was a way to get the evidence quashed. After thanking Queenie for the refreshments and the information, I walked to my car and called Nate's office. He wasn't available and I asked Katrina to have him call me back; it was important, but not urgent.

Martha Jo's car was in front of her house along with the pickup. She wasn't out on the deck. I had knocked three times and was deciding what to do next, when she came to the door. She was wearing a white terry cloth robe.

"Mr. Ryder," she said. "Sorry if you've been standing out here. I just got out of the shower. What's so funny about that?"

"Nothing," I said. "Just reminded me of something I heard a little while ago."

"What're you doing here?"

"Are we going to have a conversation out here or are you going to invite me in?"

"I didn't know we were going to have a conversation. That's why I asked what brought you here."

"Touché. I'm still working on the murder and was just up at Queenie's. Since I was in the area, I wondered if anything else may have occurred to you that you think might be helpful."

"Well, let's see. Oh, yeah. My husband committed suicide. That help?"

"Maybe," I said.

"Oh, really?"

"You never know."

She narrowed her eyes at me before finally saying, "OK, come on in." She sent me out to the deck while she put some clothes on. It was impossible not to think of possibilities.

She came out wearing white short shorts and a relatively demure halter top. I took her up on an offer of coffee. Five minutes later she appeared with a carafe, a bowl of sugar and a small pitcher of half-and-half. She reclined in a lounge chair and lit a cigarette. I sat in the shade at the umbrella table. The sun was well over the yard-arm and I was surprised I detected no odor of alcohol.

"You're a dancer, aren't you?" I said after we'd settled in.

"Used to be. Out at the Dolls House. Saw you out there a couple of times."

"You saw me?" I was always chagrined when this happened. I didn't go there very often, half a dozen times since I'd moved here and it's not the kind of thing you put on your resumé.

"Yeah," she said. "You kind of, you know, stick out in a crowd. I mean, I didn't know who you were, just there was this one-armed guy used to come in once in a while. You're the one they said killed that girl, what was her name? I never met her, she came after I left. And then they closed the club after all that went down."

"Wait a minute," she said, standing abruptly.

She was back in three minutes having added four inch stiletto heels and a long black wig with short straight bangs to her attire.

"Remember me?"

I couldn't stifle a chuckle.

"Yeah, I do. What did you call yourself?"

"Mandi."

I laughed some more.

"Funny?"

"Debbie, the young woman who was murdered, told me it was in the Universal Strippers Contract that all dancers' names had to end in 'i'."

"Yeah. Don't hear of many strippers named Martha Jo, do you?"

I sipped my coffee. It was remarkably good. I don't know why that surprised me.

"You want something to go with that coffee? I mean like a muffin or a bagel or something?"

I thanked her and told her that I'd had something earlier.

"Did you like it?" I asked.

"Dancing? Well, the money was good. Turns out I'm kind of an exhibitionist. Not that you ever would have noticed. I liked dancing, the attention. For a while, anyway. There was a lot I didn't like."

"For instance?"

"Oh, don't be a jerk. You know what that business is like. You really do get sick of yourself after a while. Why so many of the girls do drugs. I'm kinda glad they shut it down. I know that was how those girls made a living but ..."

She shrugged and lit a fresh cigarette.

"So, Stan came and took you away from all that," I said.

"Something like that. Actually, I'd already quit and was living off some savings when he came around to where I stayed. He'd always liked me at the club and was respectful to me, something you can't say about many of the assholes who went there ... present company excluded, of course. He told me he missed seeing me and, get this, asked me to marry him right then."

"Whirlwind romance," I said.

"Yeah. I said 'no,' and he asked me to dinner. So we dated a while. He brought me up here. I made him fix this place up. After a few months I thought, what the hell. He's ... he was amazingly good in the sack."

She was leaning back, like she was talking to the sky. I couldn't tell if that last was said for effect or if it was just a matter of fact. Then she sat up and said she was getting another cup of coffee and asked if I wanted a refill. I said anymore and I'd float but I would like to use the bathroom.

What I could see of the house as I passed through appeared clean and tidy. There was a dog-eared Harlequin romance and a People magazine in the bathroom.

"Who do you think killed Stan?" I asked when I rejoined her on the deck.

Her expression turned quizzical, like she was thinking of an answer. As if the right one had popped into her brain, she sat a little straighter and said, "He killed himself. Why'd you ask that?"

"I guess Brian's murder is on my mind, so I'm just thinking in those terms."

"Well, shit. He shot himself," she said, her temper rising.

"OK. Sorry," I said, holding my hands up in surrender.

She glared at me.

"It's probably time for me to go," I said.

"Yes," she said. "I think so."

I stood and thanked her for the coffee. She nodded, her expression neutral, her eyes narrowed like they were before she invited me in. I walked off the deck to my car.

My cell phone had buzzed twice while I'd been chatting with the widow. A call from Nate and one from Audrey. I called Nate first. Katrina put me through.

"Whadaya have for me, homey?"

Out of the corner of my eye, I saw Martha Jo get up and go inside.

"Did you know Queenie used to grow marijuana?"

"Uh oh."

"So you did."

"I think I remember hearing something about it."

"Oh, don't be coy, Nate."

"Long time ago, bro, long time ago. She never got busted or anything. There's no public record as far as I know."

"Well, Nate," I said, "apparently the sheriff's boys and girls carted away a couple dozen books about how to grow the stuff. I think it's about to become part of the public record."

"Doesn't seem to have much to do with murder."

His nonchalance was infuriating. "Except the scenario seems to be that she was growing marijuana and Brian was helping himself to the fruits of it ... which, by the way, does seem very probable, the helping himself part, not Queenie growing it ... and, the theory goes, she killed him because of it. Or because she was afraid he'd wind up getting her busted. Something along those lines. Isn't that the narrative for this over at the court house?"

"Seems about it," he agreed.

"According to Queenie," I went on, "all the books were written before 1970, before sinsemilla came into vogue. She thinks that shows they have nothing to do with what was being grown out there."

"Hmm. Not sure a jury would appreciate the distinction."

"That's what I said."

There was a pause. I assumed he was consolidating the information.

"Any good news?" he asked.

"Well. I'm not sure this means anything, but I asked Martha Jo, wife of the deceased ..."

"Yeah, I know who she is."

"I asked her who she thought killed her husband. She paused a few seconds like she was thinking about it, before she seemed to remember that he committed suicide. Then she went off on me for suggesting it might not be suicide. Methinks the lady doth protest a bit much."

"You think now we've got two murders to solve?"

"Isn't that what the cops are supposed to be doing?"

"In an ideal world, my friend. See, this is where us darker skinned people have an advantage over you pale folks. We understand from the get-go that we do not live in an ideal world. Gotta run. Keep in touch."

The phone went quiet. I knew this was not an ideal world. If it was, I wouldn't have private detective work to keep me busy.

27

Audrey's call confirmed our meeting. Her car was already in the parking lot when I got to the café where we'd lunched before. Her knees were crossed under the table, exposing a pleasing expanse of thigh beneath her pale blue dress. I slid in across from her. A modest degree of cleavage was on display. Her hair tumbled down to her shoulders. I couldn't kid myself about why I had agreed to meet.

She was sipping from a glass of white wine.

"I'm still pissed, you know," I began.

Her face reddened.

"I'm sorry," she said.

"So, what's up now?"

When the waitress came, Audrey ordered her standard large salad. I got the scallops.

"So?" I repeated, keeping my gaze at eye level.

"I'm kind of freaked out being watched by the cops."

"Want to call them off?"

"I think so."

"If you do, you're never going to get them back, you know."

"I hope I don't need them. Maybe you've scared away whoever it was."

"Could be. People who do this kind of thing typically aren't your real brave types. Even with a gun, I knew he was harmless. Although my leg still hurts."

"What did he do to your leg?"

"He didn't do it. I slammed his arm into it to get him to drop the gun. I may be stronger than I realize."

I didn't think I said it for effect, but her eyes widened.

"Do I get any of my money back?" she asked.

"Afraid not."

"Seems like a lot of money for the little ..."

"Hey. I had a gun pulled on me. Even though I didn't think he'd use it, that still qualifies as dangerous work. And if it got him to go away, I completed the assignment. If he comes back, I'll come back. That's how the retainer thing works."

"OK," she said, averting her eyes, like the guilty little girl again. "I'm sorry."

"Nothing to be sorry for. That's just the way it is."

The food came and interrupted our awkwardness.

"How's work?" I asked, tacking toward calmer waters.

"Busy."

"What is it you do, exactly?"

"I'm an account manager."

I nodded as if I fully understood what that entailed. "And you like the work?"

She shrugged. "Beats digging ditches. That's what my father used to say. He ran a small manufacturing company and some days he'd complain about all the idiots he had to work with, and then he'd say, 'but you know, it sure beats digging ditches.'"

She leaned slightly toward me. I maintained eye contact.

"So, how's the investigation coming?" she asked, her voice suggesting we were engaged in some clandestine operation.

"I can't talk about other work I'm doing, just like I couldn't talk to anybody else about my work with you. Haven't we had this conversation before?"

"Well, it's in the papers, you know."

"What I'm doing isn't."

"I think it's kind of cool that old lady was growing pot."

"That's an allegation. Not a fact."

"You don't think she did it?"

"Audrey. I'm not going to talk about it."

The waitress came and we declined dessert. We said nothing for two or three minutes until she asked how I lost my arm.

"A car wreck. I was eighteen." I didn't tell her I was drunk and killed someone. Or that I'd stayed mostly drunk for a long time afterward.

She was silent, as if waiting for me to go on. Then she said, "That first time I saw you? In the coffee shop? I didn't even notice it right away. You seem to do OK without it."

"I've had a long time to get used to it." I didn't talk about all the things that are a pain in the ass like tying shoes or a necktie or opening jars. And no two-handed backhand. I had almost forgotten why I had agreed to come to lunch other than the pleasure of seeing her.

"So, are you going to call off the cops?" I asked.

"I think so."

"They won't take you very seriously if this guy starts showing up again and you want them to do something about it."

"It wasn't really my idea to have them follow me."

"I thought you called them for help back before you first called me but they wouldn't do anything because there wasn't any evidence of a crime. It wasn't until the guy pulled a gun on me that they could do anything."

"It's just creepy, that's all."

"I wouldn't want cops following me around all the time, either.

I get that. I'm just pointing out that if you really want something done about this guy – and maybe it's already been done – if you send them away, they're unlikely to come back."

"Would you?"

"Would I what? You mean, tail you again?"

She nodded.

"I just told you," I said, not masking my irritation. "I still have your retainer and I'm not giving you a refund. I don't think this guy's going to show up again. But if he does, we'll take it from there."

Although I had no appointments, no place I had to be, I pulled the cell phone out of my pocket making a display of checking the time. I said I had to be going. She settled the check and we walked to the door. Outside, she got a box of cigarettes and a pack of matches from her pocketbook. It took me by surprise.

She had trouble lighting it because of the wind.

"Here, you cup your hands and I'll light the match," I said, having perfected the one-handed match-strike thing back when I still smoked.

After the cigarette was lit, I started to hand the matchbook back to her when I read the printing on it: NORTH REALTY, along with Pete Haywood's name and contact information.

"Where'd you get these?"

She looked at the pack and gave a shrug. I was sure I saw her eyes shift, just slightly, before she said, "I don't know. Just picked them up somewhere."

My phone buzzed and displayed "Pete Haywood" on the little screen. I excused myself and answered the call.

"Rick. Pete Haywood here. Got your messages. Been out of town a couple of days. Tied up the rest of the day, but I'd have some time tomorrow morning if you want to go driving around the mountains."

We agreed on nine-thirty.

"Now there's a coincidence," I said, re-pocketing my phone.

"What?"

"That was Pete Haywood."

She looked at me with what I interpreted as studied indifference.

"North Realty. Company on the match book."

"Oh. Yeah."

"Yeah," I repeated.

"Are you mad at me or something?"

"Just confused."

"About what?"

"There are things going on right now that I don't understand. And you're one of them."

A hand went to her chest.

"Moi?"

"Yes. You lie to me about people you've been out with. I have a guy pull a gun on me while I'm following you. I wonder if you haven't made the whole thing up just to create some drama in your life."

Her jaw was set, eyes glaring.

"I have enough drama in my life. I don't have to go making things up."

"I'm sure that's true. OK. I've got to go. Let me know if you're being followed again."

"You are infuriating."

I wanted to say, I'm infuriating? I let it alone and smiled as she turned in a huff and walked to her car. I watched to see if anybody was obviously making an effort to get behind her. She was out of sight when I went to my car and called Kathy's office.

Her young assistant answered.

"Warren, this is Rick ... Fine, thanks. I wonder if you could you do me a favor. Check with the folks who do your advertising, see if they know who handles North Realty, Pete Haywood's outfit ... Yeah, North Realty ... Just gimme a buzz if you find out. Yeah. ... Tell Kathy I said 'hi.' Thanks."

I was still in the parking lot, mulling over possibilities for the afternoon, when my phone rang again. It was Bobby Headley.

"I was just on my way to the coffee shop and wondered if you wanted to come out."

Although it meant a trip back out into the county, my afternoon social card was empty. I said I'd be there in twenty minutes.

The full name of the establishment was the New Mountain Café and Readery and it was run by a transplanted Yankee couple. They had learned the gourmet coffee business in New York and found a local roaster to supply them. The used book business was pretty much a wash, money-wise, they'd told me. But, they'd always wanted to own a bookstore and this was a way to indulge their two great passions. Two old sofas and some overstuffed chairs provided seating around a half dozen coffee tables. Bookcases lined the walls. Well-worn Oriental rugs covered most of the floor.

Taylor, a pleasant-looking woman given to wearing floor-length skirts and peasant tops, was about my age. Mickey, her husband, was a few years older. They both wore their hair in pony tails, his solid gray, hers a little more salt and peppery. His attire tended toward white painters' overalls, a holdover from an earlier livelihood. Locals assumed they were hippies, and nothing in the shop discouraged the notion. They were the people who'd suggested Bobby Headley might be helpful when I'd been investigating the disappearance of a teenage girl out that way.

Bobby was sitting on one of the half-dozen stools that lined the counter, chatting with the proprietress, when I walked in.

"Hello, stranger," the woman said.

"Hi, Taylor."

"Gotta wait for an invite from Bobby before you come see us?"

I held my arm up in a silent mea culpa. "My travels haven't brought me this way for a while."

"It's OK." She turned and called to the back. "Mickey. Come on out."

The tinkling of a beaded curtain announced his arrival from out of a back room.

"Rick. Nice to see you." He looked at Bobby. "We get to see this old coot fairly regularly." He turned back to me. "Looking for more runaways?"

"Wish it was as innocent as that. This is another murder. Maybe two, actually."

I gave him the Cliff's Notes version of what had transpired.

"Did you know they found a bunch of books on marijuana growing at Queenie's house?" I asked Bobby.

He laughed. A guffaw, actually. "Ah, that's our Queenie. I'd forgotten all that. Yeah, she was the queen of pot up there back in the day."

"That how she got her name?"

"Queenie? Nah. That's her given name."

"She seems to think because these were old books, from back in the sixties, they can't be used as evidence that she's been growing anything up there recently."

"Well, now, isn't that some coincidence," Taylor said. Bobby and I looked at her.

"Queenie?" I asked.

"No. Books on growing pot. Some lady brought a box of books like that just, oh, when was it Mickey?"

"Few days ago."

"Yeah. End of last week, maybe. But these books didn't look old. Names like, Growing Primo Pot, and How to Grow Sinsemilla. I didn't look inside them but, on the outside, they were in good condition."

I asked what the lady looked like.

Taylor looked at Mickey with a grin. "You tell 'em."

"Nice looking lady," he said. "Thirty-something."

"Oh, come on, Mick. You were practically drooling."

"Well, she wasn't dressed in a way that would mask her, mmm, attributes, shall we say."

Bobby looked at me. "The Widow Dillingham?"

"Sounds like it. Strawberry blond, five-five-ish?"

Mickey nodded.

I asked if they'd bought the books. Mickey looked at me like I was out of my mind.

"You kidding? It's hard enough convincing people we aren't a front for drug dealing."

Three teenagers, apparently high school students, came in and up to the counter. Bobby and I moved to one of the sitting areas. He closed his eyes as if he were awaiting a revelation.

"OK," he said. "So, Stan's growing the stuff. Has a small reference library. Probably doesn't keep it out in the open, you never know who might show up. Has it stashed somewhere the law doesn't find it when they look the place over after he has offed himself."

I thought it sounded like a reasonable scenario. He went on.

"Why on earth would Martha Jo try to sell them? I don't know her, but my understanding is she's no dummy. Made her living on her looks for a while, but still has a brain. I don't get it? Why wouldn't she just toss them in a dumpster?"

We sat in contemplation for a few minutes.

"Say she's a toker," I said. "Her supply – and her supplier –

are gone. She's one of those who thinks Mickey and Taylor are running a front for drugs. She brings the books in as a way to announce herself. You know, 'I'm one of you,' a way to hook up without coming in and saying, 'You guys know where I can find any pot?'"

Bobby mulled that over for a minute. "Could be. Still pretty risky. And if she and Stan were growing the stuff, surely they'd have had connections. People who are buying from them would probably know other dealers."

"Yeah, but everybody's real skittish. What with the bust and the murder and the supposed suicide, everybody's staying away from her. It's a stretch, I know."

My spook mind liked it.

The students had gotten their coffee drinks and were cruising the used books. They were enjoying themselves, laughing occasionally, showing one another what they'd come across.

Bobby's phone rang.

"Shit. There's a brush fire out in Sandy Mush and it got away from the locals. Gotta go give 'em a hand. Let me know if there's anything I can do to help the investigation."

Mickey returned to the back room. I thanked Taylor for the coffee and information. My phone went off just as I approached the Honda. It was Jay.

"What's up, comrade?" I asked.

"Oh, get off that, will you. Just because I think the corporations will be the downfall of our society doesn't mean I'm a Communist."

"Just messin'. What's goin' on?"

"I'm out at that Ivey woman's place, the lady you talked to Zella about?"

"Yeah?"

"She's gone."

"Off to town, maybe?"

"No. I mean, gone. The place is cleaned out. It's spooky, almost like nobody ever lived here."

28

Jay was standing on Maisie's porch when I pulled up. The front porch rocking chairs were gone. Hair on the back of my neck stood.

"I just got the shivers," I said as I walked up to my former colleague.

"Like I said, it's spooky. Like a horror movie right before the evil force appears. I don't know why. It's just an empty old house."

We toured the place in silence. He'd been right when he said it was empty. Not a stick of furniture, nothing in the kitchen drawers or cupboards, nothing in any of the tiny closets. The only clues that someone had once lived here were the places on the walls where things had hung and wallpaper and paint had faded around them.

Upstairs, Jay stood in the middle of what presumably had been a bedroom.

"How long ago were you out here?" he asked.

"Last week. Thursday, I think."

The floors were dusty, but not more than you'd expect in an old house after a few days of inattention. No other detritus. Not even old wire clothes hangers, something that in my experience always seemed to get left behind.

"I wonder if Queenie knows anything about her moving out," I said. I tapped her name on my cell phone display. Her machine picked up. I had begun leaving a message when I heard the buzz announcing an incoming call. I took it.

"Just heard the phone as I walked in," Queenie said. "Was down at Martha Jo's."

"And how is the widow this afternoon?"

"Not so good. She'd had a few drinks, not unusual, of course, but she was going on about 'those sons-of-bitches' and how they weren't going to get away with it."

"With what?"

"She didn't say, nor did she say who the sons-of-bitches were. But she was sure worked up about it."

"She was holding it together pretty well when I was down there this morning," I said. "It was almost noon and I don't think she'd had anything to drink."

"Maybe that was the problem."

My memory flashed to the time before I'd gotten sober, when I'd try to go a day without a drink and how crazy I'd be before finally giving in to the craving.

"Could be. Anyway, I'm out here at Masie Ivey's place. The old bird seems to have flown the coop." I explained about Jay's call and finding the empty house. "Did she say anything to you about leaving?"

"Unh-uh. Haven't talked to her in a little while, but it's not like her to just up and go like that. Unless, of course, she decided to sell the place after all, and was embarrassed to tell me after going on about how she'd never do that. Still, don't seem right."

"When I talked to her, she mentioned a nephew. Seemed like that might be her only relative. Got any idea where he lives?"

"I remember her talkin' about him. Why don't you come on up, have some tea, I'll try to get my brain a-workin'."

"Got time to run up there?" I asked Jay. "She'd probably like to see you."

"See me? Why?"

"I believe she thinks you're cute."

He rolled his eyes.

"Thanks."

He followed me up the mountain, past the trail we'd taken when we found Brian. I shivered again. My phone rang. I remembered back when we didn't have mobile phones and somehow did alright without being in contact with the rest of the world every minute. The phone ID'd Audrey. I ignored it. The afternoon was slipping away, the sun hiding beyond the west side of the ridge.

Queenie looked relaxed in a rocker, holding a glass of clear amber liquid, when we walked onto the porch. I took her free hand in mine and held it to my lips.

"Ms. Weaver."

"Mr. Ryder. I'm so glad you brought your associate." She held her hand toward Jay. "Mr. McIntyre. So good to see you again." He made a slight bow toward her.

"Queenie. And nice to see you, as well."

"Now we got all that out of the way, you boys want some refreshment. I know Rick'll stick to the tea. I've got something I'll think you'll like, Jay?"

She returned with a bottle of ale for Jay and tea for me.

"Wilson," she said as soon as she'd sat back down.

"Wilson?" I said, making a display of looking around for something I'd missed.

"Yeah. Neal Wilson, that's the nephew's name. Last I remember her saying, he was living in Old Fort."

"In McDowell County?"

"You know another one?"

"Just clarifying."

"You think he had something to do with Ms. Ivey leaving?" Jay asked.

"Let's hope she's just moved out," I said. "She did mention to me that this nephew coveted the place. Actually, she thought it was the nephew's wife more than Wilson himself. Maybe they finally talked her in to letting them have it."

"Yeah, I do remember about that boy. She'd have to have had a real change of heart to give it to him from the way I remember her talking."

"Maybe something happened," Jay said, "like she found out she had terminal cancer or something."

"Maybe. But she wouldn't have gone off without telling me."

"Maybe I should go see this guy Wilson," I said.

I felt a buzz in my pocket. I thought about ignoring it, then reconsidered. I put my drink down and yanked the phone out of my pants. The little screen showed "Audrey 2" meaning it was the second unanswered call from her. I excused myself and walked down the porch steps.

"This is Rick Ryder," I said, as formal a response as I could come up with.

"Oh, hi." She sounded surprised, as if she expected me not to answer again.

"Hello, Audrey."

"Oh now, Rick. Don't be so cool. I wondered if you'd like to have dinner with me tonight."

If I'd had two hands, I might have pulled my hair with the free one.

"What?"

"You heard me. Come to my house for dinner. I know I've been an aggravation and I wanted to make it up to you."

I didn't feel like trying to sort out what might really be going on or coming up with an excuse.

"Can't make it."

"You sure?"

"Yup."

"Well, if you change your mind, let me know. I probably won't eat before seven."

"OK."

"Oh, lighten up," she said before hanging up.

Walking back up the porch steps, I thought that she must have known Kathy was out of town, something I didn't remember telling her.

"You look flustered, Rick," Queenie said as I returned to my chair.

"A different case," I said. "Or, at least I think it's a different case."

"What do you mean, you think it's a different case?" Jay asked.

"Just that paranoid part of my personality that tends to see connections in everything."

"Everything is connected," our hostess waxed philosophically. "Didn't you know that?"

"Thanks. That helps."

We chatted some more until Jay said it was time for him to be getting back and I supposed I ought to be running along as well, although there wasn't any place I had to be. I'd go home, throw some dinner together and make an eight o'clock AA meeting. My phone rang again as I approached the Honda. I wanted to throw the thing away until I saw it was Kathy. Maybe she was coming home early.

29

"They want me to do a presentation to the whole staff at their monthly meeting," Kathy said after we exchanged greetings. "They're anxious to move on this thing. The downside is, the meeting isn't until five-o'clock tomorrow afternoon."

"Hell of a time for a staff meeting."

"I don't have much control over that. Anyway, we won't be done until seven or so and you know how I feel about driving that far at night."

I learned in therapy about fear-fight-flight responses when people feel threatened. I was doing all those things. I was afraid. I wanted to yell. I wanted to hang up. I took a deep breath.

"So, you won't be home tomorrow night."

"That's the short of it."

I didn't say anything.

"It's been almost two years now, Rick. You can't hang onto it, or it's going to kill us."

She was right. But it was like asking a child who was afraid of dogs to go up and pet a Great Dane. It was hard enough for me to deal with her absences when they were part of a plan. When the plan changed, I got suspicious. I couldn't help it. And I knew this was important for her work, for her career.

"I can't help it," I said.

"Yes, you can. You wallow in it, you know. This, 'Oh my god, is she going to be unfaithful again' thing. The victim. It's not endearing."

"Wallow?"

"Rick. I'm staying an extra night. I'll be on the road first thing Wednesday morning. I'll be home by noon. Go to a meeting or something."

She hung up.

The reasonable thing to do, the grown-up thing, would have been to stick to my plan, go home, eat dinner, and, go to a meeting. I know it now and I knew it then. Instead, I called Audrey.

"That invitation still good?"

She said we'd be having pasta so I stopped and got a bottle of red wine. When I arrived, she was dressed modestly in a pair of snug black slacks and a sleeveless cream-colored shell. It all accentuated her figure, a good figure, close to a ten, although revealing much less skin than previous outfits I'd seen. When I handed her the Merlot and she gave me a peck on the cheek, I wondered what the hell I was doing there. She was all smiles.

"I'm glad you changed your mind."

I was glad she didn't ask why. I didn't want to tell her I was mad at my wife. She led me into the kitchen and chatted away about the meal preparation, how she'd gone and bought fresh Italian sausage for the sauce, she hoped I wasn't vegetarian, she could scoop the meat out but she knew that wasn't really acceptable to real vegetarians, was relieved when I said I wasn't one. Leaning against a counter, I did my best not to obsesses when she bent over to check on the bread heating in the over. She directed me to the drawer where I'd find a corkscrew. I said she'd have to open the bottle. She blushed.

"It's alright. It means you weren't thinking about it."

It took two trips to get everything to the table. When she began to pour me a glass of wine, I told her I didn't drink.

"After I lost a body part in a drunk driving accident, I decided I was better off without it."

I didn't go into the part about killing a young woman or that it had taken several years after the wreck to finally quit.

Over dinner, I asked about her job.

"It's okay. Pay's pretty good compared to a lot of things. It's not really what I intended to be doing. I actually have a degree in fashion design. But I went to a job fair during senior year at college, and these guys made the advertising business seem glamorous. And, I liked the idea of coming to Asheville. What about you? How'd you get into being a private detective?"

"When I was an attorney with the state's environmental protection agency, I got bored pushing papers around. I really wanted to be out in the field. I saw an ad for a private detective training school. Seemed like fun. I took the class, passed the test and got my license but never used it till I moved here."

"So, how's the murder investigation coming?"

I sat up in the chair, threw my arm up in the air and stared at her in disbelief.

"I know, I know. You can't tell me anything about it."

I shook my head. To change the subject, I said, "The pasta is very good, by the way."

"Thanks. Old family recipe. And I still am fascinated with what you do." She leaned forward before she asked, "Do you have a gun?" as if this would be classified information.

I thought for a moment before answering. "Yes, I do. Although I rarely carry it. My experience is that guns tend to beget guns."

"Have you ever been shot at?"

She was flirting and I decided to enjoy it. "Yes."

"Oooh. Ever shot anybody?"

"Shot a car once."

"A car?"

"Yeah. Guy'd been following me. I was tired of it. Shot out the windshield and the front tires. Felt good."

"You shot a car."

"Yup." I was afraid my stock might have dropped a few points. Probably a good time to change the subject again but she asked her next question before I had a chance.

"You have any suspects?"

"Audrey! What part of 'I can't talk to you about it' don't you understand?"

She was pouring a second glass of wine. "Oh, fiddle."

In spite of my annoyance, I laughed.

"What's so funny?"

"'Oh, fiddle'?"

She smiled. "Yeah. Something my father used to say."

"Along with 'beats diggin' ditches.'"

Her eyes widened, the smile got broader. "You remembered."

"You must like him a lot."

The smile cracked. She held a hand to the side of her face and looked away. After a minute, she turned back. Her eyes had a sheen to them.

"He died when I was eleven."

"I'm sorry."

"You're right, though. I liked him a lot."

I had finished my meal. According to an old Hamilton clock sitting on a buffet at the side of the room, it was seven-twenty, plenty of time to make the eight o'clock meeting.

"I probably ought to be going, Audrey. The dinner was very good. But there's somewhere I have to be in a little bit."

It wasn't quite a glare she gave me, but close to it.

"You can't leave me like this," she said, making a show of wiping her eyes. "Anyway, I bought some cannoli and you've got to help me eat them."

I said, "OK. But then I have to leave."

We cleared the table and she got the dessert out of the fridge. She said she had some really good coffee, too, and I said I'd pass on that.

At the door fifteen minutes later, I thanked her. She thanked me for coming. Then she put an arm around my neck.

"You're cute," she said, and kissed me on the lips. A light kiss, not unlike the one Zella had given me, although fraught with more possibilities.

There's an expression people around here use to describe a feeling of being off balance. Swimmy headed. That's how I felt walking to the car. Swimmy headed.

The meeting was just about to get underway when I walked into the Fellowship Hall at the church. My sponsor came over while I was getting a cup of instant decaf.

"You OK?"

"Yeah. Why you ask?"

"I don't know. You look a little weird."

"Actually, I've been feeling a little light-headed," I said.

He suggested I probably ought to sit down and we walked to the rows of folding chairs.

Driving home after the meeting, my mind was still in a muddle. I tried not to replay the earlier part of the evening, but couldn't stop myself. I started to get annoyed all over again remembering her attempt to get me to talk about the investigation.

Clarity descended on me when I pulled into the drive, maybe the effect of being on home turf. When the subject of what I was working on had come up at our earlier lunch meeting, she mentioned the old lady growing pot. I never told her I was working that case. Or the murder.

30

Kathy's call came predictably at ten. "I'm sorry I hung up on you," she began. "It's just that ..."

"I know. I'm sorry I was a jerk about it."

"I don't think I've ever given you a hard time when you've gone out of town," she said.

I wanted to say, "Well, I never slept with anyone when I was out of town." Instead, I said, "I know. I'm sorry. So, what did you do for dinner?"

"Went to nice little Thai place. It was very good. And I know you're wondering if I went alone. I didn't. I went with a man from the department."

My teeth clenched. I thought about telling her I had dinner with a client. I didn't know if my desire to tell her that was because I wanted to counterpunch or because I wanted to be honest. Because I wasn't sure, I didn't say anything. Silence hung between us like dirty laundry.

"I love you," she said at last.

"I know. And I love you. And I'm sorry I do this."

We said our good nights. She said she thought she'd be home around noon. If I wasn't tied up, she said, maybe we could have lunch.

I called Jim, my AA sponsor.

"If there was a bottle of Scotch in the house, I'd probably drink it," I said after explaining what was going on.

"You going to tell her about your dinner?"

"I probably need to or the guilt will be having me all weirded out and she'll know I'm all weirded out and then she'll be really pissed because she'll know there's something going on I'm not talking about."

"You seem to understand that scenario pretty well."

When I woke up at 6:25, I was surprised I had slept soundly given the turmoil in my mind. By eight o'clock I had exercised, showered, dressed, and eaten some breakfast. I was on the deck with a second cup of coffee when the phone rang. It was Pete Haywood confirming our 9:30 rendezvous. I was out of the house a little after 9:00. Half-way to the offices of North Realty, the phone rang again. It showed Kathy's office number.

"Hi, Rick."

"Morning, Warren."

"Sorry I didn't get back to you yesterday. Got tied up filling orders, yadda, yadda. But, I did find out what you wanted to know. An outfit called HPA does North Realty's marketing."

I worked that over for a couple of seconds.

"Would that be the same as Hensley, Presley and Associates?" I asked.

"Yeah. They went hip a few months ago. Now they just go by the initials."

"Like ATT and 3M," I said.

"I guess. Anything else I can help you with?"

I said there wasn't and thanked him. He really was a nice lad.

I wondered why Audrey would lie about the matchbook, unless she didn't want me to know she knew Pete Haywood. Which begged the question. A couple miles farther on a light bulb went on. If I had been in a comic strip, the name "Presley" would have been in the balloon above my head. It could simply have been coincidence. There were, after all, all those Presleys and variations thereof in the phone book.

The Reverend Haywood was on the porch when I pulled into the parking lot. He greeted me with a large smile and an assertive handshake. I responded in kind.

"I like a man with a firm grip," he said. "Shows character. Hate those dead mackerel types."

"I had lunch with someone you might know," I said after we climbed into his SUV and headed north.

"Oh? Who's that?"

"Audrey Hollingsworth."

For a split second, his expression was blank. Then, his brow curled.

"Audrey who?"

"Hollingsworth."

"Doesn't ring a bell."

I didn't think saying, you're full of crap, Reverend, would advance my investigation and instead said, "I'm surprised."

"Why is that?"

"Because she works for the outfit that does your advertising."

More furrowing of the brow.

"Oh. Audrey. Nice looking girl."

"Very nice looking girl. I'm surprised you wouldn't remember her."

"I really don't have much direct contact with the staff over there, you know. Sometimes I review copy, that kind of thing. But mostly they just do what they do."

And, I thought, Audrey could merely have had a pack of North Realty matches because there were some lying around the office. Maybe I was making too much of it, the workings of my conspiratorial world view.

I let it go. We moved into a discussion about the environment.

He was all for it, he said. "But you can't have progress if you're gonna worry about every tree that gets cut down."

"What worries me isn't a few trees coming down. It's when acres come down all at once."

"Rick," he said in the voice I imagined he used with his congregation, teaching them some important universal truth, "you can't make an omelet without breaking a few eggs."

We would not, it seemed, be having a significant philosophical discussion about conserving the planet.

The property he showed me was as he had described it. A modest two-story frame house sat just below a ridge line with a spectacular view from the front porch. There were woods surrounding it on three sides and an open field in front. Near the road, a portion of the land was terraced.

"Old tobacco allotment," Pete said. "Be a nice garden space. Of course, there are pictures of all this on the Internet, but I thought you really had to see it to appreciate it."

It was a nice spot, a little over-priced, but I was sure that was negotiable. If the market hadn't been so soft, it probably would have been sold soon after it was listed.

"I'll talk to Kathy about it. Although, I have to tell you, Pete," I said, improvising a story for why I wouldn't be following up on this, "she's kind of backing off the idea of moving. She moved a lot as a kid and is beginning to feel rooted to where we are."

"I know how that is, Rick. Women get settled; they like to nest. I'm pretty sure the sellers would entertain a reasonable offer. If you think there's any chance you might want it, we need to move. I don't think it'll be on the market much longer."

"I'm sure you're right, Pete. I probably shouldn't have wasted your time coming out here this morning. I will tell Kathy how nice the place is. Maybe she'll have a change of heart."

"Let me know," he said. I'm sure he would not have admitted to the irritation I heard in his voice.

My phone had buzzed me three times while I'd been occupied with Haywood. According to the call memory, they had come within minutes of each other. Bobby Headley, Queenie, and Jay. I listened to the messages in the order they'd come.

Rick. Bobby. I thought you'd want to know that Maisie Ivey's house burned last night.

31

I was so disconcerted I didn't get the next part of the message and had to replay it.

I'll probably be out here most of the morning if you wanna come out. It's seems kinda interesting, this happening with all the other stuff going on. What's that you say about coincidences?

The messages from Queenie and Jay were essentially the same. I called Queenie after Bobby's phone rang busy.

"What happened?" I asked.

"Don't know. Sonny started barkin' about five this morning. There was an orange glow above her place and I went on down. By the time Headley's crew had got there it was pretty much to the ground except for the fireplace. It's kind of miracle the woods didn't catch on fire."

I could smell the smoke before it was visible from the four lane. Queenie's pickup was on the outer fringe of a cluster of sheriff's vehicles and fire trucks when I pulled into the drive. I was immediately told to get my car out of there. After leaving the Honda on the old logging road, I walked back to the house. Queenie and Bobby were on the front lawn, talking and watching while water was pumped from a nearby creek onto the embers.

I repeated my "what happened" to Bobby.

"Can't tell yet."

"Natural causes, you think?"

He gave me a "what part of 'can't tell yet' didn't you understand" look.

"Another coincidence," I said. "They just keep piling up."

"I was just telling him about Maisie's rather abrupt departure," Queenie said.

Bobby nodded. "Does give you cause to wonder."

She looked at me. "You wanna come up for some coffee, engage in wild speculation about what might've happened? There's not much else I can do here 'cept'n give the chief advice he doesn't need."

The morning sun was still below the line of trees sheltering Queenie's house. Although the prevailing breeze across the ridge top kept the smoke away, the smell of smoldering lumber permeated the air. We sat in silence on the porch with our hot drinks, gazing out to nothing in particular.

She broke the silence. "Whaddaya think?"

"Let's say it's not a coincidence and the fire was intentional. Who stands to gain? Not Maisie. She would have gotten more for selling the place than she'll get in insurance money."

"If she's still around," Queenie said.

"You mean, if someone hasn't, uh, disposed of her?"

The old woman nodded. "What if they killed her, moved everything out, then brought her body back and burned her up with the house?"

"Why do that? Why not just kill her in the house and burn it. It would seem more likely that an accident could happen if someone was living there than if it was vacant."

Our collective consciousness returned to the middle distance between the valley and the far mountain peaks.

I intruded on the quiet this time. "Maybe it's time to visit, what's his name? Wilson? Neal Wilson, you said?"

"That's him. You gonna ask him if he killed his aunt?"

"Maybe be a little more subtle than that."

We went into the kitchen to freshen our cups. When we returned to the porch, we resumed working on our gazing technique.

"You find out any more about that company's been buying up all the land around me?" she asked.

"HPB Holding, LLC? No I haven't. I ... well, damn."

"What's that?"

"Coincidences. The advertising agency Audrey works for and that handles Pete Haywood's North Realty account is HPA. Formerly Hensley, Presley and Associates. Audrey seemed not to know they handled Haywood's account, and when I first mentioned Audrey's name to Haywood, he went quiet, then denied he knew her until I described her and he reckoned as how he had met her. Now, Audrey's one of those women you really don't forget."

"Kinda like me."

"Yes, Queenie, kinda like you. Although, for different reasons. And the detective who has shown up a couple of times, one of which I am sure was in the recently cleared pot field, is named ...?"

"Presley," she said.

"Bingo. Well, there's lots of Presleys hereabouts. OK. Maybe that really is just coincidental. But then there is the ..."

Again, she filled in the blank. "HPB and HPA."

"Yeah."

"Looks like there'd be some work for a detective in all of that," she said.

"Seems like it," I said. "So. Say this nephew somehow gets Maisie out of her house. They don't kill her. She gets the insurance money for the house when it burns to the ground. Then, there's no reason for her to keep the property. The people who want the property don't care about the house, anyway. They've got bigger plans for the area, so the loss of the house doesn't significantly affect what they'll pay for the land."

"But if Maisie's still alive, how does that help the nephew?" Queenie asked. "And his wife? She's the grubby one of the two, I understand. Leastwise, that's what Maisie thought."

"Maybe they figure Maisie's not got many years to live, they can wait her out. They are, supposedly, the only heirs."

"Doesn't necessarily mean they'd automatically get it all. There could be a will givin' it to someone else."

"So," I said, "if they know someone's been talking to Maisie about a land trust, they'd want to do something about it soon. Like, now."

32

Queenie's nature was to be laid back and I thought she might not grasp the real danger that could be confronting Maisey. There was, indeed, work for a detective and there were several lines of crumbs to follow: confronting Audrey about her connection to Pete Haywood; talking to Martha Jo about the book collection she was trying to peddle; finding out who the principals in HPB and HPA were. But the smoldering embers of Maisie Ivey's house seemed akin to a bush burning in the desert, saying "I want your attention."

I didn't want to unduly upset Queenie. It was possible, after all, that there was no evil intent behind all that had transpired, from the drowning of a young man and the burning of a house to phantom stalkers and people lying about knowing each other. After thanking Queenie for the coffee and conversation, I waited until I was at the car before calling Kathy.

"I know you'll have been on the road several hours," I said, "but do you want to take a ride down to Old Fort?"

"What's in Old Fort?"

I told her about Maisie's house and the nephew and his wife who seemed to be her only living relatives.

"The old Nick and Nora Charles thing," I said. "Without the martinis."

Kathy had accompanied me once before when I had traveled out of town during a murder investigation. The case blew wide open. Shots were fired at people as well as at automobiles. It was scary. I was glad she had come along.

"You going to be packing heat this time?" she asked, already in character.

"I don't think it's risen to that level yet."

She was still an hour away from home. That gave me time to check in with the Widow Dillingham. Neither vehicle was in sight when I pulled up and no one responded at the front door. I thought it was strange that both vehicles would be gone.

Not spending time with the Martha Jo meant I had time to spare. I picked up sandwiches at the Downtown Bakery on my way out to the house. Kathy arrived home a few minutes after I did and we ate on the deck before heading out of town. It would be a twenty minute drive down Old Fort Mountain on Interstate 40 into the town of the same name.

While Kathy drove, I talked to an information operator and found there were two likely possibilities for the man we were looking for – an F. N. Wilson and a Neal Wilson. She gave me the addresses listed for both. I figured the second was the most likely and called the first to do a rule-out. When a woman answered, I asked for Neal and she said I'd gotten a wrong number which meant the address I'd gotten for Neal was the right one. I punched 52 Maplewood Road, Old Fort, NC into the Infiniti's guidance system.

"What are you going to say to him, if he's even home?" Kathy asked.

"Oh, I'll make something up."

"You know," she said, "I'd have to kill you if we worked together all the time. I don't know how you can go into these situations and not know exactly what you're going to do. I have to go over and over and over whatever I'm going to say when I'm meeting with anyone."

"Yeah, I guess it's a good thing we only do this once a year or so."

At the foot of the mountain, we were guided to U.S. 70 and through the small downtown to the east side and then a quarter mile off the main highway to Maplewood Drive. It was an older developed neighborhood of modest brick ranch houses. Some had car ports, a few had bricked-in garages. None had front porches, just walks leading from the parking area to the houses. Most had foliage of some kind along their front walls. Tiger and canna lilies were popular. A sheriff's car was parked in front of 52.

I let out a "hmmm."

"Change your strategy?" she asked.

"I don't think so. I wonder if they're here for the same reason we are – looking for Maisie."

A woman answered the door. Forty-ish, pleasant-looking in a skirt and blouse, hair in that kind of perpetual permanent she could have been wearing when she graduated from high school.

"Neal home?" I asked.

Her gaze went to the space in which an arm didn't exist and quickly moved back to my face. I thought she felt too awkward to ask who I was.

"Neal?" she called into the house, waited a few seconds and repeated the name. "Neal! Someone here to see you!"

"Who is it?" came back, the caller unseen.

"Didn't say."

"Well, why don't you ask?" the voice said as the speaker came into view. It was a man in a sheriff's deputy's uniform.

"Mr. Wilson," I said into the house.

"Yeah?" he said, now at the door alongside the woman I assumed was his wife.

"Hi. I'm Rick Ryder," I said as I leaned in with my hand

outstretched.

He took it in his and we shook as he said, "Do I know you?"

"Don't think so. I'm a friend of Queenie Weaver." I felt the air around us thicken. "She knew I was going to be in the area today, and asked if I'd stop by and check on Maisie. She figured with the house burned and all, Maisie'd probably be staying with you."

It's fun to watch people get speechless, trying to decide if they should deny knowing anything you're talking about or figuring out what story they can make up on the spot.

"She's not here," he finally said.

"Oh. Can you tell me where she is? I'd like to take her some flowers, give her Ms. Weaver's greetings."

"She's at a nursing home. She's not taking visitors. She was pretty shook up. They had to sedate her pretty heavily. That's why we had to take her there."

"Oh, that's too bad," I said. "Which one is it? We'll just go by and leave the flowers."

"She's not supposed to be bothered. It would probably upset her more to hear from the Weaver woman."

The last was said in a tone suggesting Queenie was not their favorite lady of the mountains.

I was afraid Kathy and I might have to scour the county, looking for all the nursing homes, not even being certain she wasn't locked up in a back room there on Maplewood Drive.

"Oh, tell him, Neal," the wife said. "It can't hurt if he just leaves the flowers."

He didn't look at the woman, but his expression was of one who has to put up with this kind of crap all the time.

"It's the Marion Family Home, out on U.S. 70."

I said thanks, tipped my head in the direction of the woman and turned around.

"Not going to be able to see her, you know," the man called

behind me.

I nodded my head, then stopped and turned back.

"How long you been on the force, Neal?"

"What?"

"How long have you been working for the sheriff?"

You could almost see all the little gears inside his head whirring around, trying to figure out what this had to do with anything and whether or not he should answer or if he should just tell me to fuck off.

"Four years. Why?"

"Just wondered. Thanks."

I got back in the car and said, "We've got to go find some flowers."

Kathy pulled into the next driveway and turned the car around, heading back toward downtown. When I looked back at #52, Neal had come a few steps into the front yard. I was sure he got our license plate number.

Kathy remembered passing The Olde Fort Flower Shoppe. "Kind of name that sticks in your mind," she said.

I sat in the car as Kathy ran in. She came out with a bouquet appropriate for an elderly convalescing woman.

Highway 70 paralleled Interstate 40 and was the old main drag between Old Fort and Marion. A mix of old homes, small businesses, and churches was interspersed with the occasional light manufacturing plant along the easy rolling terrain. One furniture plant was still in operation back near town, but for the most part that industry along with the textile business that had supported this town and hundreds like it across the state had disappeared. It seemed a minor miracle that Old Fort managed to hang on, probably helped along by a lot of commuting up the mountain to Asheville.

The Marion Family Home may have been named for an actual Marion Family or they adopted the name of the neighboring town to the east. The building sat up on a hill, a large lawn rolling out in front of it. In spite of its name, it looked like the home of no family I knew, apparently built to meet state nursing home code requirements. One story concrete block with a ramp up to a front porch lined with rocking chairs painted white to match the whitewash on the building. No one was seated outside. Four small boxwoods struggled to soften its appearance. I noticed a crumpled cigarette box on the ground among the shrubbery. The building was longer than it was wide. I imagined a corridor down the middle with rooms to either side.

The nurses station was straight ahead of us. A TV was playing in the room to the left where half a dozen people sat in wheelchairs, some asleep, the others apparently mesmerized by what was on the screen. The room to the right had four tables, set for a meal like a small restaurant. The odor of urine mixed with disinfectant was pervasive.

Our entry had disturbed a bell above the front door and a minute later a man in healthcare whites came down the corridor and stood behind the counter. He was big, probably a foot taller and a hundred pounds heavier than me. He had high cheek bones, ruddy skin and black hair pulled into a pony tail. He looked to be in his mid-40s. I thought of The Chief in *One Flew Over the Cuckoo's Nest*. I was not so naïve as to assume Deputy Wilson had not called ahead of us or that they'd be glad to see us here.

"Yeah?" he said as he might to someone on the phone, as if we were already in mid-conversation. Nothing about him suggested he might have a sense of humor, the kind of guy you didn't want pissed off at you.

"Hi. We're here to see Maisie Ivey," I said with an air of nonchalance I did not feel.

"Can't."

This guy was going to make the late Stan Dillingham seem loquacious by comparison.

"Why not?"

"Orders."

A woman in more chic pastel nurse's garb appeared behind him.

"Problem, Jerrod?"

"Nope. Just tellin' this gentleman – and the lady – they can't see Ms. Ivey."

"That's right, sir. She's not to have visitors."

Looking down the corridor behind these two, we could see another line of people in wheel chairs. Afternoon med time, I assumed. None of them looked as if they had any interest in the world around them and the meds weren't going to change that. The woman second to the end of the line looked familiar although her drooped head made it hard to be sure.

"Maisie?" I called.

"Sir," the uniformed woman said.

I repeated myself, louder.

"Maisie!"

"Hey, Mack. Keep it down. You can't talk to her."

I gave it one more shot before The Chief came around the desk.

"MAISIE!"

I thought I saw her head rise. No recognition registered on her face.

"That's enough, Mack."

He was along side of me, reaching for my arm. I snatched it away, went into a crouch, bent my elbow and slammed it back into his groin as I came up. He bent over with a loud groan and slowly went down to the floor.

"Let's go," I said to Kathy. We double-timed it back to the car. I could see the nurse in the doorway, a cell phone to her ear as we pulled away.

33

"My God, Rick, are you trying to get us killed?" Kathy said as she started the car.

I assumed her question was rhetorical and, after I caught my breath, said, "We better get out of Dodge. Head east when you get back to U.S. 70."

We rode in silence as Kathy guided us away from the small town. My body trembled from the adrenalin charging through my blood stream. My teeth were on edge and my skin felt too tight.

"So, why did you do that?" she asked, breaking the ice.

"Smack him in the gonads?"

"Yeah. Kind of over-the-top, don't you think?"

More than one therapist had suggested that I had been angry at my father for a long time and, then, even angrier at myself for killing the girl in the car wreck and losing my arm. Although I didn't look for opportunities to act out the rage, I often didn't try to find alternatives. When I stopped drinking, adrenalin had become my replacement drug.

Kathy knew this stuff, and I didn't think now was the time to dig back into it, so I said, "Instinct, you know. I am under-armed in any physical confrontation and that guy was huge and menacing."

"After you yanked your arm away from him, we could have

just run. Like we did anyway. Some day that instinct is going to get you into serious trouble. It may already have."

I knew she was right and didn't say anything.

"So, where're we going?" she asked after another cool spell.

"You up for a little tour around the foothills?"

"You think Deputy Wilson will be looking for us?"

"Along with the rest of the McDowell County Sheriff's Department. He knows we came from Asheville, so he'll probably have someone looking for us on I-40. I think we should head east to 226, go south to 64, west to Hendersonville, and, thence, home."

"Think they'll come up to Asheville after you?"

"They'll be looking for you, too, you know. And they could, I suppose. Wilson doesn't have any reason to doubt my cover story. But it wouldn't take a lot of work to find a name for the one-armed guy who knows Queenie."

I noticed her checking the rear view mirror every few seconds.

"If he does start asking questions," she asked, "how long would it take before he also finds out you're involved in the murder investigation?"

"And if he does? How would he link that with Maisie?"

"That's what you're trying to find out, isn't it? Assuming, as you are, there is a connection, it could make him, them, whoever they are, kind of nervous, don't you think?"

The adrenalin began to wear off, leaving behind an ache in both arms. It had taken me a long time to get used to that, the phantom feelings where there used to be an appendage.

Kathy kept the Infiniti near the speed limit as we cruised along the gently rolling hills, glad we were early enough not to get caught in school traffic on this two-lane road. Corn and soybeans filled the fields, and it seemed like everybody had their little patch of tobacco. On the approach to Marion, the county seat, there was a little Italian restaurant near the intersection with U.S. 226. If Wilson had alerted the sheriff's force to be looking for the Infiniti, it would be good to get off the road and let the alarm die down. Kathy parked in back, out of sight of passers-by.

"What did we learn for our effort?" she asked after we'd been seated.

Although the dining room was almost empty, we leaned in toward each other and spoke in hushed tones, not knowing who might be paying attention to the two strangers in this place.

"Wilson was at the sheriff's department at the same time Presley was there."

"And ...?"

"Could be just another coincidence. But, if we assume that attempts to buy up the mountain, including Masie's property, are somehow related to the death of Brian McFadden – and maybe to the death of Stan Dillingham – then I think it's a reasonable assumption that Wilson and Presley are connected in some way other than that they just happened to work for the McDowell County Sheriff at the same time."

Kathy raised her head, signaling that someone was coming our way. It was our waitress. I guessed she was in her fifties and possibly had worked here since the place opened, the kind of waitress who keeps her pencil in her hair, calls all the guys "sweetie," and doesn't attempt to get on a first name basis with unfamiliar customers.

After she'd left with our order, Kathy said, "I still don't get it."

"Buncombe County Sheriff's Deputy Presley shows up repeatedly around Queenie's place. Deputy Presley used to work with McDowell County Sheriff's Deputy Wilson. Wilson's Aunt Masie's house is on land that some developers want. She has refused to sell, just like Queenie. Maisie's disappears, her house mysteriously burns to the ground, and she turns up in a nursing home, apparently placed there by aforementioned Deputy Wilson. As for the pot connection, it seems likely that the late Brian McFadden knew about the marijuana and had helped himself to some, or maybe some was given to him. And, after Stan dies, a bunch of books about growing marijuana surfaces."

I broke off again when the waitress came by to freshen our drinks.

"And Presley – I'm sure it was him – shows up out where the marijuana had been grown and was not, apparently, there as part of the investigation."

"Seems pretty convoluted," Kathy said. "And you think Presley and Wilson are in league with the people who are trying to buy up the land?"

"That's my theory."

"What do you think's going to happen to Maisie?"

"I don't know. But I think a call to the people who license nursing homes is in order. An inspector might not find violations they can take action on, but it might make it harder for Wilson and his buddies to do anything else to the old woman."

"Like cause her early demise."

"Exactly."

She shivered.

Our lunch was delivered. We had ordered a couple of specials and I dug into Mama Pavone's Special Recipe Eggplant Parmesan.

Kathy watched me. "I'm surprised you can eat," she said.

"I'm famished. Probably the result of the adrenalin rush wearing off. Kind of like back in Columbus, how we all would go to White Castle for a dozen of those little burgers after a night of drinking."

"As I recall, we'd never just been chased by seven foot nurses."

I shrugged. She picked at her ravioli; I cleaned my plate.

The lunch crowd had long gone and we didn't feel rushed to move on. In an hour or so, they'd be changing to the dinner menu. We had coffees but skipped dessert.

"Well, Watson, you ready to see what nefarious deeds we can thwart?" I asked when our table was being cleared, trying to inject some levity into the afternoon.

"I thought we were Nick and Nora Charles. I'm not sure I'm comfortable with you as Sherlock, with that cocaine habit he had."

We headed south into Rutherford County. A light cloud cover moved in making for perfect driving weather. The elevations were gentler here, more Piedmont than Foothills. I fiddled with the radio, landing on a classical music station out of Charlotte.

Halfway to Hendersonville, where we would turn north to Asheville, I said, "I think I'm ready to give it up."

"Give what up?" Kathy asked.

"My jealousy."

"Just like that? Poof?"

"Doesn't seem to do me much good. I mean, I don't expect the feelings to never come up again, but I don't have to hang on to them. It's like resentments. We – I – feel morally superior when I'm counting the score against someone. That someone being mostly you. It's just like another drug. I feel good, justified. I'm the right one. All that stuff. Well, it just makes me miserable."

She glanced over at me. When she leaned in my direction it was like a magnet drawing me toward her. She gave me a peck on the cheek. "My knucklehead," she said.

The rest of the trip was uneventful enough that I nodded off a couple of times. At the house, the cats appeared to be glad to see us until they'd been fed, then dropped the pretense. We had a light supper on the deck. I would have thought the recent adrenaline drain would have left me with no energy for bedtime athletics. We were pleasantly surprised to discover otherwise.

There was a message on the answering machine from Nate when I surfaced from the basement after my workout the next morning.

"This is your mouthpiece calling. Call me back."

I did.

"So what kind of mischief were you up to in McDowell County yesterday, Counselor?"

"Boy, that was quick. What do you hear?"

"That there's a warrant for your arrest for trespassing and assault. Involves the Marion Family Home? What're you doing, beatin' up old ladies for their meds?"

I described the visit to Deputy Wilson and our attempt to see Maisie.

"The guy was almost seven feet tall, Nate. Probably close to three hundred pounds. I think when a one-armed guy a good foot shorter and hundred pounds lighter than him shows up at court, someone's going to be amused at the idea of me assaulting him. Frankly, I would think the guy'd be embarrassed."

"OK. So, figure the assault charge goes away. What about the trespass?"

"Oh, I don't know. Someone might mention to the people at the Marion Family Home that it appeared there were several violations of the terms of their license, having to do with unsanitary conditions and over-medication of patients. See what they do with that. And, by the way, I'm impressed with the speed with which you found out about all this."

"Yeah. Old friend is a magistrate down there."

"How does he know you and I have a connection?"

"Like I said, he's an old friend. A colleague. When I was

defending you against your previous criminal charges, he was someone I talked to a lot. So, when these guys come into his office to get a warrant for the arrest of Rick Ryder, he gives me a call, thinks I might be interested. So what was it you hoped to accomplish with your little David and Goliath act?"

"That wasn't the purpose of the trip, Nate, although I have to admit, there is some satisfaction in being able to tumble a seven foot behemoth. I really went down there to check on this Wilson character, who I was able to confirm worked with Buncombe County Deputy Sheriff Aaron Presley. And, to see if we could find Maisie Ivey."

"Remind me, who's Maisie Ivey?"

"The woman who disappeared from her house out near Queenie's before her house mysteriously burned down. She's Deputy Wilson's aunt."

"And now she's in a nursing home?"

"Yeah, put there by her nephew. And I believe Presley and Wilson are in cahoots with this whole land-grab-murder thing."

"So, you're gonna bill me for all the time you spent on your little escapade."

"Fact-finding mission, Nate."

"Yeah. Right. OK, I'll give the folks at the nursing home a call, see if I can't work things out so I don't have to go down there to keep your ass out of the McDowell County jail. And you probably want to watch your back. If you're connecting the dots between all these people, they might decide you know too much."

We talked a minute about the case against Queenie. Nate thought the DA's office was being particularly close-lipped prior to going to the grand jury.

"If she gets indicted for murder, we might not find out what they have until the discovery process before trial. It's possible they don't have anything and are playing this out as long as they can, hoping something'll surface to incriminate her. Those books on growing pot don't help."

"But they don't suggest murder, do they?" I asked.

"They suggest she was not law-abiding."

I told him about Martha Jo trying to sell similar, although apparently newer, books.

"Don't think that helps Queenie. Stan worked for Queenie, after all. Then killed himself. It does suggest he was involved in the pot growing and maybe more, but doesn't exonerate our girl. Of course, a defense attorney might make the case that Stan was a lone wolf out there. If his investigator would bring him some more evidence showing that was so."

"Lone wolf or in the employ of other parties?"

"Either would do."

34

Kathy walked by and gave me a light kiss on the lips. When I got off the phone with Nate, I poured a cup of coffee and joined her on the deck where she was finishing up a bowl of granola and some orange juice. She was dressed in slacks and a light sweater, ready for work.

"Nate?" she asked.

"Yeah. He implied his investigator hasn't been doing his job."

She raised her eyebrows.

"Oh, not really. Just giving me a hard time. But I do need to get out to Queenie's, see how she's holding up and go have another chat with the Widow Dillingham. Maybe have a conversation about her reading material."

I walked off the deck and strolled the back yard while I calling Bobby Headley.

"Got any more of an idea of what had happened to Maisie's house?"

"Arson guys are coming today. I think the fire was set. The timing's suspicious, for one thing. As is the rate the fire seemed to move through the house. Granted, it was old and dry as tinder and all that. Even so, it appears there was more of an explosion than a naturally expanding fire. The arson guys'll sort it out."

I told him about the previous day's escapades.

"I'm worried about Maisie," I said. "I wish we could spring her from that place."

"You mean, like, kidnap her?"

"I've thought about it."

"Really?"

"Oh, I don't know, Bobby. I do know I don't feel good about leaving her down there."

He told me to call him if there was anything he could do.

Kathy was just about to get into her Infiniti when I came into the garage. I told her to wait a minute. When I went over to her, we engaged in what, in public, would have been considered an unseemly display of affection.

Queenie was enjoying the mid-morning quietude on her porch when I pulled up a half-hour later. Low clouds rested like layers of cotton in some of the valleys but overhead it was a flawless blue, the color of the chicory that would soon be lining the roadsides.

We went inside while she fixed coffee.

"She could stay with me," Queenie said, after I'd brought her up to date.

"We'd have to kidnap her, Queenie. The authorities look askance at that and you're already considered a scofflaw."

"Can't just let her wither away down there."

"Nate's going to call the Morgan Family Home about possible violations of their license. Maybe I oughta just call the state people myself."

"The people who run that place are gonna know who made the call."

"So?"

"Might get physical."

"Already got physical."

"So you said. You know, for a guy with only one good wing, you sure don't do much to avoid trouble, do you?"

She brewed some coffee and we took our now familiar perches on the porch.

"You know," Queenie went on, "if the state people do go in there and make too big a fuss, she's just going to wind up back with that nephew."

"I have to admit I've been thinking about how it might be done," I said.

"How what might be done?"

"Liberating her."

"I think you're crazy, Rick. Probably why I like you."

"Thanks, Queenie. I'll take that as a compliment."

It was time to visit the widow Dillingham again. As much as I tried not to anticipate seeing her in some mode of undress, the tape of our first encounter replayed in my brain.

If she heard the Honda pull into her yard, she made no attempt at modesty. She was, again stretched out on the lounge chair on the deck, apparently her default mode. When I got close enough to see that she was wearing even less than she had at our first meeting, I called to her.

"Martha Jo."

Her head rose from the lounge chair.

"Hey, Ryder. What you up to?"

"Thought I'd see how you were doing. Want to put something on?"

"Not really. You want me to?"

A minor skirmish played out in my psyche.

"Yes, I think I do. I'm rather easily distracted."

She sat up and pulled on the terry cloth robe I'd seen her in a couple of days ago.

"That better?"

"Yes. Thanks."

"Didn't realize you were such a prude."

I shrugged and took a seat at the umbrella table at the corner of the deck. With the rest of her covered, I was able to focus on her face. It looked older, weathered. Could have been the sun. She had a drink in a large plastic tumbler. Ice cubes clinked when she held it to her lips.

"How's widowhood?" I asked.

Sunglasses kept me from being able to read her eyes.

"Good days and bad days. Kinda what you'd expect, I guess. You know, he was a good old boy. I mean that it in the best sense. For the most part, treated me good. When he wasn't obsessed with the idea I was seeing other men. Kind of laughable when you think I was holed up out here most of the time. He liked me, you know. And not just for the same reason a lot of other men had liked me."

I started feeling like her confessor or therapist.

"Do you like me, Ryder?"

I thought for a second. "Yes, I do, Martha Jo," I said, knowing it was true.

"What is it about me you like? Other than the obvious that makes you squirm."

"You're bright, funny."

"Bright. What does that mean?"

"Smart. Clever."

She tipped her drink to her mouth, upending the container.

"Want something to drink, Ryder?" she asked as she got up. The robe had not been pulled tight in the front and came open when she stood. It was hard to tell with a woman used to being unclad in front of an audience whether it was purposeful or accidental.

"Have any unsweetened tea?"

"Matter of fact, I do, Ryder. Good base for Long Island iced tea. Ever drink those?"

"Long time ago."

"Oh, that's right."

It was like we were warming up for a friendly game of Ping Pong. Lobbing soft shots to each other. If I wasn't going to get serious, I might as well leave. She must have had similar thoughts.

"So, why are you really here, Ryder?" she asked when she returned to the deck with the drinks. "You didn't come just to pay a social call." The robe parted just below the waist, at eye level. I looked up and thanked her. She returned to the lounge chair.

"I heard about the books you tried to sell Mickey and Taylor."

Her face pulled taught, as if she were working her brain hard. She sipped her drink.

"Oh. The hippies. Yeah. Found those books out in the shed. Didn't think it'd look good if the law found them."

"Could be construed as destroying evidence."

"So you've come out here to give me legal advice?"

"I've come out of curiosity. You might imagine that a person tasked with finding evidence that would exonerate his client of murder would be intrigued by the existence of this material."

"Stan did like his pot. What can I say?"

"Enough to grow a field of high end sinsemilla?"

"I don't know anything about that."

She was lying, of course. I presumed that she knew I knew it.

"I'm also curious about why the police didn't find the books. I presume they searched the area after ..."

"He shot himself?"

"Yeah. After that."

"I guess that is curious," she said.

The tea was good, tasted like it was brewed, not instant. She'd put a lemon wedge in it. I would have liked to have stayed a while, batting the ball around. But too much of her game depended on deception. I wasn't going to get any further, certainly not win any points.

"The tea is excellent, M.J. People ever call you that? M.J."

"Stan did all the time."

"Oh. Sorry. Anyway, I think it's time for me to be on my way."

"Day's early, Ryder. You oughta stick around. See what comes up."

"Got other people to see, I'm afraid. I am a working man, after all."

"Unlike the poor widow woman," she said. "All she has to do is lie around getting snockered. Well, y'all come back, ya hear," she said, taking on a twang and holding her drink toward me.

"I'll probably do that," I said, thinking I probably would.

Having nothing urging me anywhere else, I headed down the "back" way, the way Stan and I had gone to find the pot patch. Just over the boundary of Queenie's property, past where one tine of the fork in the road went back up to where the marijuana had been growing, a brown sedan approached, the unmarked kind used by sheriff's people.

35

My eyes locked on him as soon as he appeared around a curve. He didn't look at me. I thought it was a conscious avoidance. I slowed and kept my gaze on him as he passed. Sunglasses. A khaki jacket over a white shirt. I couldn't say for sure it was Presley, but I would have bet my remaining arm on it.

A little further on, a creek paralleled the road. At the first chance, I pulled over. I tried to get the geography right in my mind, wondering if it was the same body of water that crossed Queenie's land, along which Weaver's Falls thunders and Brian McFadden's body was found. An old cabin was visible on the other side sitting in the midst of a small space cleared out of the forest. A pickup truck sat in a graveled driveway. My investigation had uncovered activity involving land sales only back on the other side of Queenie's place. That didn't mean nothing had been happening on this side of the ridge as well. I got back in the Honda and started looking for a way across the creek.

A small wooden bridge, of a kind common to the area, came up quickly. If I hadn't seen the truck on the other side, I might have worried about how much it could hold. A sign posted on a railing advised trespassers that they were not welcome. No one accosted me with a weapon when I pulled into the drive behind a surprisingly new pickup truck with an oversized cab. I started calling as soon as I got out of the car.

"Hello? Anybody home? Hello?"

A woman came out as I approached the small porch. I'd been expecting someone older, some Beverly Hillbillies stereotype. Instead, she was young, maybe late teens, early twenties. A redhead, cute, in jeans, and a T-shirt imprinted with picture of The Raconteurs. Her bare feet were the only part of the picture that fit the stereotype.

"Who're you?" she asked.

I told her my name and handed her one of my P.I. cards.

"I'm looking into the fire that burned the Ivey house. Did you hear about it?"

She looked at me as I imagined people around here once looked at the revenuers who came to bust up stills.

"I don't think you had anything to do with what happened. But Ms. Ivey had been offered a lot of money to sell her place and had been threatened when she wouldn't. Anybody been around talking to you about selling this place?"

"What happened to your arm?" she asked.

I liked her immediately in spite of the non sequitur.

"Car wreck. Long time ago. I didn't get your name."

"That's 'cause I didn't give it to you."

"Care to?"

"Sarah Jean."

"Nice name. Who all lives here, Sarah Jean?"

"I'm not sure that's any of your business."

"OK. Can you tell me who owns the house?"

"Me."

I let that register, hoping my surprise wasn't obvious.

"Owned it a long time?"

Before she answered each question, she ran her hands through her long, wavy, hair. It was a fetching habit. I believed Sarah Jean was shy.

"A year. Since Momma and Daddy were killed in a car wreck. Was my granddaddy's and my great-granddaddy's 'fore that."

For its age, the house looked to be in good shape. The chinking between the logs was intact; the tin roof appeared relatively new. A kitchen garden stood off to the right and azaleas lined the front of the porch. The girl smiled when I said it looked like she took good care of the place.

"So, Sarah Jean, has anybody been around, talking to you about selling the place?"

She was still standing on the porch. I was on one of the flagstones that led to the drive.

"Wait here a minute," she said and went inside. I turned around to look at the creek that divided the property from the road above. I bet the place was cold in the winter but it sure was a pretty spot. She reappeared and handed me a business card.

North Realty, Pete Haywood, Realtor.

"He come around a few weeks ago. Wanted to talk to Daddy. I didn't tell him Daddy was dead. None a' his business. None a' yours, either. But you seem like a nice guy. He seemed kinda, you know, sleazy. I don't know. You know he's a preacher, too?"

I said I did know that and asked if they'd heard anything else from him since then.

"He called a couple of times to talk to Daddy, asked if I'd given him the card. I just told him Daddy wasn't home. I think he was getting maybe suspicious that Daddy isn't really around at all."

"Since you have decided I am a nice guy, are you ready to tell me who all lives here?"

She cocked her head, put a hand on a hip, assumed a severe look.

"Me and my brother."

It was impossible to keep that other stereotype out of my mind.

"See. That's why I don't tell people. Y'all think it's some sick thing. Well, I was married for three years and my husband died and my brother got his leg shot off over in Eye-rack and I take care of him. There. That OK with you?"

I was chagrined. Seriously.

"You wanna come in and meet him?"

I said I would and followed her into the house. He was a nice-looking young man, sitting in a wheelchair, a blanket covering him from the waist down. He was reading a James Patterson thriller but looked up when we walked in, his eyes going immediately to my left shoulder. I understood why his sister was so nonchalant asking what had happened to the arm that wasn't there. We shook hands.

"Arlo," he said after I'd said my name.

"Like the folk-singer," I said. He nodded.

"Would just as soon they'd called me 'Woody.' But what're you gonna do?"

"I was talking to your sister about ..."

"Yeah, that asshole Haywood. Seen him on TV on a Sunday. Thought he was an asshole then. I hope I'm not offendin' you."

"You're not."

"You know, people come around here, we live in this little cabin, they think we're some kind of Appalachian low life. Now, if we were Yankees and had bought this little place, people'd think it was cute and quaint. 'Love what you've done to the place.' That kind of thing. That Haywood character was just so sorry for us, you know. Like he was taking pity on us, offering to sell the place for us. Didn't even occur to him that we might like it here, prefer it to some cookie cutter condominium somewhere. Just arrogant, you know."

I repeated the story of Maisie Ivey and said that I was also working for Queenie and thought she was being framed for murder.

"Yeah. Heard about that. Now, she's a curmudgeonly old broad. But she's no murderer."

"How well did you know Stan and Martha Jo?" I asked.

"Stan used to come around when Daddy was alive," Sarah Jean said, "back before he married that woman. I think you could say him and Daddy were friends."

"They talked about hunting and fishing and what was wrong with the government," Arlo said. "I fished with him and Daddy a few times. Quiet guy. Then he got married and Momma and Daddy got killed. He did come around a few times after the wreck to see if we needed anything. I think I made him uncomfortable. I make a lot of people uncomfortable. You probably understand that."

The morning was sliding away. I wasn't sure what I was learning here that would lead my employer to believe I'd been earning my keep. Perhaps confirmation that someone was trying to buy up the whole mountain. It did occur to me that if the operation was that big, there was more information to be found out about it somewhere. I thanked Sarah Jean and Arlo for their time and asked that they let me know if they heard any more from Haywood, or anyone else, about selling the place. Sarah Jean told me to wait a minute and went into the kitchen, returning a few seconds later with a plastic grocery store bag filled some leafy green material.

"Leaf lettuce," she said as she handed the bag to me. "Only so much of it two people can eat. Take some to the church down the road, but even so ..."

I thanked her again, thinking of the bounty of Kathy's garden and the annual dilemma of how to dispose of surplus homegrown produce.

Turning the car around in the yard, I faced the same choice I had when I'd first seen the cabin, whether to see what was going on back up at Martha Jo's or go on down the mountain. Back across the bridge, I sat for a minute, deciding on my next move, when my cell phone rang. "Audrey" was in the caller ID space. I hit the return-call button.

36

"Hi, Rick," she said, sounding altogether like we were best friends. "How are you?"

"Just fine, Audrey. What can I do for you?"

"All business today, huh?"

"I do have work to do."

"Gotta have lunch," she said. "Want to have it with me?"

Two almost simultaneous thoughts flashed in my mind. One said that this was not a good idea. The other said it was an opportunity. I went with the opportunity. We agreed to meet in an hour at what had become our usual spot. I had enough time to get to her office before she left. And I wanted to make another stop before that.

"McDee," I said to the car phone, verbal shorthand for MCDE, the Mountain Center for the Defense of the Environment.

A woman's voice said, "Mountain Center."

"Hi, Carole. Zella in?"

"Hi, Rick. Sure. Just a sec. Nice to hear your voice."

Within a minute, my erstwhile boss was on the line.

"Could I borrow your Prius for a little while this afternoon?" I asked. "I need to be in a car that won't be recognized as mine."

"Sounds intriguing. Sure, you can have it, I'm not going

anywhere until the end of the day."

The offices of HPA, formerly Hensley, Presley and Associates, were in a free-standing three-story building identified by the name of a bank, on the outskirts of downtown. I was there in forty-five minutes with Zella's car, looking for a place from which I could see Audrey leave without her seeing me. Her car was parked about twenty feet from a side door. I found a spot near enough that I'd be able to see her coming out of the building but far enough away that she was unlikely to notice me. Ten minutes later, the man who had once held a gun on me came out of the door I was watching, got in a smallish blue coupe and pulled away. Less than a minute later, Audrey appeared. Sometimes my instincts surprised even me.

I wondered what kind of a story she would have if I told her what I'd just seen. Probably deny knowing anything about it. The blue car driver could have been doing business in the bank. Except he didn't come out of the bank entrance. I decided I'd skip it and avoid the scene that would follow if she thought I was accusing her of something. I gave her a small lead before pulling out.

When she turned into the restaurant's parking lot, I went on by, coming back after she'd had time to get inside. She was seated and talking to a waitress as I walked up.

"She just took my drink order," Audrey said. I said I'd have unsweetened tea. I'd adopted the southern habit of not specifying "iced" since that was the default way tea was served. It was only if you wanted it hot that you had to be specific.

"To what do I owe the honor of your company today?" I asked.

"Oh, nothing special. I just thought it would be nice to see you."

"People might begin to wonder," I said.

She smiled, as if that was exactly what she hoped people would do.

"My wife might be one of them," I added.

"Oh," she said, as if that hadn't occurred to her. "Is there something to wonder about?"

I believed 'coy' described this behavior and checked on it when I got home. Artfully or affectedly shy or reserved; slyly hesitant; coquettish. That would be Audrey.

Her silky white blouse was close to opaque, but didn't entirely mask the white bra underneath. Her hair was presented in the usual mannered-unkempt style. It was hard to stay mad at her since what she displayed was not quite real, like being mad at a character in a movie. And, I wasn't really mad. Just curious. She was being dishonest with me. But, unlike Martha Jo, she didn't know that I knew she was being dishonest, and therefore, I had one up on her. My sense of moral superiority was narcotic.

"So," I said, steering the conversation, "any more mystery followers?"

"Well," she said, "I didn't want it to seem like I only wanted to see you because of business, but I think he ... or somebody, may be following me again."

"The white Miata?" I asked, knowing that was unlikely.

"No. It's not even always the same car. It's just I have the feeling someone's watching."

"The feeling."

"Yes. It's hard to explain."

"No, not really," I said, playing along. "I think we have senses that can pick up on that kind of thing."

"You do? So, you don't think I'm crazy?"

"Well, the one doesn't exclude the other."

Her mouth was pursed, her lips shifting to the side, wondering.

"So, just because it's not crazy to think someone's following me, that doesn't mean I'm not crazy. Is that what you mean?"

"It was a joke, Audrey."

Her eyes narrowed. She turned her head away. I thought there might be some real human emotion there, as if she'd really been hurt.

"A joke," I repeated.

She turned her face to me. A flat expression turned quickly into a smile.

"It's too bad you can't tell me about the murder investigation." I must have appeared as exasperated as I felt because she held up a hand and said, "I know, I know." The smile disappeared. Her eyes went to the table top. At first glance, it appeared she was pouting before I realized it was disappointment.

"I can tell you this," I said and she looked up and her eyes widened, although the smile did not return. "All investigations, at least all that I've been involved with go pretty much the same way. You clump along until you find something that opens a door, somebody says something, or something is left behind somewhere, or people start showing up in unexpected places. Pretty soon, you have a list of things and then it's a matter of connecting the dots."

I didn't say, like white Miatas showing up at the office of the guy who's trying to buy up a lot of land in the mountains and then showing up in the parking lot of the company that does that guy's advertising and employs the woman who accused the driver of said Miata of stalking her, said driver also having pulled a gun on the guy looking into the woman's charges that the guy was stalking her. And the guy who drove the Miata coming out of her office building but into a different ... I wasn't sure what it all had to do with murder. Maybe two murders. And, more than likely, arson.

"Do you have any suspects?"

A laugh erupted before I could squelch it. "You just don't give up, do you?"

That brought the smile back along with a shrug.

"I once heard a cop say that, early in an investigation,

everybody's a suspect."

"Does that mean I'm a suspect?"

I smiled. I may not have done coy as well as she did but I could play in that same league.

"Since you are one of everybody, I guess you are."

"Oh, my!" She sounded like some over-stuffed matron in a Victorian melodrama. "Why would I be a suspect?"

And there it was, like playing Tetris when the pieces start falling into place. Clunk, clunk, clunk. The people she worked for were somehow connected to the whole land acquisition-pot growing-murder business. That's how she knew I was investigating the murder. I wasn't trying to hide it. A lot of people around town knew what I was up to. Including, it seemed, her employer. Her job was to find out what I knew. No wonder she'd been relentless. She was the bait. I was the fish that wasn't biting. Maybe I'd nibble the line and see what happened.

"Oh, Audrey, I don't think you murdered anybody."

"How do you know?"

"I'm a detective. Remember? And why on earth would I suspect you? Really. What could you possibly have to do with it?"

"Me? Nothing. That's why I wondered what you meant when you said everyone is a suspect."

"And you really thought that meant you were a suspect?"

"I don't get it. First you say I am a suspect, then you say I'm not."

I thought I'd made her squirm. I hoped so.

The waitress came with our drinks and took our food order.

We were silent for another minute until she said, "But you don't know who did it?"

"Actually, there is not just one 'it' that has been done. Several 'its' have been perpetrated."

Her eyebrows shot up.

"Oh? Do tell."

"No, we've been over this ground before. I can't tell you or anyone other than my employer and, if appropriate, the authorities, about any particulars in a case."

"Except you know I didn't murder anyone."

"Anyone in this particular case."

"Now what's that supposed to mean?"

"It means that's all I know about. For all I know, you may have body parts of dead people stashed in your freezer."

"On, now you're just being silly. And sick."

Her mouth pulled up in a moue making her look like a child who's had the pieces of a game she'd been playing taken away.

"I think you're mean," she said.

"Oh, come on, Audrey. You invite me to lunch and ask me stuff you know I can't tell you and then get mad because I won't tell you."

"And then practically accuse me of murder."

"I didn't accuse you of anything. I just suggested that I don't really know anything about you prior to you calling me up a week or so ago. I have no idea what you've done in your life...." I almost added, "... just as you don't know what I've done in my life," but I was afraid that would lead her to ask if I'd murdered anyone and, although, technically, it was manslaughter and not murder, I didn't want to open up that box.

"But, you do think I could have murdered someone, theoretically."

"I think, theoretically, we could all murder someone under the right conditions."

"You could murder someone?"

"I might have to kill you if you keep this line of conversation going."

The food came and we attended to that for a few minutes.

She mostly shuffled the greens around in her Chef's Salad while I enjoyed my fried oysters. It seemed that, with the discussion of my investigation off the table, we had little else to talk about. In the silence, I thought about dragging the line out some more.

"Mr. Presley," I said. She perked up like a dog hearing a bag of treats opened.

"What about him?"

"What's his first name?"

She looked as if she was debating the pros and cons of answering me.

"I'm just curious," I said. "I came across the Presleys in the phone book the other day. Did you know there are over two hundred Presleys there?"

She paused a few seconds. "He's Web."

"Web?"

"Short for Webster. His whole name is Chester Webster Presley."

"Guess Web is the best you can make of that," I said.

"Yeah. And you don't ever want to call him Chester. Or Webster for that matter."

"Kind of distinguishes him from the other hundred and ninety-nine."

"I guess."

The rest of the meal was cordial, as if she'd never been annoyed with me. We talked about the coming high summer when tourists would ascend into the Blue Ridge and Smokey Mountains seeking relief.

When everything was cleared from the table except for coffee, she said, "I'm sorry I got mad at you."

"I take back what I said about having to kill you."

As we got ready to leave, I said, "If that sense you have of being followed becomes more than just feelings, if there is a real person or vehicle I can lay eyes on, give me a call."

Her smile stretched across her face. It seemed sincere. She pulled me into a hug before I could hold my hand out for a less intimate good-bye. When I extricated myself, I said I needed to go back inside and unload some of the caffeine I'd just loaded up on.

I waited until she was out of the parking lot before I went to the Prius. I hadn't gone more than a half-mile back toward town when I noticed the small blue car behind me. It stayed the same distance back whether I sped up or slowed down.

37

He must have been lurking somewhere near the restaurant, watching me as I left. The Prius hadn't fooled him for long. I was approaching the neighborhood in which Kathy's office was located and it seemed like an opportune time to drop in.

Her space was in a two-story edifice about halfway back to downtown with parking for the upper level off a side street. I turned right off the four-lane, keeping an eye on the rear-view mirror. He followed, coming up the street as I turned into the parking area. He went on past the parking lot, turned right at the street just past a church, and was soon out of view. My guess was that he would turn around, come back until he could see where I'd parked, and wait. I had no real interest in losing him, not right now, and wondered how serious he was about tailing me.

Warren was at the reception desk when I walked in. We exchanged greetings before he told me Kathy wasn't in. I don't know whether people who are good at reading other people are drawn to detective work, or if the work brings out that trait. I thought the young man was holding something back.

"Gone to lunch?"

"Yeah."

"Some place I might meet her?"

"I'm not sure where she went." He paused a fraction of a second. "She's with a client."

His expression turned into, I don't know what else I can tell you.

"Any idea when she'll be back?"

He looked down toward the bottom right corner of his computer screen where the time would be displayed.

"Maybe an hour. I don't know. She just left a few minutes ago."

I was considering my options, when he said, "She's with a guy who builds indoor water parks. He wants Kathy to represent his company."

It poured out of his mouth, like something foul he needed to get rid of. I wondered if he was uncomfortable because there was more to it or because of how he thought I might react upon hearing it.

"It's OK, Warren, really." And it was. Really. It was like when I gave up drinking. One day I just didn't want to drink anymore. Today, I didn't want to be suspicious and angry and jealous. It is true that I relapsed once on booze, with fairly dire consequences, and I knew my sick thinking could return as well. But, for today, I felt relief. I thanked Warren and told him to tell her I stopped by.

Instead of leaving the way I came in, I took the stairs to the lower level. If my follower was waiting for me, I counted on him having his eye on the upper door. The office building across the side street had a layout similar to Kathy's building. I went in the lower level, out the upper, and kept walking up and around the church on the next corner. Coming back toward the side street, I saw the blue car parked facing the four-lane, where he could pick up my tail when I left. I continued to approach him from the rear, taking note of the license plate, although I suspected it did not legally belong to the vehicle. I sidled up to the driver's side.

When I was just to the rear of the driver's door, I leaned over and rapped on the window. If he hadn't been belted in, his head would have hit the ceiling. Once he saw my face – or maybe it was the missing arm – he immediately turned the key in the ignition and sped off down the street.

By the time I'd returned to my car, the rush had passed and I realized I'd been getting high on a game. If all I'd wanted was to get the guy off my tail, I could have gone straight up to him. He would have left when he saw me coming, but that wouldn't have been as much fun. So far two people had died in this case, an elderly woman's life was probably at risk, and I was acting like a kid playing capture the flag.

Sufficiently chagrined, I decided it was time to find out more about Chester Webster Presley, HPA, and HPB, LLC. Once back into town, I left the car in a parking deck and carried my laptop to Malaprops Bookstore and Café where they had good wi-fi and a decent cup of coffee. I put my gear down by an empty stool at the counter with a view out onto the street, got a half-caf latte and went to work.

Anybody with a computer and access to the Internet can now do much of what a contemporary private eye does. Information that once took hours of schlepping from place to place to find can be unearthed in minutes anywhere an Internet connection is available. Fortunately, for those of us who make a buck at the work, people are still willing to pay for someone else's time and expertise.

I had low expectations for finding any interesting personal information about Chester Webster Presley on HPA's website. C. "Web" Presley, as he was identified, was a civic minded sort, sitting on the boards of local non-profit agencies, being active in the United Way Campaign, and garnering numerous awards from various trade organizations. He was also the Chamber of Commerce's representative to a county-wide economic development consortium. By itself, this latter piece of information was insignificant, a pro-development stance being the norm for people in his line of work.

Then I googled him, wondering, as the computer was searching, when it was that "Google" had become a verb. Nothing came up for Chester Webster Presley, probably because that was not how his name appeared on anything about him on the Internet. There were, however, many pages of listings when I typed in 'Web Presley,' most of them relating in some way to Elvis on the World Wide Web. I was just about to give it up as a lost cause when I saw a link to HPA that took me back to their website. This lit a spark of hope and I returned to the 'Web Presley' listings. A few pages farther in, there was a link to Citizens for Freedom, an organization of which Web had been the Chairman a few years back. This group's purpose had been to prevent the county commissioners from imposing zoning, the predominant position among pro-development sorts at the time.

My gaze wandered out onto the street and was quickly captured by two young women dressed in very short skirts and tube tops. Not much was left to the imagination. A middle-aged woman walked into my line of vision, looked into the window and smiled at me. I returned the smile and lowered my head back to the computer screen.

I was just about to click ahead when the listing on the bottom of the page caught my eye. "... C. WEB PRESLEY ... indicted for fraud and extortion..." The link at the bottom of the citation was to our local daily newspaper. It was a four year old article that began, "The principals in the business HPB Holding, Inc., were indicted yesterday for fraud in connection with their participation in the High Winds development ..." It went on to relate that High Winds had been described in promotional material as a planned community to be built in Western North Carolina around a golf course designed by a notable golf professional. The principals in HPB were identified as Marshall Hensley, C. Web Presley, and Morris M. Beatty.

I leaned into the stool's back rest and began playing a drum cadence on the counter with my fingers. This, I thought, is how a mathematician must feel when an equation works out for the first time. I knew I should avoid feeling smug, the kin to hubris, a sure setup for a crash. There was an article in the newspaper's archives which had appeared six months after the original one. The criminal charges against the HPB principals had been dropped at the same time that civil suits brought by several property owners in the area of the proposed development were also settled. As a condition of the civil settlements, no details would be made public. HPB denied any violations of the law. Conversations with those property owners might prove interesting.

A web service to which I paid a modest amount every month for detailed criminal records disclosed no information about fraud or extortion for our man under any of the permutations of his name. There were, however, two assault convictions and one for spousal abuse for one Chester Webster Presley, resident of Asheville, NC.

I went outside with my cell phone and called Nate. Katrina answered, her deep Slavic tones sending chills down my spine. "It have big news for the big man," I said.

"I vill see if he is available," she said, just like Natasha on *Rocky and Bullwinkle*.

It took five seconds for her to put me through.

"What's up, Counselor."

"Know a Web Presley, Counselor?"

"Sounds familiar."

"He's the 'P' in HPA, the advertising firm that Audrey

Hollingsworth works for and that has Pete Haywood for a client. He's also, it would seem, the 'P' in HPB, LLC, the outfit buying up the land around Queenie's place. Quite the civic type. But maybe not so nice a person."

"I've got a client waiting in the lobby. How about coffee in the morning?"

It was almost five o'clock. When I got back to my laptop, I felt drained. It had been a good day with several high notes: Martha Jo's naked body; the guy I assumed was one of the Presleys in the deputy's car; Sarah Jean and Arlo; lunch; accosting the guy who'd been following me; the information I'd found on the Internet. In the very recent past, finding that Kathy was lunching with some guy would have been a serious downer but I was unruffled by it.

It seemed like a good time to call her. She didn't answer and no one answered at the office, understandably, as it was past closing time.

I was halfway to my car when my phone buzzed.

"I was in the middle of a conversation when you called," she said. "Might have some more business. Something very different."

"Warren told me about the water park thing."

"I'm down outside Hendersonville now, looking at one being added to a wannabe resort hotel. It might be more than I want to chew right now, but I'm going to think about it. What are you up to?"

"Just leaving downtown. I wondered if you wanted to get a bite somewhere. I'm not really up for cooking. Or, I could bring something home."

We agreed on the latter since it would take her about forty-five minutes to return to the county. There was no answer at MCDE or on Zella's cell phone when I called to make arrangements with her for swapping back cars. I left a message saying I'd get it back to her in the morning unless she really needed it tonight, in which case I'd come back into town.

I picked up a couple of meals from a little Thai restaurant on Merrimon Avenue. About half way out Cove Road, I happened to glance up into my rear view mirror. I couldn't tell much about the car behind me except that it was blue.

38

I'd had people follow me to the house before. I didn't like it. If I'd had my gun, I would have tried to shoot out his tires. Not a good idea, since they can arrest you for discharging a firearm in the city limits. But it's what I felt like doing. Instead, I stopped the car, got out, and began walking towards him. He made a fast K-turn and left rubber on the pavement as he sped away. I drove on to the house, left the food in the kitchen, fed the cats and walked out back and up into the woods. In less than ten minutes, my heart rate returned to near-normal and I returned to the house. I was on the deck with a glass of tonic, lime wedge, and ice, listening to the creek as it tumbled alongside the house on its way toward the Swanannoa River when I heard a car door shut in the garage.

In my mind, I saw Kathy coming into the kitchen, opening the refrigerator, getting the bottle of white wine, pouring a glass. I was looking at the sliding glass doors when she appeared, wine in hand. She came over and kissed me on the forehead before taking a seat.

"To water parks," I said, raising my glass.

"Let's not get carried away, yet," she said as our glasses clanked. "But thanks for the thought."

"So, what's the deal?"

"This outfit manufactures material for water parks and they want me to represent them in the southeast. Seems like the indoor water park attached to a free-standing resort is the coming thing."

"Sounds good."

"Really?"

"Sure. Isn't it?"

"I don't know. It'd mean a lot more traveling. I thought you'd be all, you know, like you get about that."

"I may be getting over it."

"Really?" she repeated.

I shrugged. "When Warren told me who you were with – and he was pretty freaked out about having to tell me – something didn't happen. A button didn't get pushed. The 'what is she really up to?' thought did land in my mind. There still are old tapes playing around up there. But I was able to turn them off."

"You're not just making this up so I won't get on your case about it?"

"It just wasn't there today. Still isn't. It's kind of nice. Some people think addicts are as hooked on the drama of being addicts as much as they are on the drugs themselves. Keeps the excitement going."

"Adrenalin addicts," Kathy said.

"Yup. And, as you so kindly pointed out the other day, that's going to keep getting me into trouble. I don't know. Maybe living with you is good for me."

"Knucklehead." She got up, leaned over and kissed me on the forehead. "I'll go fix dinner."

In this case, "fixing dinner" meant moving the Thai food I'd left on the kitchen counter from the cartons onto plates. It smelled so good, Gladys and Wilbur even joined us on the deck. While we were eating, the wind picked up. Before we'd cleared the table, lightning was crackling in the west and thunder caromed around the hills. If our bedroom theatrics that evening didn't match the heaven's in intensity, it wasn't for lack of effort.

If Kathy and I paid more attention to weather prognosticators, a favorite hobby of people hereabouts, we would have known that what we'd heard and seen on the porch that night had been the harbinger of a hurricane sweeping up from the Gulf of Mexico. Overnight, many local creeks and rivers, including Cove Creek, had swollen beyond their banks, creating chaos with the morning commute into the city. Half of Cove Road was underwater in several places, slowing traffic to a cautious crawl and making me late for my meeting. I lucked into a space at the curb near the Downtown Bakery, grabbed an umbrella, fed the meter, and hustled the half block to the café.

Nate was already ensconced in a booth, dressed for work in a black, well-tailored suit, white shirt, silver and gray tie, stogie clamped between his lips. If a casting director came to town looking for someone to play an African American mob boss, all Nate would need was a black shirt and he'd be a shoo-in for the role. I'd known him for over ten years, and I was still struck by how big a man he was. Not corpulent. Just big.

"'Morning, Counselor," he said as I approached with a scone and coffee.

I nodded. "Counselor."

"You found something interesting," he said as I slid in across from him. No idle chit chat this morning.

"Things may be starting to fall together," I said, and I filled him in on what I'd found in my computer search. "I'm surprised they're still operating under the same name."

"Maybe they think things have quieted down enough so no one will be paying attention and don't want to go through the paperwork to establish themselves as something else. Might be some financial stuff tied up in the name." He shrugged. "As you know so well, Rick, people don't always do what seems to make sense to someone on the outside looking in." He rolled the foreshortened cigar between his teeth for several seconds before removing it from his mouth. "It would appear as if they're engaging in the same strong-arm tactics that got them in trouble before. Might even say it's a modus operandi. It's the way these people are. Be interesting to talk to those neighbors of Queenie's who did sell their property, see how that all went down."

"The Jenkins and the Pruitts," I said. "Queenie didn't seem to know where they went. Maybe I could track down some relatives. I also thought about finding the people who sued HPB, see what their experiences were."

"You know, I'd love another cup of coffee," my employer/colleague/good friend/attorney said, "but I don't feel like dragging the old body around this morning to get it."

"At your service, boss."

After I returned with freshened cups, I told him about the previous day's experience with Audrey and the blue car.

"I think her job is to use me to find out what's happening with the investigation, maybe help them know how worried they should be. It's pretty clear that she and at least the one of the Presleys – and probably both – along with Haywood and the Miata-slash-blue car driver are all of a piece, like tentacles on some otherworldly beast."

"Don't go getting all melodramatic on me," he said. "You think they're trying to get Queenie off her land so they can have the whole mountain to do what they couldn't do on the other side of the county?"

"'That's what it looks like."

"Got a theory yet about the murder?"

"I do."

"Pray, tell."

"This outfit wants to build a high-end residential development around a golf course. Mega big bucks. They failed in this county once. You'd think they'd go elsewhere, so they must have resources here."

"Resources meaning people?"

"That's my guess. So they go about buying up the land they need. They've got their eyes set on an area that Queenie's property is key to. She's not interested in selling, but they are able to get a couple of other families to sell. They run into a stumbling block with Maisie Ivy. We'll pick that back up later. Now to Queenie's. I think old Stan was probably growing pot up there for a long time. Martha Jo and Aaron Presley go back to her dancing days. She's the connection between Stan and Aaron. Aaron is a relative of Web Presley. I'm making that up at this point, but they are too close in this thing not to be. Don't know how it all goes, but they come up with this scheme to set Queenie up for growing pot. The narcotics guys'll impound the land which will subsequently wind up with HPB after the usual courthouse shenanigans."

I sipped some coffee, looked down the aisle between the bakery case and booths toward the front door. People came in, shaking off umbrellas and rain hats, making proclamations about the weather that would be repeated ad nauseam all day.

"They're ready to wage a war of attrition out there. Not in a big hurry. The bucks are big enough to wait for. Then, young Brian shows up and stumbles onto the pot patch. Oh. Yeah. I think in the process, Stan and whoever all he was in with figured out they could also make a bucketful of money growing high-end sinsemilla. Anyway, Brian finds it. Helps himself. Maybe he sees Stan tending the crop. Stan and whoever figure the kid might go to Queenie. Or, if they manage to get her busted, Brian would testify that he never saw her around the stuff but did see Stan."

"So," Nate said, "they have to get rid of him and figure Queenie'll take the fall. So to speak."

"That's what I'm working with, anyway."

"And what about the Ivey woman?"

"Aaron Presley worked with her nephew, Neal Wilson, back in McDowell County. They may have been scheming how to get the old lady's land back then. Now, this other thing comes along, and the nephew figures he can make out better by selling the land to developers. Gets her out of there and the house mysteriously burns down. No reason for the old lady to go back. Got her medicated out of her mind in a nursing home. He can get power of attorney. Yadda yadda yadda." I stopped talking for a moment, then remembered something Nate was going to do. "Did you talk to the people at the Morgan Family Home?"

"Ah, yes. And the woman I spoke with, who identified herself as the director, apologizes for any misunderstanding there was about your intentions and assured me that Ms. Ivey will get nothing but the finest care."

"Yeah, well, I still don't trust them. I haven't given up on the idea of springing the old lady."

"I don't think I want to know about that," he said while making an ostentatious display of holding an arm out and letting his shirt sleeve slide up to display a gold Rolex. "I've got to be in court. Got a kid who decided to take a gun to school. They have no sense of humor about those things these days. So," he said as he began his slide out of the booth, "what do we do with all that? No smoking gun in there. The grand jury sits next week. If they indict, it sure would be good to have a defense."

"Think we can build on the theory that HPB was trying to get her land?"

"Maybe. Rather have something that more immediately exonerates her."

"Did I tell you I saw a sheriff deputy's car going up the back way to Martha Jo's the other day?"

He stopped as he was about to stand up.

"Don't think you did. And …?" he said, hovering at the edge of the booth, encouraging me to fill in the blank.

"I think it was Presley."

"Presley the cop or Presley with HPA and HPB?"

"I am impressed with your memory, Counselor. Presley the cop."

39

Clouds drifted through the valleys and glens, hung over creeks and rivers, masked and revealed dark woods. I stopped at Queenie's to see how she was holding up. Sonny was standing sentry at the top of the porch steps. He barked once and trotted down to greet me when I got out of the car, then returned to his post. I slipped my poncho on and walked up to the closed front door. After three unanswered knocks, I tried the handle. It was locked. I walked around the house and saw no sign of her or the truck. I realized then that if I'd just paid attention to Sonny, I would have known she wasn't home.

Down at Martha Jo's, the only vehicle in sight was the old pickup. Three knocks there got the same response as they had back at the big house. I grabbed a tail of my poncho to use as a barrier between my fingers and the door handle. The door opened. After calling her name a couple of times, I was satisfied no one was home. It was an unlawful entry and, depending on her reaction if she found me, it could be a crime. I made up a story to explain my presence if she did show up.

After shaking water off on the small tiled space inside the door, I let my eyes wander around. The room was clean and tidy. On a shelf over the fireplace, there was a framed photo of Martha Jo and Stan in beach clothes. She looked terrific and the old boy was remarkably trim, not a bad looking older man. They were smiling, holding drinks. Scanning some more, I saw what looked like photo albums on a shelf under the coffee table. I took a seat on the couch and lifted them up. The first one I opened looked like a recap of her dancing career. The apparel got skimpier as the years progressed. There were some nudes at the end, although the dancers at the Dolls House didn't dance like that. Not for the public, anyway. I had to have a conversation with myself before I put the book down.

The other book was a wedding album. It appeared that the ceremony proper had taken place at Weaver's Falls with Martha Jo, Stan and a minister on the rock at the top, the place from which Brian had presumably been launched into the river. Martha Jo was resplendent in a figure-embracing, blue knee-length dress with a great deal of décolletage. Stan was wearing dress slacks and a white shirt. The rest of the documented festivities went on around this house, tables and chairs set up in the yard, and a three piece country or bluegrass band judging by the instrumentation. It looked like the event was attended by a couple of dozen people, including Queenie. I didn't recognize anyone else until I came to the last page. I had to pull the picture out of the album to reduce the glare. The guy was in the background so it was hard to make out his features. It was, I was sure, the guy I'd seen coming up the back way the day before.

After taking care to put the album back as I found it, I got up and went to the front window. The rain had lightened up. What I was thinking about doing next was riskier than staying put in the living room, but I couldn't pass up the opportunity.

There were two bedrooms, the master having its own bathroom. A framed photograph of Stan and Martha Jo stood atop a dresser next to one of Stan by himself. I pulled a couple of tissues from a box on a night stand to use in the place of gloves as I walked around. A quick glance in the closet revealed an absence of men's clothes, the same as in the dresser drawers. There was a fairly extensive collection of lovely unmentionables of which I kept my hands off.

I stepped into the bathroom. Medicine cabinets can be very revealing. There was Tylenol and Pepto-Bismol. Baby aspirin I imagined was for Stan as he was of age to be at risk for heart attack. Some outdated penicillin. Antibiotic salves. Uninteresting stuff. Ambien for Martha Jo. That was interesting. Usually prescribed for sleep but also a minor tranquilizer. And, Paxil for Stan. An anti-depressant. Nothing else worth noting.

Sitting on the edge of the bed, I poked around in a night stand. A vibrator and a dildo sat on top of the stuff in one drawer, along with a tube of lubricant. I pulled the whole drawer out for ease of moving things. Underneath the sex toys was a gun. My mind went immediately to Stan. Surely the cops would have searched in here after he was found dead. The gun wasn't necessarily evidence of anything except maybe someone taking precautions out here in the boonies. But if the police found it, they'd want to keep it to see if it was related to the killing. Unless the person searching this room knew what was in here and chose not to reveal everything he saw. I set the gun beside the playthings. Lying on the bottom was a small, white, office envelope, the size you might mail a check in.

More photos. The first few were variations on the ones in the living room, individual shots of Stan and Martha Jo, some of the couple taken by a third party. Another four photos were similar to the others taken at the beach except there was another person in them. The guy I'd identified as Presley in the wedding photos.

The next few pictures were of Martha Jo in various stages of undress. Breathe, keep going, I told myself. My hands began to shake when I got to the next one. A nude picture of Martha Jo and Presley standing in front of a mirror. I thought I was going to drop the whole lot when I uncovered the last one. Another self-photo, this one of the naked couple coupling. My fingers felt sticky and it took an act of will to put the pictures in order and back in the envelope. I thought about taking one of them for evidence and then thought better of it. Adding theft to the list of crimes I'd been committing didn't seem like a good idea.

When I had everything back in the drawer, I gave it a look. It would be hard to tell that it wasn't exactly as I'd found it. As I slid it along its tracks, the sound of gravel crunching out front got my attention and I moved as fast as I could to the guest bathroom off the hallway.

I timed the flush to the sound of the front door. She was standing firmly planted as I entered the room.

"What the hell are you doing here, Ryder?"

"I came by to see you and waited for a while in the car, 'till I needed to take a leak. The door was open and I didn't want to stand outside in the rain so I took the liberty."

"There's a law against that you know."

"Oh, a couple I can think of."

She looked at me like she might at a box of something she'd lifted off a shelf at the supermarket, trying to decide if she should take it or put it back.

"What do you want from me now?" Before I could answer, she said, "Want a drink?"

Apparently, I was not going to be surrendered to the law.

"Oh, that's right," she said, again cutting off an answer. "The AA guy. OK. Tea, Coke ..."

I was reminded of the old 'coffee, tea, or me?' line. "Glass of water would be good."

I followed her into the kitchen where she fixed herself a whiskey. She took a carafe of water from the refrigerator and poured a little in her glass before filling a tumbler for me.

"As far as what brought me out here today, I wondered if

you'd thought of anything else that might help in finding out who killed Brian."

"You're sure Queenie didn't do it?"

"As sure as you were the first time I talked to you about it."

Her expression suggested she'd forgotten that episode.

"That story," I went on, "is just to protect who really did it. So, of course I want to know who needs to be protected."

"Well, like I also told you before, I don't really know much about what goes on out here."

"Right. Stan grew a little pot. That's all you know."

"Yeah."

"You're lying, Martha Jo."

She looked at me like she'd just been slapped.

"What?"

"You're lying."

"Well, fuck you, buddy. You better leave, before I do call the law. Jeez, Ryder, you just keep being more and more of an asshole. Go. Get out of here. Don't bother coming back. I don't have anything else to say to you."

I raised my hands in defeat and turned toward the front door.

"You know, for a while I thought you were a nice guy," she said. "Turns out you're a prick like all the rest."

I wondered who all the rest included. I wanted to ask her about Presley but had already overstayed my welcome. When I reached the door, I looked back, and wagged a finger at her. "I know you're in this thing up to your eyeballs, Martha Jo." It was the old "get 'em thinking you know more than you do" tactic. Get them nervous, get them to react, to point fingers. And hope they point at each other and not the one stirring the pot.

She turned toward the side like a baseball pitcher and hurled her drink glass at me. Her aim was good and I had to duck. As it shattered against the wall behind me, she yelled, "Get the fuck out of here!"

I did.

Although the rain had almost ceased, small gullies were still being etched out of the dirt road coming down from Queenie's. Sonny was lying on the porch, head between his paws. He looked up as I drove by. I waved. Her truck was still gone. As I began to make my descent down the mountain, the phone buzzed in my pocket. I pulled over to answer it and saw it was Nate's office

"Hi, this is Rick."

"Hello, Mr. Ryder. Mr. Chatham says he can meet you at twelve-thirty in the coffee shop at the court house."

I said I'd be there.

It wasn't yet noon and I had time to swing by the offices of the Mountain Center for the Defense of the Environment to return Zella's Prius. Carole, the office manager, greeted me with a hug, saying how much she missed me around the place. Jay came out of Zella's office and greeted me with a handshake.

"How goes the investigation?" he asked.

"Slower than I'd like. But some pieces of the puzzle are beginning to fit together."

Jay looked directly into my eyes, an annoying habit he had, like he was looking into your soul.

"There's something else on your mind," he said. "I can hear the gears grinding."

"Yeah.... How free are your evenings this week?"

"Nothing special going on. Just hanging out with Zoey."

"How is she?" I asked. "You guys gonna get married, or what?"

"Not now. It works okay the way we're doing it. Think we'll just keep it at that."

"Tell her I said, 'hi.' The reason I ask about your schedule is, I'm thinking of taking a little road trip down the mountain some night soon. Maybe tomorrow. Could be tonight, but I don't really have things worked out, yet."

"Sounds mysterious."

"And it might not be ... hmmm ... strictly legal."

"Oh, I'm surprised," he said, grinning. "How unlike you."

"Yeah, yeah. I know. And, I'm going to need some help."

"Let me know. Sounds like fun."

Zella came out of her office. We hugged and bussed each other on the cheek.

"Nice car," I said, as we exchanged keys. "Things didn't go quite as I had planned, but the outcome was just as good."

I told Jay I'd get back to him, waved at Carole on my way out, and reclaimed my Honda. On the drive to the courthouse, Maisie Ivey came to mind. A plan began to take shape. It was insane. Big trouble could ensue. I couldn't leave it alone.

40

District and federal courts were in session and I had to park three blocks away, grateful the rain had taken a recess. The coffee shop in the basement of the old building evoked a bygone era with its Formica-topped tables and off-white ceramic coffee mugs. Although crammed with a sampling of all those who had business in the building – dark-suited lawyers, uniformed officers of the law, civilians in everything from Sunday-go-to-meeting attire to jeans and Harley Davidson T-shirts – it was impossible not to notice my friend as soon as I walked in and thought of Adam Clayton Powell holding forth in some Harlem restaurant. Two tables had been pushed together, a dozen people crowded around, all African American, all impeccably dressed. I started to drag another chair over when he waved at me.

"These folks are just leaving," he called as the entourage rose, as if on cue.

"Counselor," he said when I took a seat.

"Counselor," I said.

"Gonna eat?" he asked.

"About that time."

"Want to grab me a tuna sandwich while you're up there? And a milk."

I smiled. He was so matter-of-fact in his presumptions. "Not much of a lunch."

"Doctor's telling me I gotta be careful or my ticker's gonna explode. I try to be good at least twice a week."

After returning with the food, I told him about the pictures of Martha Jo and Aaron Presley.

"Presley's the deputy sheriff, right? Used to work for McDowell County."

"And," I said, "Asheville P.D. before that."

"Left Asheville under, uh, cloudy conditions, if I remember correctly. And now out there consoling the grieving widow, you suppose?"

"I had a more sinister thought. Bear with me here. Say that Stan's always been jealous of Presley. Not too much of a stretch. Guy seems to be around a lot. Stan's also taking a prescription drug for depression. What if Martha Jo and Presley did their little picture taking before Stan died. Martha Jo leaves them where Stan can see them. He sees them and it sends him around the bend."

"Intriguing idea. Kind of flimsy evidence to go on."

"I told Martha Jo that I knew she was involved in all this."

"After you'd illegally entered her house."

I smiled.

"You do like to get out there on the skinny branches, don't you, counselor?"

"I think my ADD is kicking in. I'm getting bored, Coach. I need some action."

"Just don't get yourself thrown in jail again, will you? It's one thing when you're freelancing. But when you're in my employ, it doesn't look good for me. You know, there are people downtown who still think I'm an uppity nigger. They don't need much ammunition to come after me."

I cringed a little inside my shell, thinking of my plan to go to

McDowell County.

He finished his sandwich and milk and was rolling the stogie around in his mouth as if it were dessert. A large round clock on the wall, the old-fashioned kind with the big second hand marking the inexorable passage of time, showed 1:15. He caught my gaze.

"Gotta be somewhere?"

"Just thinking about what to do next."

"Finding something concrete that exonerates our client would be good. And keeping your name out of the papers would be another plus." He tossed his napkin on the table. "Better be getting back upstairs. My client's a little nervous."

"What happened this morning?"

"Got the jury empaneled. The high point was when the prosecutor got lectured for needlessly protracting the process. Doesn't mean the judge is on our side, but it sure didn't help the other guy."

I rode the elevator with him to the first floor. Before we declared a War on Terror, you could leave from a side door in the basement. Now the basement was "secure" and you had to go out the main door upstairs.

When I stepped outside, I thought maybe I'd done a Rip Van Winkle. It was a different day. The rain had stopped. The sun appeared to be drifting between the clouds, sporadically breaking through and turning water-drenched leaves to glitter.

I have discovered in sobriety that when in doubt about what to do next, more caffeine is usually called for. I headed out to see my friends at the Country Café and Readery. Maybe check again on Queenie while out that way. There was a new sign outside the small shop. It read "Country Coffee Roasters and Café." When I stepped through the door, the aroma lifted my spirits. Prior to its recent incarnation, the store smelled of coffee mingled with the musk of old books. Not an unpleasant experience, but today it was all coffee. Taylor, the distaff half of the store's ownership, was behind the counter, standing over a large canvas bag of coffee beans.

"What's goin' on," I asked as I approached.

She stood and turned.

"Oh. Hi, Rick."

"Where're the books?"

"Ah. Kind of hard to compete with the downtown used book places, unless you're willing to deal almost exclusively in crap. Stuff you'd find at the Goodwill. There were a few people who appreciated what we were trying to do, but mostly we were a dumping place. Friends of ours who operated the roasting business where we'd been getting our supply decided they'd had enough entrepreneurialism in their lives and gave us a good deal on their equipment and the business. That's the short of it."

"So, now you'll have not only really good coffee, but really fresh coffee."

"You got it. What brings you out here today?"

"Just that. A good cup of coffee. My brain's kind of fried so I thought I'd refuel. Might go out to see Queenie, see how she's holding up."

"She was by here this morning. Seemed to be doing fine, although it did seem something was on her mind. But you know Queenie. Not the kind to be blabbing for the sake of conversation." As she worked on a latte for me, she asked how the investigation was going.

I knew that, unlike Audrey, she was just making conversation, like a bartender asking, "how's work?"

"Finding stuff out," I said. "Not sure how it all hangs together. I feel like the guy in that Dylan song, one that goes, Something is happening here, but you don't know what it is, do you, Mr. Jones."

"It'll come," she said.

"You're optimistic."

"It's right, that's all."

"I hope it comes in time to keep Queenie out of prison."

The chimes announcing a customer rang just as she put the coffee in front on me.

"Speak of the devil ..." Taylor began.

"And she appears," Queenie finished.

I turned to see my client.

"Hey, Rick. Saw that Honda and figured it had to be you."

"Taylor said you'd been by this morning."

"On my way to see Maisie."

My eyes widened involuntarily.

"Wanted to make sure they were treating her right down there. Told 'em I was an old friend and had heard through the grapevine where she was."

"Little risky," I said, "since they haven't exactly broadcast her location."

"Old Fort's a small town. Information gets around. Even with all that privacy stuff, what's it called?"

"HIPPA?"

"Whatever. People are still people. Gossip is currency."

I knew that was true. It was the currency detectives, public and private, dealt in.

"I'm surprised they let you see her," I said.

"I think I took 'em by surprise. They didn't have time to think about it."

"How is she?"

"Like you saw her. Pretty doped up. Didn't seem to recognize me. Probably a good thing or she could have blown my cover. You know, blurting out, 'Queenie.' Not that the staff would understand anything by it, I guess. Anyway, we gotta get her out of there."

"My thoughts exactly. Got any ideas?"

"I've been thinking about it. Wanna come outside? We can chat in my office."

Taylor put my drink into a to-go cup and I followed Queenie out to her truck. It was raining off to the east, but the sun was out and there was a rainbow toward the horizon. I took it for an omen.

"How about someone calls," Queenie said when we were settled in the cab. "Says they're from an ambulance service – we'd have to find out the name of one down there – and are going to be transporting her. Can they have her ready in half an hour. Just matter of fact."

"And if they get suspicious and call Deputy Wilson?"

"Guess we'd be up Shit Creek."

After a beat, as if we were both waiting for each other's comment, we burst into laughter.

"Yeah," I said, "that would probably describe it."

41

"See you in a couple of days," I said, stepping out of the pickup. As I opened the door to the Honda, my phone rang. People had been trying to convince me of the advantages of programming my cell phone with caller-specific ring tones so I'd know if I had a call I didn't want to bother with, a real help, they said, given the relatively few appendages I had to work with. It seemed like technological overkill to me. I pulled the phone out of my pocket. It was Kathy.

"Want to meet for dinner?" she asked. "I'm buying."

"Ooh. Feeling flush are we? Did you take the water park offer?"

"Just wait."

We agreed to meet at Pete's, a little Greek diner where the proprietor's mother made fresh spanakopita three times a week.

Immediately after I started the car, I saw Maisie, head drooped, sitting in the wheelchair in the hallway of the Morgan Family Home. The picture in my mind was as clear as if I was standing at the nurses' station. It wouldn't take much of the right kind of drug – morphine, for instance – to stop her breathing. I mulled over a plan. It was simple and for that reason alone might be successful. I didn't, however, know what we'd do with her once she was liberated.

The rain had quit altogether and the blacktop glistened under the glare of the late afternoon sun. I gave up solving the 'where to stash Maisie' problem in order give my attention to driving on the slick pavement. A few minutes down the road, like that instant when those old Polaroid pictures came into focus, it came clear. Zella. There it was. She had no connection to Maisie. A thorough investigation over time could lead to her as my ex-boss. But I hoped we wouldn't have to hide the old woman away for that long, just long enough for whatever she was doped up with to clear her system.

I called "Zella" to the car phone.

"You want me to be an accessory to a kidnapping?" she said after I'd explained the caper.

"I prefer to see it more in terms of a life-saving intervention."

"Like CPR?"

"Exactly."

"I'm not sure the law would see it that way. You know, I am a lawyer. So are you, for that matter. The bar frowns upon its members engaging in criminal activity."

"Once all the drugs clear her system, she'll be able to tell people what really went on."

"But if they've had her declared incompetent, it won't matter, will it? The family will just ascribe it to the rantings of a crazy woman."

She was right. I didn't care. I knew we had to get Maisie out of that nursing home.

"So, will you do it?" I asked, as if I hadn't heard what she'd been saying.

"When are you planning on doing this?"

"Next day or two."

"I'll call you. If I do it, you'll owe me big time. I mean, BIG time."

I was on the bridge going over the French Broad River when the car phone rang again.

"Bobby Headley," the voice said. "Thought I'd give you an update. It's not official and not surprising, but the arson guys are pretty sure the fire at the Ivey place was set. Now they're working on the 'who done it' part. They're probably gonna want to talk to you since you had some conversations with the woman."

"Am I a suspect?"

"You know how it is, Rick."

"Everybody's a suspect," I said. Although I knew I wasn't, really.

I was seated at a booth at one end of the small building when Kathy came in. The restaurant was mostly a lunch spot and at this hour we shared it with one other couple. The waitress was Pete's daughter, Angelina, a dark-haired beauty upon whom her father doted. If a guy got fresh with her, it only happened once.

"Two orders of spanakopita and two small Greek salads," the girl said without prompting, "and one glass of red wine and one unsweetened iced tea."

"We're pretty predictable, aren't we?" I said to Kathy.

She dropped her chin and looked out at me from the tops of her eyes.

"I guess if we look over the long term there are some recurring patterns," she said.

Our drinks came.

"Santé," she said, holding her glass toward me. I reciprocated. An auspicious beginning.

"To water parks?" I asked.

"No. To us," she said. "I spent a lot of time thinking today. The water park thing has opened up some new possibilities for me. So, I have to decide, how far do I want to take this. You know, I've already had offers to go to work for a couple of states and some big cities and have turned them all down because I don't want to leave Asheville. I know you don't, and I'm not leaving you. Even though you are a knucklehead." She smiled and tipped her glass toward me, again.

The salads came. I started to say something and she held up her hand. "I can do this new thing out of my office but it will involve a lot of travel. I've thought about what you said the other night, about letting go of old stuff. I realize I have to do it, too. Ever since the thing with that dancer, and in spite of my over-the-top way of trying to balance the scales back then, I have hung on to a sense of moral superiority. Just a little. But it's still there. I remember you saying it takes two people to make a relationship not work. I've never been sure I got that until now. If I don't think things are right, I can do my part to make it right and if that doesn't work, I can get out. And I don't want to get out. And you're doing your part to make it work. So, I will, too."

She took a bite of salad. "That's it."

"Whew. You know, sometimes I'm not sure I deserve you."

"None of us deserve anything, Rick. We are not owed by the universe. Sometimes we're able to make the most of what we've been given. Sometimes we screw it up. It's like my business when I lose a contract or don't get one I'd like. I've too much time and effort invested to chuck the whole thing. I have to work harder on the next one. That's how I feel about us. I know it can be hard living with me. I can get cold and distant. And holier-than-thou."

Angelina brought the food. I didn't even ogle her as she walked away.

Between bites of salad and the feta and spinach pie, I explained what I had in mind for Maisie.

"Sounds simple. What ever could go wrong?" she said with the slightest roll of her eyes.

"Probably, the worst that could happen is if a family member is at the nursing home when we arrive. Or, someone makes a call to the family when we get there."

"Then what would you do?"

"'We.' This is a 'we' thing. We'd scram. But before we do anything else, we need to reconnoiter the place one more time."

"When you talk about 'we,' kemo sabe, to whom are you referring?"

"Me and my sidekick. The good guy always has a sidekick along. You know, for backup and comic relief. And, someone who might – just might – keep me from acting egregiously stupid."

"I do have some experience," she said. "Friend of mine has let me come along on some capers."

I reached across the table and shook her hand.

"Partner."

We finished up, paid the tab, said goodbye to Pete and his daughter, waved to Mama in the kitchen. The break in the weather had been a momentary reprieve and we ran to our respective vehicles through heavy rain.

After setting the alarm for one o'clock, I fidgeted until giving up the idea of a nap. I fixed a pot of coffee and woke Kathy before the buzzer went off. My nighttime sleuthing outfit consisted of blue jeans, black sweatshirt over a long-sleeved T-shirt, black knit cap, black shoes. Kathy dressed in similar attire. Her clothes were snug and she was almost intolerably sexy, reminding me of Diana Rigg as Emma Peele on the old Avengers TV series. Adrenaline raced through my veins as if I'd mainlined it. If we weren't under time constraints, I would have ... Well, I would like to have, anyway. We threw matching black slickers in the back seat of the black Infiniti. We would be in Old Fort by two AM, a time when things should be very quiet.

Fog and rain closed around us before we reached the top of Old Fort Mountain. The descent in near-zero visibility could have been managed with one hand, but I was glad she had two on the wheel. Once on US 70, the weather turned from nemesis to ally, providing cover as we reached the Morgan Family Home.

Kathy cut the headlights and turned slowly into the drive. The Infiniti glided silently on the pavement as we headed toward the back of the rectangular building. We noted a side door to check on our way out. There were three cars in the rear parking lot in, presumably those of third shift staff. Steps led up to a loading dock and door at the back of the building. Kathy steered left, drove to the end of the lot and turned the car around, ready for a getaway. A pale yellow glow shone on the far side of the building. I grabbed my slicker out of the back and flipped the dome light switch off before getting out.

A gently sloping concrete ramp led toward dim light illuminating a doorway. I was squinting through the drizzle when a door opened, spilling light onto a small landing. I froze for a second, then stepped off the ramp to huddle against the outer wall of the building, counting on the elements to make me invisible. The door closed, briefly, before another figure appeared, then closed again. A point of light flared, quickly replaced by a tiny red glow that moved back and forth between the two figures. I guessed they were smoking something. Probably not tobacco. Perhaps it was the weather that made their break short, but it hadn't been more than three minutes before the red dot disappeared and the two figures reentered the building.

Water dripped off the front of my rain gear as I waited another two minutes before making my way up the ramp. The door handle didn't move when I tried to turn it. Returning to the back of the building, I climbed the stairs at the loading dock and encountered another locked entrance. There was only one more chance if my idea was going to work. Kathy guided the car slowly, turning right, down the driveway, back the way we'd come in, while

I walked. A short ramp led from the pavement to the door we'd passed earlier. I stepped up to the door, grabbed the handle and turned. The handle turned with me. I pulled slowly. When it was open far enough, I looked inside. No alarm went off. The lights were down. Nobody was moving where I could see them. There was a fire alarm pull within arm's reach. I closed the door, stepped back outside and into the Infiniti.

As soon as we turned onto the road, the front porch light came on. I hoped that, if they had noticed us, they would assume someone had used the drive as a turn-around. I was sure they wouldn't be able to get a license plate number.

Had it been up to me, I would have put the rest of the plan into play the next morning. Kathy suggested we wait until Monday, take the weekend to work out the details, contingencies, possible snafus. I was afraid we might think it to death and decide it wouldn't work, but Sunday night came, and everything and everybody was go.

42

At eight-thirty Monday morning, I walked out of Kinko's with two matching magnetized signs reading Mountain Health Transportation Services, the most generic name I could think of that didn't have a listing in the phone book. The signs also had a phony address, phone numbers (land and cell), website, and a drawing of a wheelchair. I took them with me to the offices of Blue Ridge Ambulation, where I rented a van equipped with a wheelchair lift. The white background of the signs blended well with the healthy looking white paint of the vehicle. I left the Honda in their parking lot and drove the van to Western Uniform Rental and Supply, my last stop in preparation for the afternoon's enterprise.

The rain had moved on toward the coast, leaving a clear Carolina blue sky in its wake. Queenie was waiting on the porch when I pulled up at two o'clock. Sonny barked at the van until I'd turned it around and he could see me in the driver's side window. He ran down to greet me, then sulked back up the steps after Queenie got in and we pulled away.

At MCDE, Jay took the uniform I gave him into the restroom.

"Halloween's early this year," Zella said when Jay reappeared, looking like central casting's idea of a hospital orderly.

"We should be back at your place about five-thirty, six o'clock," I said to my ex-boss. "If everything goes all right."

"And if it doesn't?"

"You can come visit us in the McDowell County jail."

I took Queenie to Zella's house while Jay drove on to Kathy's office. I had explained to Queenie that a home health nurse would be arriving there about four. "All the agency knows is that an elderly lady is being transported here from a nursing home and that she's a distant relative of Zella's. The nurse might have some questions about Zella, with her mahogany skin and not-from-around-here accent, being related to a very white and very southern country woman, but I assume she will have the good manners not to say anything about it."

When I got to Kathy's office, I gave Warren the other uniform I'd rented. "I appreciate you and Jay doing this," I said. "I feel much better with a couple of people no one down there has seen before."

Jay gave me the keys to his Toyota before he got in the van. Kathy would be driving and Warren had claimed shotgun. I led the way down the mountain in Jay's old Corolla, getting off at the Old Fort exit and pulling over to the side of the road. Jay pulled in behind me. After making sure everybody had taken a pair of rubber gloves from the box I'd gotten at the uniform supply place and that our watches were synchronized, I got back in the Toyota and headed for the nursing home. Kathy would follow two minutes behind me. While waiting, she would call the home. We anticipated the conversation would go something like: This is Kay with Mountain Health Transportation just reminding you we'll be there in a few minutes to pick up Maisie Ivey.

The person answering the phone would pause and say he or she didn't know anything about it.

Well, I'm sorry about that, but we're on our way. Please make sure she's ready to go and that her medications are ready.

Seven minutes later, I turned into the driveway of the Morgan Family Home, drove into the back parking lot, turned around, and pulled up to the door on the north side, the one I had reconnoitered the night before. My cell phone rang.

"We're on our way in," Jay said. He would carry his phone in a holster and keep the connection open. Mine was in a pocket and I listened through ear buds. I pulled on gloves and stood by the side door, counting slowly to keep my mind on something other than the somersaults my stomach was doing. I got to twelve when I heard Jay say, "Hi, we're here to pick up Maisie Ivey." I turned the side-door handle and pushed it open. A man in scrubs was walking down the hall away from me. When he reached the intersection with the main hall, he turned right, out of sight. I leaned in far enough to yank the fire alarm pull. The noise probably wouldn't wake the dead, but it was extremely obnoxious and insistent. As it screeched, I got back in the car and drove out onto the street, listening to the commotion inside.

"Well, damn. Now what?" a woman's voice yelled. "Y'all will just have to wait a minute."

"Why don't we just get her out of here? One less for you to worry about," Jay said.

"Well, there she is."

"Meds?" I heard Warren ask.

I watched in the rear view mirror as Kathy drove the van past the driveway, stopped and backed in so that the sliding side door of the van was directly across from the bottom of the ramp coming off the porch.

I heard a woman say, "Sign these." I presumed they were releases for Maisie and her drugs. There was a whole lot of scurrying going on in the background as they rounded up the residents to evacuate them from the building.

Jay's voice came through in a loud whisper. "We're going to go for a little ride."

By then I was out of sight of the nursing home, headed to the Interstate.

Ten minutes later, the fake Mountain Health Transportation Services van pulled up behind me on the shoulder of the on-ramp to I-40, headed back up Old Fort Mountain. I got out and removed the phony identification signs from the sides of the vehicle. Jay got back in his car and I joined Kathy, Warren and Maisie in the van.

The old lady looked as she had when Kathy and I had seen her. At least she was alive.

"How'd it go?" I asked as our mini-parade headed back to Asheville.

"A little scary." Warren said. "I wouldn't have been at all surprised if they hadn't let us take her. The fire alarm distraction is what did it. Kathy had the side lift down so we could wheel her right on in when we got to the bottom of the ramp, so they didn't have time to think about it too much. We had to mess with the chair tie-downs in the van and by the time we got out of there, they were lining up wheelchairs in the drive."

"About two minutes down the road, we heard sirens," Kathy said. "I thought it was the police coming after us before we saw the fire trucks."

That we might be pursued wasn't a farfetched notion, and Jay kept watch out the back window for signs of McDowell County Sheriff's vehicles. We got off I-40 just over the ridge into Buncombe County and took the state road through Black Mountain and on into Asheville.

By the time we arrived at Zella's, the adrenaline buzz I'd been working on since early in the morning had long since worn off. I was exhausted. It was only after I'd let myself down into an easy chair in Zella's living room that I wondered how long it would take before McDowell County Sheriff's Deputy Neal Wilson, former colleague of Aaron Presley, heard that his Aunt Maisie had been shepherded away from the Morgan Family Home.

43

The home health nurse who had come to help at Zella's was a blanket of calm and sympathy woven with threads of "I'm the Nurse and you're not." She followed as Jay and Warren carried Maisie up to a second floor bedroom. Her name was Helene. I was sure Zella and Queenie could handle her.

Jordan Granville, Ms. Ivey's family doctor, had agreed to come see her. He would assess her medications and put her on a regimen to decrease anything that was keeping her doped up and was not also life sustaining. He would also check for signs of abuse.

I called the team together in Zella's music room out of earshot of the nurse.

"Every one of us could go to prison for this," I said. "I know I tend to go off on adventures purely for the sake of the rush, and I thank all of you for giving me the benefit of the doubt. I imagine you've talked to each other about whether or not this was just another of Rick's cowboy escapades. I do think we saved a woman's life. I also take it as a good sign that we've not heard anything from McDowell County."

"Couldn't they be looking for her and we don't know it?" Jay asked.

"Nate ... you all know Nate, except maybe you, Warren, and I imagine you know about him ... He has a friend who's a magistrate down there. When I smacked the big guy at the nursing home, Nate knew about it within a couple of hours. When Neal Wilson does find her missing, I'm sure Nate will get word that they want to talk to me."

"When do you suppose that will happen?" Jay asked.

"Third shift will probably just take the report that Maisie was picked up at five o'clock and transported somewhere. They're not going to do anything about it at that hour, just pass it on to first shift. Whoever's the honcho on that shift – probably the nurse Kathy and I met the other day – will have a fit that no one knows where she is. Then the phone calls will begin."

In the van on the way back to Kathy's office, she asked me what I was going to say when they came to talk to me.

"I doubt I was seen, so I don't think they can get an arrest warrant. If they try to find Mountain Health Transportation Services, they'll come to a dead end unless someone got the license plate. Pretty unlikely, in all the commotion. The other person they might go after is Queenie and she can honestly say she can't tell them anything about the abduction since she wasn't there. She's not going back to her house for a while and I doubt they'll make the connection to Zella."

"But," Kathy pursued, "what if they ask if you have any information regarding the whereabouts of Maisie, point blank."

I had to think about that.

"Might have to lie."

By the time I'd returned the van and driven home, stars were competing with the remnants of daylight for space in the evening sky. Kathy scrabbled together some leftovers and we ate on the deck as the light exited the stage. I followed her upstairs after we'd cleaned up the kitchen. We were pretzelled together when I fell asleep.

The room was flooded in sunlight room when I woke up. Kathy wasn't in the room. The clock read 7:30. She must have turned off the alarm so it wouldn't wake me. Sounds of someone puttering in the kitchen climbed up the stairwell. I made a trip to the bathroom and had returned to the bed when I heard her feet on the stairs.

She was in a bathrobe and carrying a tray with two English muffins, butter and blackberry preserves, two glasses of OJ, a mug of coffee and one of tea.

"I know you don't like to eat before you do your exercise, but these are unusual times and I thought you might make an exception to your rule."

The scene was so domestically tranquil that it was possible to forget for a few minutes that we had been involved in a kidnapping the day before.

"Nate called," she said when I came out of the bathroom after my shower.

"You talk to him?"

She shook her head. "Just saw the name."

"I think it begins," I said, as I pushed the button to return the call.

Katrina answered.

"The Boss available?"

"For you, Mr. Ryder, I think he is especially available."

"Counselor," he said when he got on the line.

"Counselor," I parroted.

"I don't suppose you'd have any idea as to the whereabouts of one Maisie Ivey, do you?"

"Mmm. I may want an attorney present before I answer that."

"Point taken. The reason I ask is that my friend the magistrate down in McDowell County – you remember me mentioning him?"

"Yes."

"Yeah. So, anyway, he calls me and says that the aforementioned Ms. Ivey has gone missing from the Morgan Family Nursing Home."

I did not point out that the correct name of the facility is the Morgan Family Home – without the Nursing. Seemed like a pointless cavil in the larger picture.

"Your name has come up, given the outcome of a previous visit to said Home."

"Mmm hmm," I mumbled.

"Now, no one is saying they saw you there. But, needless to say, Deputy Sheriff Neal Wilson is screaming for a warrant for you. Thinks your prints are all over this, metaphorically speaking."

I repeated my mumble.

"If I were you, I might want to make myself scarce today. If you talk to Queenie, you might pass that along to her, as apparently her name has also surfaced. Someone thinks the two of you might be in cahoots."

"Oh, Nate, I'm shocked."

"Yeah. I know. How do people get these ideas? I need to point out that if you are involved and you need a lawyer, I'll find other representation for you. We have a conflict since, as I recall, your acquaintance with Ms. Ivey began while you were working on a case for me."

44

Knowing they might put a tail on me, I called Zella for a status report rather than drive to her house. Doc Granville said Maisie was malnourished, not in imminent danger but, given all the tranquilizers they had her on, she could have died if we hadn't intervened. He ordered an I.V. and gradually reduced her Valium. She was in remarkably good shape, all things considered. Bruises on her arms were not distinguishable from the normal bruising of people that age, but he was concerned about some on her abdomen, like she'd been punched. He thought there was easily a case for neglect and probably for outright abuse.

"Isn't he required to report that to Social Services?" I asked.

"Yes, he is and he is also an accessory to a kidnapping," she said. "He's going to call his lawyer."

"There's a lot of that going around. I hope we haven't overly imposed on the man."

"He was very clear he was doing this because of his concern for Maisie and that he understands the implications. I also get the idea he is beholden to Queenie."

"I'd be surprised if a lot of people out that way aren't beholden to her in one way or another. Might also be why some people want to see her brought down. Maybe too many people owe her too much."

"Do you know anything about that or are you just making it up?" Zella asked.

"Just making it up. But I don't think it's beyond the realm of possibility. Tell her I'll be going by her house to feed Sonny and make sure everything's in order."

While I was on the phone, Kathy gave me a peck on the cheek and a finger wave, announcing her departure. I believed that one reason our relationship had weathered numerous assaults was that we valued each other's inclination for separateness. That morning I would have liked her company. Someone to sit out on the deck and drink coffee with. It seemed as if others were moving merrily forward from yesterday's drama, but I was beat. I dragged around the house knowing I ought to get going in case the gendarmes were looking for me.

I was measuring out coffee for a new pot when my cell phone rang. Audrey. I really and truly didn't feel like getting back into that drama, but I answered anyway, trying to keep annoyance out of my voice.

"Want to have lunch?" she asked.

Something was different in her voice, nothing I could articulate, a softness, none of that coy, flirty thing. My annoyance lifted. I considered. Why not?

She suggested the Dogwood Café on the east side of town at eleven forty-five, before the height of the lunch crush. That would leave the rest of the morning to go out to Queenie's and check on Sonny, maybe go up the back way and visit Arlo and Sara Jean, see if Pete Haywood had any more contact with them. I could check out Martha Jo's house, see if a sheriff deputy's car was there, then go on up to the big house.

I was still standing in the kitchen when the phone rang again. It was Nate again. I doubted it was good news.

"You near a TV?"

"Yeah, there's one here on the counter."

"Turn it on to the local station."

The fuzz on the little thirteen-inch screen took a few seconds to resolve into a picture. The woman talking looked familiar. I had to lean in close before I recognized her as the nurse from the Morgan Family Home. The Chief was off to one side.

"Two white men," the woman said into a microphone, "both in their late twenties I'd guess. They had a van with a wheelchair lift and everything. Just came in and said they were here to take her, just like that, in broad daylight."

"Did they say where they were taking her?" the reporter asked.

"No. Someone called earlier to say they were coming. But they never really said who they were or where they were taking her."

I thought, and you didn't ask? They were trying to build a case against us, but they sure didn't look good themselves. Criminal negligence was the phrase that came to mind.

"They just acted like they knew her. We thought they were going to take her to a doctor's office maybe, or even to the hospital. She's not very well."

"If she's not very well, why'd you let her go with people you didn't know?" I realized how lucky we'd been that they ran such a slipshod operation. Then again, if they ran a quality place, we wouldn't have had to do what we did.

The camera shifted to the right to take in a man in a sheriff's uniform.

"Deputy Wilson, do you think her life is in danger."

"Absolutely. She was very fragile and on a lot of medication. I think the shock of moving her would be terrible. I don't know who these people are, but we will find them and they will go to prison for this."

"Do you have any idea who would do this?"

"We do have some leads," he said.

"That was McDowell County Deputy Sheriff Neal Wilson whose aunt, Ivey Maisie, was abducted yesterday from the Morgan Family Home in Old Fort. For News Thirteen, this is Tracy Bennett reporting live, from McDowell County."

The scene shifted to the studio in Asheville.

"Thank you Tracy. We will be following this story and will bring you updates as they come in. Anyone with knowledge of the whereabouts of Maisie Ivey should call the McDowell County Sheriff's Office."

"You've got one in the wringer now," Nate said when I got back on the phone.

"Just one?"

"Yeah, 'cause there's a page two to this. Seems a Doctor Jordan Granville has filed a lawsuit in McDowell County this morning alleging elder abuse by the Morgan Family Home, Neal Wilson and unnamed others. He is asking for a restraining order to keep the family and staff of the nursing home away from her and for an injunction to prevent any actions against anyone who was involved in rescuing her and asking that he be given temporary custody of Maisie Ivey until the case is resolved."

"That was quick. Covered a lot of bases, too."

"I've heard of this guy. Old Doc Granville. He's kind of a legend out Leicester way. If he were filing in Buncombe County, it would probably be a slam dunk for him. But ... well, he's not a local hero down there. He does have a good lawyer, though."

"Let me guess. Another friend of yours."

"We've broken bread a few times. Another one of those old rabble-rousers they couldn't run off in the sixties. Been there long enough to be an institution himself."

"Kinda like you."

"With the added advantage of being of the Caucasian persuasion. 'Course, if he wasn't, they would 'a lynched him down there a long time ago. Anyway, if this thing's got a chance at all, it's because of him. But you've got him going up against a member of the Sheriff's Department, another force to be reckoned with. It's gonna be a mess before it's over. Then there's Facilities Services, the state agency that regulates nursing homes. I have a feeling they're gonna be down on that place like white on rice."

I wondered if some other "they" would come down on our rescue party for kidnapping, conspiracy to commit kidnapping, accessory after the fact, and who knew what else.

45

It was time to vacate the premises. I rounded up my wallet and keys, fixed a mug of coffee to go, and set off for the hinterlands.

Sara Jean's truck was gone when I got to the little cabin on the creek. Arlo called for me to come in after I'd knocked and announced myself.

"Gone to town," he said when I asked after his sister. "Probably getting her a little. I hope so. Damn. I love her to pieces and she's been real good to me, but she can sure be a misery if you have to be around her all day. Probably shouldn't be talking that way about my baby sister. Anyway, what brings you back here?"

He waved me toward a chair. A soccer game was in progress on the TV. The push of a button muted the sound.

"Still trying to get Ms. Weaver off the hook for murder," I said in answer to his question. "Just came up the scenic route."

"I'll bet scenic. I've heard about how the Widow Dillingham comports herself."

"There's that, too. But I did wonder if you've heard any more from Pete Hayworth."

Arlo reached in his shirt pocket. I thought he was going to extract a business card left by the preacher, but instead he retrieved a perfectly rolled joint. It looked like one of those little pencils they give you to keep score at miniature golf. He fired it up and handed it toward me. I declined, graciously. He inhaled like he was taking air for the first time, held his breath, and slowly exhaled, coughing slightly.

"Good shit. Sure you don't want some?"

"I'm on the job. Need my wits about me."

There was a pause. Not a pregnant one with the implication that something's going to come sooner or later. This was one of those that could go on for a long time. His attention meandered back to the soccer match.

"So," I repeated, "hear anything from Haywood?"

"Oh, yeah. That's why you came knocking the first time, isn't it? Yeah. Sumbitch finally figured out Daddy's been dead this whole time. Kinda pissed him off. Like we had some obligation to be honest with him. Like real estate people are always straightforward themselves. And don't get me started on all that self-righteous preaching crap, either."

"Okay," I said. "It's a deal."

"What's a deal?"

"I won't get you started on all that self-righteous preaching crap."

"Oh. Anyway, yeah, he came around. Acted, you know, like it was all a big joke at his expense, but you could tell behind that pasted-on grin of his that he would like to have torn my other leg off."

After another hit, he went on. "He said again how much money we could get for the place and we told him we still weren't interested. He started getting all, you know, y'all'll be sorry when they develop this place and you're left out. 'Left out of what?' I said. 'Once they get what they need, you won't get shit for the place.' That's exactly what he said. 'You won't get shit for the place.' I said, 'that's some fine talk for a preacher.' 'It's just the plain truth,' he said."

"They must still think they're going to get Queenie's spread," I said.

"And why is it again they think that's going to happen?"

"Because even if she doesn't go to prison for murder, they're still counting on the pot charges to stick and that she'll forfeit the land and it'll be auctioned off. They think they have it greased and they'll be the ones to pick it up when it's on the block. Maybe before it gets that far."

"Yeah. And how's that lookin'?"

I held my palm up and shrugged.

"All this War on Drugs B.S." I said, slipping into rant mode myself, "it's one area where there's very little of the 'presumed innocent' thing. If they find stuff on your land, you pretty much have to prove it's not yours instead of them having to prove it is. Presumptive, know what I mean?"

"They presume you're guilty."

"That's it. And it's hard to prove the negative, that you're not. That's the Catch-22. It was on her land. They've sent aging grandmothers to prison because somebody grew a couple of pot plants on their property without them knowing about it."

"Yeah. I've heard about that. I smoke the stuff because a doctor recommends it for pain." He looked at me. "Do you get that? Chronic pain where your arm used to be?"

"Used to," I said. "Took a lot of drugs for a while but started to get in big trouble. Wouldn't stop drinking and the meds and the booze didn't mix well. Or, mixed too well. Anyway, seemed like I when I quit taking the meds, the pain started going away. I mean, I still have days, and sometimes it seems like the arm's still there and aches like hell."

"Phantom pain."

"Yeah. But, mostly, it's OK."

"So maybe there's hope," he said. A smile broke out. "But,

then I wouldn't have an excuse to smoke the stuff."

"You ever worry about getting busted?"

"Since there's no legal medical marijuana in North Carolina, I could. But I'm counting on them being too busy going after old ladies to bother with us crippled folk."

I liked Arlo's dark sense of humor and thought he'd probably be fun to spend some time with, although when this case was all over, I doubted I'd have much occasion to come back this way. "Ought to be heading on up to Queenie's," I said. "Gotta go feed the dog for her."

"Where's she off to?"

"Ah, there's another long story you don't want to know about."

He shrugged.

"Well, when you see her, tell her I said, 'hi.'"

I said I would and was about to let myself out the door, when I turned back.

"Stan didn't happen to be the one you got this pot from, was he?"

"I'm not one to speak ill of the dead," he said, the grin returning to his face.

It would be disingenuous to say that the possibility of seeing Martha Jo on her deck au naturel didn't occur to me, although I doubted I'd be greeted as warmly as I had in the past, whatever her manner of dress. I didn't want to push my luck since she could still file charges for criminal trespass. All the scenarios I could make up turned out to be moot, anyway, since her car was gone from the front and there were no signs of life evident to the casual passerby.

With the exception of Sonny, it was equally as quiet at Queenie's. He greeted me as if I was the one person in the universe who could make him happy. I had the key to the house and went in to find food for him. As I filled his bowl in the kitchen I thought if he wiggled any more the skin might shake off his frame. Walking down the steps to my car after I'd closed up the house, I felt the way I've heard parents say they do when they leave their kids on the first day of school. The combination of reproach and forlornness as he sat at the bottom of the front steps, head cocked to the side as if asking "where are you going, when will you be back, do you have to leave?" caused an ache in my chest. I thought about what I was doing the rest of the day, got out of the car, opened the back door and called him. He hopped in. The thing about dogs is they have no short term memory for perceived affronts, unlike cats, who will carry resentments for days. For months. Forever.

We went home to Cove Road and I led Sonny onto the back deck. Later, the cats would probably let me know how they felt about this intruder. I wouldn't have been surprised if we didn't see them again until he left. I knew he could find the creek for water but filled a bowl for him anyway. It never occurred to me he'd run off.

At eleven-thirty, I was parked across the street from the bank building housing the offices of HPA. My phone rang. It was Audrey.

"Would you mind if we took a walk before lunch?" she asked.

I was intrigued. We agreed to walk along the Swannanoa River where it ran along the edge of a nearby youth sports complex.

46

Five minutes later I saw her come out of the building and get in her car. A nondescript green car got behind her as she exited the parking lot. I fell in line. While we were in traffic, I got close enough to read the green car's plate number. I called out "Dominic" to my phone.

"Dom," I said when Nate's other investigator answered. "I've got another license plate for you to track, although, I'm guessing it's going to be another stolen one." I called out the numbers.

"I'm on it," he said. "Get back to you ASAP."

At this time of day, the parking area for the ball fields was largely unoccupied. Audrey turned off the approach road and turned left. The green car followed and turned right, parking about fifty yards away. I pulled in alongside Audrey.

When I walked up to her, I held out my hand, as I would in greeting any friend. She took it, leaned close and gave me a kiss on the cheek.

I wasn't sure what the appropriate response to that gesture was but was relieved of an obligation to make one when she said, "Thanks for coming."

"I think your people are following you," I said, falling in alongside her as we headed down to the river.

"What do you mean, 'my people'?"

"People you work for. The people who you claimed were following you but actually have been keeping tabs on me."

She stopped mid-stride and looked at me.

"You knew about that?"

"I'm a detective, Audrey, remember? And that guy you had following me? I hope he has another line of work."

"I didn't have him follow you."

"Whoever."

A large rock outcropping that spilled into the river made a nice waterside seat.

"God," she said, "I can't believe I'd gotten myself all worked up to tell you what's been going on and you knew all along. I'm such a ninny. That's what I wanted to talk about. And to tell you I'm leaving."

"Leaving what?"

"Leaving here."

"Asheville?"

"Yes," she said, annoyed. "If you knew, why did you keep meeting with me?"

"Because I enjoyed your company. You know, at first I thought you were a phony. Then I figured out you were only being phony, playing at it, acting a part. I wanted to find out what was beneath that. I have to admit it was fun knowing you were playing a game and you not knowing I knew."

"That's mean."

"I suppose. And I could have told you what I suspected. But this way, I felt I was in control of things. And, like I said, I enjoy your company."

I thought I detected her face reddening although it could have just been the way the light reflected off the water.

"Well, I think you're nice, too."

"Why tell me about this now? And why leave?"

She shifted so her whole body was facing me. "I'm afraid something bad is going to happen. I had no idea what was going on when Chet suggested a little game with you. That's how he talked about it. Our little game. I knew he had an interest in the land out there. He said they were afraid all this murder and pot business was going to mess up their plans. When he found out you were working for Nate Chatham, he thought I could get you to tell me what you knew about the investigation. It didn't seem like a big deal. And it was kind of fun, being a detective, like you. I felt special, doing it."

She turned away again, like she was looking for something in the river.

"But then, when I couldn't find out anything, he started to get mad. Threatened to fire me. This wasn't even part of my real job. That's when I realized there was more to it. I don't think I'm any dummy, but it did take a while to dawn on me that they were involved in the stuff at Ms. Weaver's and that's why they wanted to know what you knew and why Chet was freaking out."

She turned back to me.

"I'm sorry, Rick. I really do like you. You ... Well, you were nice to me. Even when I was being a bitch. And you did seem to like being with me. That wasn't an act, was it?"

"No. I told you. I enjoyed – do enjoy – your company."

"Will you come see me?" she asked.

"Where?"

"Charlotte."

"Ah. The big city."

"Well, bigger, anyway."

"What are you going to do?"

"I'm going to design clothes for a woman who owns a boutique down there. I don't know if I can make any money at it, but it's what I want to do. I've got a degree in textile design. I was recruited into advertising and I thought I could make a lot of money fast and then go do what I wanted to. In a way I'm glad things turned out like they have or I might have stayed there thinking someday I'd be making a lot of money."

"Did you tell Presley you were going to tell me what was going on?"

"God, no. I haven't even told him I'm leaving."

"When are you going?"

"Friday."

"This Friday?"

She nodded.

"Friday's a long time. You know that whoever is driving that green car is going to report to Chet and he's going to wonder what's going on, why you're seeing me when your're not on assignment for him."

"I know. And he'll be relentless in getting me to tell him and I'll eventually break down. I don't want him to know. Let him sweat a little wondering what's up."

I didn't think she should go back to work. Ever.

"What if you call in sick for the afternoon? Tell them you think it might be something you ate. I'll follow you to your apartment and hang around there for an hour or so, long enough for the guy in the green car to imagine what we might be doing. He'll tell Presley you're having a nooner with me. That'll give you cover for the afternoon."

"It'll also piss him off, since he's been trying to get in my pants since I went to work there, not so subtly implying that my career would move along faster if I had sex with him." She shivered. "Ooo. Creepy. I thought keeping tabs on you would make up for me not, you know ..."

I kept my imagination in check.

Sitting on the rock had made my butt numb. We got up and walked twenty more yards along the river bank until the path ran out, then headed back.

"You didn't say if you'd come down to see me," she said.

"If I get down there, I'll look you up. Probably won't be making a special visit."

She looked defeated, like the air had just been let out of her.

"I am a married man, you know."

"I know. She's very lucky."

"I'm very lucky," I said.

When we got back to the parking lot, I pointed to our observer.

"See, that's what I was talking about. Might as well have a sign on the car that says, 'I'm watching you.'"

As we stood there, I remembered the last young woman I befriended who wanted to change her life. She didn't get the opportunity. Maybe Audrey could extricate herself from her current circumstances without getting killed over it.

We hugged before getting into our cars. I'm not a father, so don't know for sure, but I think that's what it felt like. Parental.

I called Kathy on the drive to Audrey's place to help me stay grounded. I told her what was going on.

"So, what are you going to do for the hour or so you're there at her place?" she asked.

"I don't know. Maybe she has a Scrabble game."

The green car did follow us and parked about thirty yards away, where the driver could keep tabs on her place. He either didn't realize or care that we could also keep tabs on him.

She didn't have a Scrabble game. She did have Trivial Pursuit. Panic overtook me for a moment when she said she was going to change into something more comfortable. I relaxed when she came back wearing loose-fitting gray sweat pants and a T-shirt with a sailboat on the back and "SOUTHPORT" printed on the front. She fixed us a tuna salad with some greens and crusty Italian bread which we ate while demonstrating our collective deficit in identifying random, insignificant information.

"Want to see some of my clothes?" she asked after a while.

My eyes widened.

"Stuff I designed, I mean." She produced a half-dozen dresses and a portfolio of drawings. It looked like she had some talent although I knew little about fashion except for what appeared in the Sunday New York Times style supplements.

I recognized one creation.

"That's what you were wearing the day I met you."

"I wanted to make an impression."

"You did."

After the fashion show, I asked about her plans for Charlotte.

"I'll be staying with Jeannette – that's the woman I'll be working for – until I can get my own place. I thought I'd leave Chet a note on Friday afternoon. The guys all leave early for the weekend, out playing golf or whatever."

"It would probably be a good idea if you were gone before Chet gets the note when he goes in Monday morning. And I wouldn't give anybody a forwarding address right away, either. Get a post office box down there and have a friend you can trust pick up your mail and send it on to you. If the folks at Hensley Presley et al really want to find you, they will. But you don't have to make it easy for them."

"I'm running away, aren't I?"

"More like running toward something. Something you've wanted to do for a long time."

"Can I call you sometime? Just to talk, I mean."

I hesitated a beat.

"Sure," I said, knowing I'd have to tell Kathy that I'd said it.

We hugged again at the door. I could feel her chest start to shake.

"You're going to be OK," I said, fighting my own tears.

We disengaged ourselves and I walked to my car. Her door was shut when I looked back. The green car was still parked down the road. I waved at the driver. His return glare triggered a cold ripple through my body.

47

I called out "Zella home" to the car phone. Queenie answered and reported that Maisie continued to show signs of improvement. She'd eaten some solid food and, although she still didn't seem to know where she was, they all were optimistic about her recovery since what she seemed mostly to need recovery from was having been in the Marion Family Home.

On the way back to the house to check on Sonny, I thought about Audrey and wondered if she would take my advice to get out of town. I was glad she had a plan but I knew it would be hard to pick up and leave like that. I felt an ache in the back of my throat.

The car phone rang. It was Katrina calling to tell me that Doc Granville had gotten his injunction and the state was going to shut down the Morgan Family Home as soon as all the current patients could be placed. I knew some families had been happy to have a place like that where they could get those pesky, doddering, old fools who were complicating their lives, out of the way. It was going to be tough on other families, those who only used places like the Morgan Family Home because of the absence of alternatives.

A car was parked on the side of the road about fifty yards from my house. I slowed to a crawl. No one was visible in the vehicle. It was not a place a visitor would park. At the head of Cove Road there is a sign stating: "Pavement ends 1 mile." It doesn't say what happens after that, which is that it enters national forest property and becomes gravel and dirt. Our property is the last house on the paved road. My nearest neighbor's house is two hundred yards before you get to mine. We appreciate that the sign discourages random traffic. Occasionally, some adventuresome or clueless person heads out this way, but usually anybody on the road either lives there or has come to visit.

The vehicle could have broken down, but something about it didn't seem right. Sleuth intuition. I parked and walked back to check it out. The doors were locked. There was interesting communications apparatus inside. The license plate was a permanent one, the kind used by governmental bodies, perhaps some species of law enforcement. The only reason I could think of for parking there was to surprise whoever they had come to see. Precautions seemed reasonable.

Back in the Honda, I drove slowly past my driveway into the forest. A hundred yards in, I pulled as far off the road as I could. Keeping out of sight of the house, I walked through the woods toward my back yard, angling around so that I would come at it from the back, gambling that, if somebody was waiting for me, they would be watching the front.

My plan was to get into the basement without being noticed. Kathy and I each owned a gun. Hers stayed upstairs in the nightstand on her side of the bed. I kept mine in a cabinet in the basement. I'm not a big fan of handguns, but I thought it prudent to prepare for the possibility that if people were in the house, they hadn't come for a social call.

Standing at the back door, I glanced up to the deck. Sonny was lying on his belly watching me. I could see the tip of his tail behind him waving at me. I held my hand up toward him, the universal dog language sign to "stay." I hoped he was fluent in universal dog. I opened the door cautiously. To the right were stairs leading up to the kitchen. Stairs to the left led down to the basement. I was about to enter our code into the alarm pad on the wall, when I realized the light was shining green, meaning it had already been disabled.

Voices drifted from above, probably from the living room. I couldn't make out much of what they were saying. Names were mentioned that meant nothing to me. Some laughter. I went on down the stairs, opened the basement door, and stepped inside, pulling the door behind me before flipping the light switch. I slipped off my shoes and padded lightly into the room, past my workout equipment, to the cabinet. The revolver was where it was supposed to be. In a separate drawer was a box of .38 Special ammunition. I loaded the gun and cocked it.

Then I punched 9-1-1 on my cell phone.

Moving silently, the way my father had taught me that Indians had walked in the woods, I reached the kitchen door. I was right about where the voices were coming from. I crouched so that they wouldn't be able to see me over the kitchen counters and duck-walked toward the dining area. It sounded like they were trash-talking about co-workers, trying to outdo each other in put-downs. They were having a grand time. I let the gun lead me as I stood and looked into the living room. They were sitting next to each other on the couch, backs to me, their heads and shoulders visible.

"Raise your hands over your heads slowly. I have a gun aimed toward you. I would really hate to use it because it would royally piss off my wife, with the mess and all. But I will use it. I have used it before. You may have read about it. It was in all the papers. OK. So, up with 'em."

One of them said, "Ryder, you—"

"Shut up. I said, 'Raise your hands.'"

They exchanged a glance. I fired the gun over their heads and into the front wall of the room.

"See. Now I'm in trouble with my wife. RAISE YOUR FUCKING HANDS, YOU ASSHOLES!"

Slowly, four hands rose. Sonny came to life and began barking wildly out on the deck, defending the homestead.

"OK, gentlemen. Now, let's rise, slowly, and turn to face me."

"Ryder, you are in deep shit."

"Why, Aaron Presley, I do believe. Funny meeting you here. And, Deputy Wilson. This is a treat. You're kind of out of your jurisdiction, aren't you, Neal?"

"You are in so much shit, Ryder," Wilson said. "Where's my aunt?"

"What makes you think I would know anything about your aunt. And what brings you on this goose chase, Presley?"

Presley started to let his arms drop. I aimed the pistol straight at him.

"Don't even think about it. Like I said, I have shot a man. I'll shoot another if I have to. Of course, I only winged that guy. But I understand it hurts like hell to be shot in the arm. Who knows, you might lose the thing, end up like me," I said, thrusting my useless left stump in his direction.

Sonny continued his hell raising. I wanted to step back so I could open the sliding glass door to the deck and let Sonny in but I would have had to put the gun down to do it, so I called out, "SONNY! BE QUIET."

It worked.

I returned my attention to the two intruders.

"I am curious why you guys didn't come in uniform. Would have made it harder for me to claim I didn't know who you were. 'I had no idea they were lawmen, Officer,' I can hear myself saying.

'They just came into my house. Never did identify themselves. I didn't know what they were doing here.' That's how I imagine it will go if I have to shoot you, because if I shoot one of you, I might as well do both. And make no mistake, I will win in a shoot-out."

At that point, I was stalling for time. 9-1-1 had taken the information that my house had been broken into and the perpetrators were still on the premises. I had told them I could hear voices upstairs. Any minute now, the cavalry should appear.

"We're here to arrest you for the kidnapping of Maisie Ivey," Presley said. "You shoot us, you will be in much worse shit than you already are. You do know what they do to people who kill lawmen, don't you."

"You are so full of it, Presley," I said, reasonably sure he was, indeed, full of it. If there had been a warrant for my arrest, I would have heard from Nate. I was sure of it.

I was working out what to do next, when I heard the first vehicle pull into the drive.

48

"Presley, what the hell are you doing here?"

The inquisitor was one of two uniformed deputies in my living room. The name plate under his badge read, C. Ellington. Heavy knocks on the front door had signaled their arrival along with the announcement that they were Buncombe County Sheriff's people.

"This guy kidnapped an old woman down in Old Fort," Deputy Presley said, then turned to his buddy. "And this is the old lady's nephew, Neal Wilson."

"Yeah," said Ellington, who had established himself in charge of the proceedings, "we've heard an old lady was taken from a nursing home down there. But it wasn't any kidnapping." He was an older guy with a well-nurtured paunch, maybe had a desk job once but didn't like it or got busted back to patrol for some offense. He looked disgusted.

"What do you mean?" Wilson said. "She's my aunt. They came and took her."

"They're saying she was rescued," the big guy said, then looked at me. "And you can put the piece down."

"Rescued?" Wilson said, disbelief radiating from his face. The blood vessels in his neck were swollen and pulsing. I could see he wanted to hit somebody but he wasn't sure who that should be.

Another county cruiser came up the drive. Two uniforms got out and went around back, to come in the way I had. Ellington told his colleague to go to meet them and tell them there had been no break-in here. "Or any other crime, for that matter."

"No break-in here," he repeated to those of us in the living room. "A misunderstanding."

"There's no misunderstanding," I said. "I was coming home and I saw their car parked along the road. Nobody parks there, so I was suspicious. I and drove into the forest a little way, parked, and came back to the house from the rear. When I came inside, I heard two people talking. That's when I called 9-1-1. I got my gun from the basement and came upstairs and found these two. I was just trying to understand why they were in my house when you arrived."

"He threatened us," Wilson said. "He fired his fucking weapon at us."

"What is it you were doing here, anyway?" the deputy-in-charge asked Wilson.

"I told you," he said. "They kidnapped my aunt."

"And I told you, there's been no kidnapping."

"Okay. Then, he's the guy who took my aunt out of the nursing home without my permission."

"Yeah, well if you're lucky, they won't charge you with elder abuse and neglect, is what I hear. And Presley, you never said what you're doing here."

"Came along to support my old friend."

"Okay," said Ellington. "Here's what's going to happen. Presley. You and Wilson are going to leave and pretend you have never been here. And Mr. Ryder. You never saw these two out here today."

"I want him charged with assault with a deadly weapon,"

Wilson said.

"You forget, boy, that you were never here. Remember that now?"

"You try to do something about an alleged assault and I'll have your ass for illegal entry," I said to Presley.

Ellington was working hard to keep himself under control.

"Ryder, you also seem to have forgotten that these two were never here. Have y'all got the concept? This didn't happen. You heard some noises, Ryder, turned out to be some squirrels got in the house that were tearing around, you thought they were people making all that racket.

"You other two, I don't know how you're going to explain your absence from whatever the hell you were supposed to be doing this afternoon, but it will not involve having been out here. I hope everybody understands because if you don't, all three of you are going to wind up in jail charged with some felony. Is that perfectly clear?"

I didn't want them to get off like that but I also didn't want to muddy the waters more than they already were. The injunctions that had been issued were only temporary and, while I was confident that when Maisie regained her senses she would be a witness for our side, it was not a done deal. I did something I was not known for. I shut up.

After Wilson and Presley left, muttering between themselves as they went, Ellington said, "I'm serious, Ryder. This never happened. If I hear you've been spreading some rumor about sheriff's deputies being out here today, I'm going to be very unhappy. You do understand that, don't you?"

"Sir. Yes, sir," I said while giving a mock salute.

"And don't be a smart ass."

Ellington gathered everybody who had responded to the call out on the front lawn, presumably to make sure they were all on the same page, the one where it said that Mr. Ryder had mistaken some woodland creatures for intruders, and that no one had seen their two brethren who had been engaged in some unauthorized investigating.

I assume that Messrs. Wilson and Presley's plan had been to intimidate me or Kathy, whomever of us got home first, into telling them where Maisie was. An amateur stunt. I wanted to get them for being in my house without my permission. And I wanted to know how they got past the alarm. I wondered if, being officers of the law, they could simply call the security company that was advertised on a small sign stuck in a garden near the front door and tell them they needed to get in the house. It was the kind of thing that was hard for me to let go of. My reasonable friends and loved ones would point out how hanging onto resentments had complicated my life in the past.

I called Queenie and rehashed the events. "The good news is, they don't know where Maisie is and I hope that sheriff's guy scared them off."

"Yeah, I'd hate for there to be a shoot-out between you gunslingers out here, especially now that she seems to be rallying by the hour. She recognized me a few minutes ago, although she's still pretty disoriented. That's understandable, since Zella's house, nice as it is and all, isn't much like her old mountain house."

I had my finger on the speed dial number for Nate to ask him what he thought about trying to nail those two Keystone Kop deputies, when Kathy called.

"The guy who wants me to get into the water park business has asked us to have dinner with him."

"Us, like you and me?"

"Yes. Those 'us.'"

She suggested the Black Forest at six. I said I'd be there, and filled her in on the recent drama at Chez Ryder.

"Just a hole through the dry wall," I said.

"You and guns," she said, as if that explained it all.

I'd been pacing the living room with my cell phone since the cops left. When I finally sat down out on the deck with a glass of ice tea, my hand shook. It took a minute to realize that the aftermath of an adrenalin rush was going through my whole body. It was at times like this that I appreciated – in spite of people like Presley and Wilson and a few other unhelpful cops I've had the misfortune to interact with – what law enforcement professionals confront on a regular basis. Most cops I'd dealt with over the years – city, county, state, the feds – were straight-up people trying to do a good job. Just like the rest of us.

Sonny sat at my feet, head between his paws. I noticed that the cats had come up on the deck, while maintaining a pretense that they weren't interested in either Sonny or me. After sitting for a few minutes, I got dinner for the menagerie, showered, and dressed for the evening's outing.

I was halfway to the restaurant when the car phone rang. I called out "hello" to it.

A voice sounding as if it was coming through cotton said, "Just want you to know it ain't over, Ryder."

I couldn't tell if was Tweedledum or Tweedledee.

49

A wave of insecurity rolled over me as a Denzel Washington look-alike rose from his seat across from Kathy.

"Lemond," Kathy said, "this is my husband, Rick. Rick, Lemond Morris."

"Leh-mond," I repeated as he gripped my hand. A firm grip. I liked it.

"Yes," he said, then spelled the name to be sure I had it right. "I've never heard anybody else called it, either. It means 'the world' in French, probably picked up by the Algerians in my ancestry."

My neurosis subsided as I leaned over and got a kiss from my wife. She had a glass of white wine in front of her. Lemond was drinking Scotch, its aroma reaching out across the table to me like an old friend. I ignored it and ordered my standard tonic and lime.

"Kathy tells me you had to deal with some intruders today," Lemond said.

When I had told Kathy about it, I hadn't gotten to the 'this never happened' part. I figured Lemond was safe, but, you never knew who knew whom, who talked to whom. "Yeah, I did."

"She said you had to shoot at them."

It did sound exciting.

"I had to get their attention. I wasn't shooting at them. Just near enough so they'd know I meant it when I said I'd shoot."

"What was the outcome?"

"Sheriff came. Everybody went away. Got a hole in the front wall of the living room."

"Sounds like you don't much want to talk about it," he said.

I smiled at him and gave a little nod.

"Fair enough. Well, I've never eaten here. What's good?"

Dinner was pleasant. We talked about the water park business, how he got into it, what he saw as the future, why it would be a good move for Kathy to get involved. He talked about his family and showed off pictures of his wife and kids. When he mentioned being a tennis player, we agreed to play sometime. The energy was good. I relaxed. It was not yet seven-thirty when we said our goodbyes.

My phone rang almost as soon as I got in the car. It was from Nate's personal number, a rare occurrence.

"Where are you?" he asked. On the phone, his deep baritone always had a melodramatic quality, like Orson Wells narrating *The War of the Worlds*.

"In my car, heading home."

"Call me when you get there."

"What ..."

"Just call me."

I had to force myself to pay attention to the road as my mind wandered Fantasy Land, wanting to figure out what this was about.

Three minutes later, the phone rang again.

"What are you doing?" It was Kathy.

"What do you mean what am ..."

"You just ran the red light at Long Shoals."

I saw her in my rear view mirror.

"Oh. Thanks. I just got a disturbing call from Nate."

"What about?"

"He didn't say. Just said, 'call me when you get home.'"

"Well, pay attention."

"Why don't you get in front of me? That way I'll have something to pay attention to."

When we arrived home fifteen minutes later without incident, I went directly to the deck and called Nate.

"Sorry to be so enigmatic," he said, "but I thought you should be sitting down for this. Are you?"

"Oh, come on, Nate. What is it?"

"Audrey Hollingsworth's been murdered."

50

I couldn't make sense of it, like trying to put something into your computer that the machine doesn't recognize. After an interminable silence, he added, "She was found in her apartment about two-thirty this afternoon."

That would have been soon after I left.

"Who found her?" I asked, my voice sounding as if it came from somewhere outside me.

"Some guy works for HPA, says he'd been keeping an eye on her because of her complaints about being stalked."

My hand shook so hard I couldn't keep the phone to my ear.

"Nate. Can I call you back in a few minutes?"

"I'm here," he said.

I was crying when Kathy joined me on the deck. She didn't say anything.

"Audrey's dead," I choked.

"Oh, Rick, I'm sorry."

I was up and pacing. "Goddam it. Here I am, getting her to play games with these people, like it's some ... recreational thing. I mean ..."

"Rick. It's not your fault."

"So, whose fault is it?"

"Oh, come on. You know who's behind it. That's whose fault it is."

"But if I ..."

"Stop it! Quit wallowing in self-pity. You didn't do it. These are bad people, Rick. And I know you're replaying what happened last year. And that wasn't your fault either. Let it go. Be sad. Grieve. Fall to pieces. That's OK. But, it's not your fault."

"Hold me," I said.

Ten minutes had passed before I remembered to call him back.

"You okay?" he asked.

"No."

"I'm sorry. It gets worse."

"They think I did it," I said, thinking the worst.

"You are a 'person of interest,' as they say. Tom Henderson wants to see you in his office in the morning. LaTonya Graham and I can meet with you about eight so you can fill her in on what's been going on."

"LaTonya Graham?"

"Your new attorney."

"LaTonya?"

"You'll like her, I guarantee it. You saw her the other day in the coffee shop at the courthouse."

After telling him I'd see them in the morning, I didn't know what to do with myself. I felt self-conscious in my own house. My hand felt huge, like it belonged to someone else. I wandered back onto the deck to rejoin Kathy but couldn't sit down. I said I was going to take a walk up in the woods.

"Want company?"

"Thanks, but no."

A path we had landscaped behind the house led to a rocky outcropping hanging over the creek. I sat there and cried until there was nothing left. I closed my eyes and let the sound of the water wash over me. The sun began to hemorrhage out of the western sky.

I was still sad when I joined Kathy in the bedroom. "I gotta get outa this business."

"No, you don't. You remember that girl in Leicester you found?"

"Yes, I remember. I know what you're going to say. I might have saved her life."

"It's true. You can't go back to sitting behind a desk. You'd go crazy. Crazier."

"Thanks."

We made love. Easy. Like the two old lovers we were. The sadness returned almost immediately after she fell asleep.

Nate was installed in a booth at the Downtown Bakery when I arrived the next morning, all two-hundred seventy-five pounds of himself, the unlit stogie wandering around in his mouth. As I approached, coffee in hand, I could see only the dark hair of the woman seated across from him. When I came alongside the table, I had keep my jaw from dropping open. Although I had seen the woman in the foursome leaving Nate's table when I arrived the other day, the group had left quickly and I didn't get a good look at her. I wondered how it was I hadn't.

"Counselor, this is LaTonya Graham," Nate said. "LaTonya, Rick Ryder."

We shook hands. She smiled as if she was absolutely delighted to meet me. Her skin reminded me of polished pecan wood. I did a silent "which side of the booth should I sit on" assessment, not wanting to appear too eager to sit next to the beautiful young woman, but aware that no other adult human could fit next to Nate.

"LaTonya. Counselor," I said, my eyes going from one to the other as I slid in next to her.

"So, now the other one's in the wringer," Nate said. "Must be painful."

"You adapt," I said. "But, yes, hearing of Audrey's death was hard."

"I'm sorry," Nate said.

"Yeah. Everybody's sorry," I said. "My wife tells me it's not my fault. But I was at her house yesterday afternoon, Nate. I know that's not why they killed her. But it may have precipitated it. I can't help feeling guilty."

"Your wife's right. But, if it makes you feel better, go ahead, feel guilty."

"OK. Let's drop that. She's dead. I'm sad. And we know who did it."

"We do?" LaTonya said.

"The guy who followed me to her condo."

"Do you know who he is?" she asked.

"No. But the cops know him. I assume it's the guy who found her." I gave them a synopsis of the previous day, from the time Audrey left the bank parking lot to the time I left her apartment.

"And the green car followed you the whole time?" LaTonya asked.

"Followed Audrey," I said.

When I finished my coffee, she said, "Let's go see Henderson and get this over with."

A flood of memories washed over me when we walked through the glass doors of the police station. It didn't help that I had to be there because of the murder of another young girl although this time I was merely a "person of interest" and hadn't been arrested for the crime. LaTonya and I waved at the duty officer behind the Plexiglas window.

The door was open when we reached Henderson's second

floor office. The Lieutenant was on the phone and waved us in, signaling toward the two chairs facing his desk. Detective Lieutenant Tom Henderson was a straight-up guy. He had let me know in a number of ways that he didn't really think I was the perp of that previous murder but that he'd had to go through the motions since that's what had been expected of him.

As he was saying, "I love you, too," he was standing up. He re-cradled the phone and looked toward us. "Ms. Graham. Rick. Thanks for coming."

I knew protocol dictated that someone lower down the law enforcement food chain would ordinarily conduct this ritual. I imagined his involvement was in part to atone for how I had been dealt with in our last encounter.

"I didn't understand this was an optional appearance," I said.

He smiled.

"Well, we could have come to you."

"This is fine, thanks."

"Okay. Let's get to it."

He picked up his phone and pushed a button.

"Jennifer. Will you meet us in Interview Room 2?"

He hung up and let his gaze travel between my new attorney and me.

"She's going to record our conversation, unless you have an objection, Counselor."

"No objection, Lieutenant."

"Do I get Mirandized?" I asked.

"We're just getting a statement from you, Rick. You're not under arrest."

LaTonya and I trailed Henderson to the conference room. We were introduced to Jennifer Jenkins, apparently a civilian from the lack of uniform or rank. In the center of the small room were an old wooden table and four equally ancient wooden chairs. A couple of folding chairs were stacked against a wall. I imagined that some years earlier there would have been an ash tray. Henderson and Ms. Jenkins sat across from me and my new mouthpiece.

Jenkins pushed a button on a small tape recorder. Henderson disclosed to the machine the date, who we were and what we were there for.

"Mr. Ryder. Will you state your full name, your address and what you do for a living."

"Richard Raymond Ryder, 702 Cove Road, Asheville, North Carolina. I am a licensed private investigator. I am also licensed to practice before the bar in Ohio and North Carolina."

"Please tell us where you were from approximately noon to six p.m. yesterday."

"From about noon to one o'clock I was with Audrey Hollingsworth out at the new soccer complex off Gashes Creek Road."

"And what were you doing there?"

"Walking and talking."

"What was the nature of your relationship with Ms. Hollingsworth?"

I looked over at LaTonya. She shrugged.

"I first met her when she asked to meet with me in my capacity as a private investigator." I went on from there to describe our first and subsequent meetings, culminating in the previous day's walk and the trip to her apartment. I explained about the green car and gave him the license number. "I think you'll find that either the car or the plate or both are stolen," I said.

"Why do you think that?"

"Previous experience and detective work. When I left her apartment, that car was still parked up the road. That was the last time I saw or spoke to her."

"What time was that?"

"About 2:15. I was driving home and got a call from Nate's

office. I noted it was 2:25."

"You were driving home?"

I was about to venture onto shaky ground. I didn't want to perjure myself, but if I told him about Wilson and Presley at my house, a whole other can of worms would fly open. One that Deputy Ellington had taken pains to emphasize didn't exist. I stuck with some facts. "Yes. And I was there until about 5:40 when I left to meet my wife for dinner."

"You went straight home?"

"Yes."

"Anyone else there at your house?"

I wondered if he knew something or was just going where the conversation led.

"Two cats and a dog."

After a pause, Henderson asked, "Anything else you think we should know?"

"That's about it."

Henderson looked over at the transcriptionist. "Thanks, Jennifer." He looked back at me. "She'll be back in a few minutes with your statement typed for you to sign." When Jennifer had left, the detective said, "You think HPA is behind this?"

"No doubt in my mind."

"And it is connected to the murder of Brian McFadden out at Queenie Weaver's place."

"Absolutely. And Audrey Hollingsworth had come to that conclusion as well."

As we were walking out of the police station, LaTonya said, "You really didn't have to go into all that with him, you know. You could have just stated what you were doing that day, at the time in question, leave it at that."

"You gave me the go ahead when he asked how I knew her.

And, I have this compulsive need to explain myself. So, I really couldn't have done it any other way."

"Oh, God. A lawyer's worst nightmare – the client who has to explain himself."

She said she would let me know if she heard anything else and asked me to do likewise with her. We shook hands and she gave me another big smile. I doubted she could banter like her boss, but she was a whole lot easier on the eyes.

Standing on the sidewalk, deciding what to do next, I smelled Scotch. Looking around for the source, I realized it was a memory. I hadn't been to an AA meeting in days. I called my sponsor.

"Just checking in. Woman I knew, was working with, was murdered yesterday right after I'd been with her."

"Feel like drinking?" he asked.

"Not right now. I did last night when a guy I was having dinner with had a Scotch. It smelled awfully good."

"Been to a meeting?"

I said I planned to go at noon.

"Probably see you there," he said.

That was Jim for you. Matter of fact. No drama. When he asked if you wanted a drink and you said, "No," he would say, "Good. Go to a meeting." If you said yes, he would say, "Good. Go to a meeting." It was pretty simple with Jim. An old timer, as they say, although only a few years older than me, he'd been going to AA since he was in his twenties. It had taken me somewhat longer to get there.

By the end of the phone call, the odor of liquor had disappeared.

The private duty nurse answered when I called Zella's house. She got Queenie on the line who told me her former neighbor was talking coherently. She didn't remember where she'd been before arriving at Zella's, but said she was glad to be where she was now. She did recall arguing with her nephew on the way down to Old Fort. She couldn't understand why he was making her do that, although she was pretty sure it had something to do with him and his wife wanting to get control of her property. Queenie didn't have the heart to tell her that the house had burned down, but she knew that sometime soon Maisie was going to start asking about going back.

We had just ended the call when my phone rang. It didn't recognize the number it was being called from.

"Hi, this is Rick," I announced.

"Ryder ..."

I recognized the voice.

"Martha Jo?"

On a landline you'd hear a dial tone if the caller hung up. With cell phones, there's just silence.

"Martha Jo? ... Martha Jo?"

I held the phone out in front of me and looked at its face. "Call ended 10:17 AM."

I pushed the button to recall the number. After ten rings I hung up. I knew I should leave it alone. I thought about Audrey. I couldn't leave it alone.

51

I went out to the house to prepare for a trip out to the widow's place. Sonny was morose, lying on the deck, head in his paws. I presumed he missed his mistress. So much for the idea that dogs have no memory. The cats were on the deck with him. They were as far away on the perimeter as they could get, but still in the vicinity. I thought I might have to get them a dog when this was all over.

The revolver was where I had returned it the day before. I took it from the cabinet before calling Nate. I wanted someone to know where I was going. Katrina said he wasn't available but she would give him the message.

I called my volunteer fire chief friend, Bobby Hadley, and told him about the call from Martha Jo's number. "Might be nothing," I said. "She could have been drunk, maybe had second thoughts about calling and hung up."

"Little early in the day for that," Bobby said.

"Not so much for Martha Jo. But with what's been going on, I want to check it out."

I explained about Audrey.

"God. That's terrible. Rick, I need to call you back. We're just cleaning up here at a brush fire. I should be back at the station in about ten minutes."

I passed Queenie's house and was headed down the road to Martha Jo's when my car phone rang again.

"So, how can I help?" Bobby asked.

"I'm on my way to the Dillingham place. Know where that is, down ..."

"Yeah, I know. What's going on?"

"Not sure. You still carrying that .45 in your truck?"

"Always."

"I don't know that you'll need it, but ..."

"You never know," he said.

"You got it."

"Be there in fifteen, twenty minutes."

I pulled in alongside Martha Jo's car, reached into my glove box and retrieved the gun. Sitting there, .38 in hand, I thought I should wait for Bobby. But, if something had happened to her, minutes could be critical. When I stepped out of the Honda, I stuffed the gun in the small of my back between my t-shirt and the sweatshirt I had on over it.

There was no response when I knocked on the front door. I turned the knob, pushed the door open with a foot and stepped into the room. A voice from behind the door said, "So nice of you to come, Rick." It was a well-oiled voice, one used to greet the Sunday morning faithful.

As my eyes adjusted to the light, I saw three people in front of me. Martha Jo and Presley were on the couch. She was naked. There was a body on the floor. All three were bound with duct tape.

I turned back toward the door just as man pointing a gun at me stepped from behind it.

"Hello, Haywood," I said.

"You're just in time," he said walking toward his captives. "Things are gonna get real interesting now."

Martha Jo was sobbing. Presley was glaring. I figured the motionless person on the floor was Neal Wilson. There was a small pool of blood near the top of his head. I couldn't tell if he was alive. My best strategy was to stall and hope Bobby would get here before Haywood was able to carry out whatever perverse plan he had in mind.

"I'm impressed how all of you responded to a damsel in distress," Haywood said. "I wasn't sure it would work. I do feel real bad for Martha Jo. Really. But we had Audrey going off the reservation and these other two yahoos here haven't been taking care of business. There's just too many loose ends, things are out of control. So. We put an end to it."

"I'm trying to figure it out," I said, using up time. "Let's see. It's significant that Martha Jo is without clothes, I presume."

"Right you are," Haywood said. "Go on. I'm interested to see how smart you are."

"I'm no Sherlock Holmes, that's for sure. Holmes would have had it all figured out by the time he set foot in the door. But, I'm guessing sex is involved."

"Smart boy."

"Let's see. One of us arrives to find another one of us in bed with Martha Jo." I paused, stretching it out. I estimated five minutes had passed since I'd hung up with Bobby.

"Go on."

"In a jealous fit, the one of us who comes across the intimate couple shoots them."

"Well, Ryder, you are pretty smart. Then what?"

I listened hard for a sound from outside that would advertise a car coming this way even knowing it was premature. "He shoots himself?"

Haywood applauded by beating a palm against the barrel of his gun. "What about old Wilson?" he asked, waving the gun in the direction of the body on the floor.

"Yeah. I can't figure that out."

"Having trouble with it myself. I think one way it can work is for Presley and Wilson to have been doing a double team on Martha Jo ..."

A squeal came out from around the tape on her mouth.

"... when you come in. I mean, that would really flip you out, wouldn't it?"

"What would I use for a gun?"

"Oh, come on. Their clothes are going to be all over the place. You pick up one of their service revolvers." He looked over at the couch. "I don't know. I'm not sure that's altogether credible, although you do have a reputation for, uh, spontaneity, shall we say. You didn't think I knew who you were, did you? I didn't at first, but it didn't take long, not after hearing that the investigator Audrey was talking to was a one-armed man. Even so, I'm not sure people are going to believe you'd kill three people for screwin'. Presley on the other hand is known to be a very loose fucking cannon."

A loud "Mrrrmmph," came from the deputy.

"You know, Haywood, you have kind of a potty mouth for a man of the cloth."

"In just a few minutes, Ryder, you aren't going to have to worry about that. Like I was saying, Presley does have a reputation that would support the idea that if he found his lover in bed with you ..." He pointed his index finger at me with his thumb up. "Blam! Oops. He remembers too late that he has another cop with him. What was he thinking?" He aimed his finger down at the prostrate McDowell County deputy. "Blam! Takes care of that. Also means fewer people to get out of their clothes and into the bed. Maybe that's where we need to start to get this show on the road. Go on,

Ryder, take 'em off. Martha Jo, I think you're gonna like this part."

The guy was truly a psychopath, capable of doing what others can only imagine. I didn't move. I guessed Bobby was still five minutes away at best. It appeared I was going to have act on my own.

"I heard about you shooting the wall in your house yesterday," Haywood said. "I know you shot to miss, unlike what I will do. So, give me a reason right now and I'll do it. Or, you can stretch it out, give yourself some illusion of control over the process. Hell, I might even let you two love birds go at it. That would be the fitting thing." He glared at me. "How's that sound like a way to go, Ryder. Take. Your. Clothes. Off. Got it?"

I nodded and slipped off my shoes. "The socks are a problem. I need to sit down ..."

"Forget the fucking socks. Come on, come on." He waved the gun in my direction like a conductor with a baton.

I stood facing him and started to lift my sweatshirt.

"Now you're cookin'. Oh, yeah. I think I'll let you two love birds get in the bed. Like I said, Martha Jo's relationship with Aaron is well documented. But there's people know you've been out this way a lot yourself, Ryder. Not much surprise you succumbed to her ..."

A cell phone rang from the direction of the couch. Haywood turned reflexively toward the sound. I reached for my gun. As I was pulling it out of the waistband of my pants, the butt got tangled up in the shirt. Haywood turned his attention back to me as I got the revolver loose.

"Oh, nice try. But, we're not gonna do Gunfight at the OK Corral, Ryder. So just drop it."

Instead of dropping the gun, I dropped to the floor on my left side and fired in the direction of Haywood. It was loud. Haywood screamed. Martha Jo squealed. I rolled. Haywood shot into the space I'd just vacated, then dropped to one knee. I must have scored.

I fired again before he could get re-situated. I missed. He shot and I felt a sting on my wrist like an entire hive of yellow jackets had gotten me at once. The gun dropped from my hand.

Martha Jo launched into muffled hysterics.

"Thanks, Ryder," Haywood said between clenched teeth. "Now I've got self-defense. Too bad you decided to do it like this. You could have at least gotten your ashes hauled if you'd done it my way."

I was on the floor, bleeding from the top of my hand. Haywood limped over to me, blood dripping from his thigh. He reached down and grabbed the collar of my sweatshirt, pulling me almost to a sitting position, raising his gun to slam it into my face. My wrist hurt like hell and blood was pouring out, but my hand still worked. As he was was preparing for his strike, I swung my arm around and caught him on the chin. He fell backward, dropping his weapon and pulling me over on top of him. I looked for the nearest gun. He was bigger than me with the advantage of two arms and, even with the leg wound, he managed to roll me off and pin me by kneeling on my arm. Blood from his leg wound spilled onto my chest. His right arm was cocked, ready for another assault when the door flew open.

"What the hell?" Bobby said, looking around the room, Colt .45 in hand, at the ready.

"Ah, it's the cavalry," I said, "not quite in the nick of time."

Bobby called for two ambulances, then called the sheriff. He duct-taped Haywood's hands and feet while I wielded a gun then got the first aid kit from the truck. Haywood's wound was as superficial as mine, although you wouldn't have guessed it from all the racket he made.

After I'd been tended to, I covered Martha Jo as best I could with the robe she'd been forced to relinquish and removed the tape from her mouth.

Thus unencumbered, she said, "Get my hands loose, Ryder, and then pour me a drink, will you? Jack neat. Don't bother with ice."

I brought the drink and the bottle and proceeded as delicately as possible to unwrap the tape from her legs. She slipped the robe on and retreated to the bedroom with the whiskey. We left Presley duct-taped on the couch, his objections muzzled. Wilson was unconscious but breathing shallowly.

Martha Jo returned in cut-off blue jean short-shorts and a man's button-down shirt with the tails tied together above her midriff. In between outbursts from the over-acting Haywood, she related her version of the morning's events, beginning with the real estate man's arrival two hours earlier with a gun in one hand and a roll of duct tape in the other.

She took a long pull on the whiskey and refreshed her drink from the bottle. Her gaze fell to the glass in her lap. It stayed there a few seconds as if there were answers floating in it before looking up. There was no inflection in her voice as she continued. "He makes me call Presley the same way I called you later, just calling his name and hanging up. Aaron showed up forty-five minutes later with Wilson. A bonus according to Haywood who then held us all at gun point. All I was wearing was the robe and he makes me drop that, of course. Then he has Wilson wrap tape around me and Presley. What a pervert."

She gave out a mirthless chuckle.

"Poor Neal. He didn't know where to put the tape, you know. You'd think he'd never had his hands on a naked woman before. Anyway, when he was done, Haywood smacked him on the head with his gun, and he went down."

Wilson was still not conscious when the ambulance arrived to cart him off to the hospital. The second one took Haywood,

In spite of the law saying you can be found guilty of growing drugs on your property whether or not you know that the drugs are there, a jury failed to convict Queenie of any drug law violations. The DA quickly moved to drop the murder charge against her. I thought Stan Dillingham was the likely perpetrator in Brian's death but Martha Jo convinced me that, while Stan had his dark side, growing pot was as far as he'd push the law. I accepted that Brian had gotten very stoned on the killer weed, became entranced by the falls, wandered into the creek and got washed over the edge. Although I think I'll always have a nagging doubt.

During the dark days of winter, Kathy and I went to the pound and found a mutt puppy who looked a lot like we imagined Sonny had when he was little. We named him "Audrey," thinking he wouldn't mind the cross-gender implications. The cats seemed to think he was one of them and graciously allowed him to become one of the family.

Kathy passed on the water park opportunity and promoted Warren from Assistant to Associate. His new responsibilities included most of the out of town travel for the company. On those few occasions Kathy took overnight trips, I accompanied her. She, in turn, went with me on a couple of domestic jobs involving nighttime stakeouts. It looked as if we might become real partners after all.

I thought I was beginning to understand the meaning of serenity.

One night in early spring I answered the phone to hear Kathy's brother say, with no preliminary, "Put Kathy on."

Before she could say anything other than, "Hi," her expression turned dark. "What do you mean, 'Dad's missing'?"

Vacation was over.

that there's major drug cultivation going on out at Queenie's place, thereby setting up her arrest. I was right that they counted on the property being confiscated because of the drugs and, through some manipulation of the process, greased with a lot of Hensley Presley Beatty money, it would eventually be bought by a surrogate of theirs. Probably Pete Haywood.

"Then Brian turned up dead, which led to the property getting tied up in Queenie's bail bond proceedings. Nate says that the prosecutor is ready to drop the murder charge against Queenie but Nate doesn't want him to do that just yet since then the narcotics guys could go after the property. He wants the pot growing charges dealt with first."

"How's Queenie feel about that?"

"Says it hasn't affected her life all that much so far, so what's a little longer?"

The wheels of justice are notoriously slow rolling and it was well into the new year before everything got sorted out. Arthur Prendergast, the man who proved as inept at framing me with murder as he had been at tailing me, was charged with first degree murder in the death of Audrey Hollingsworth. Although briefly a suspect myself for that crime, I was exonerated when it was determined she had been stabbed by someone standing behind her using his left hand. Apparently, no one had bothered to explain to Arthur that I was deficient in the left hand department. Arthur, in turn, ratted out the HPB outfit for planning the crime, which netted all of them – including Haywood – convictions for murder and conspiracy to commit murder in the first degree. Haywood, who was tried separately, was also found guilty of assault, assault with a deadly weapon, and attempted murder in the duct taping incident and had his license pulled by the real estate board for being of bad moral character. Altogether, it challenged my cynicism toward the criminal justice system.

52

That evening, we gathered on the back deck, Kathy and I, the cats and Sonny. Although the sky in the west had a warm pink glow, the breeze was cool around us.

"What does Martha Jo have to say about it all?" Kathy asked

"Nothing very surprising. Stan had grown pot since he'd been living out there, just enough to keep him and M.J. supplied and have a little extra for friends and neighbors. He never wanted more than that and surely didn't want Queenie to know. Then at the end of last year, Aaron Presley, who they knew from Martha Jo's days as an exotic dancer ..."

"Stripper?" Kathy said.

"Yeah. Well. From back then. And with whom M.J. had had a ... um ... variety of relationships over the years, with photographic evidence ... that's a whole 'nother thing. Anyway. Presley suggests they grow sinsemilla ..."

"That really potent pot."

"Yeah, that stuff. Presley convinces them they can make a quarter million dollars without having to grow any more plants than they already do. What Presley doesn't tell them is that he is in league with the other Presley, Chester Webster, or that their plan includes tipping off the narcs – after most of the pot has been harvested –

but not until he and Presley had time to get into a shouting match about whose fault the whole mess had been.

When the detective from the sheriff's department arrived, Martha Jo repeated her story about the morning's events, then said, "I'm not saying anything else without a lawyer."

"I know a good one," I offered, pulling my phone out of my pocket. I scrolled to Nate's number and handed it to Martha Jo. "Might as well go ahead and make an appointment."

Pisgah Press

Also available from Pisgah Press

Letting Go: Collected Poems 1983-2003 — Donna Lisle Burton
$14.95

Unbelievable: Faith, Reason, & the Search for Truth — Joseph R. Haun
$16.00 — w. A. D. Reed

MacTiernan's Bottle — Michael Hopping
$14.95

I Like It Here! Adventures in the Wild & Wonderful World of Theatre
$30.00 — C. Robert Jones

Fragments — Martin A. Keeley
$16.00

Oscar & the Royal Avenue Cats — Martin A. Keeley
$15.00

A Green One for Woody — Patrick O'Sullivan
$15.95

Reed's Homophones: a comprehensive book of sound-alike words — A.D. Reed
$10.00

Swords in their Hands: George Washington and the Newburgh Conspiracy
$24.95 — David Richards

Trang Sen — Sarah-Ann Smith
$19.50

To order:

Pisgah Press, LLC
PO Box 1427, Candler, NC 28715
www.pisgahpress.com

Made in the USA
San Bernardino, CA
15 July 2014